MEASLE
AND THE
DOOMPIT

D1313275

Also by Ian Ogilvy

MEASLE AND THE WRATHMONK
MEASLE AND THE DRAGODON
MEASLE AND THE MALLOCKEE
MEASLE AND THE SLITHERGHOUL

MEASLE
AND THE
DOOMPIT

Ian Ogilvy

Illustrated by Chris Mould

OXFORD
UNIVERSITY PRESS

OXFORD
UNIVERSITY PRESS

Great Clarendon Street, Oxford OX2 6DP

Oxford University Press is a department of the University of Oxford.
It furthers the University's objective of excellence in research, scholarship,
and education by publishing worldwide in

Oxford   New York

Auckland   Cape Town   Dar es Salaam   Hong Kong   Karachi
Kuala Lumpur   Madrid   Melbourne   Mexico City   Nairobi
New Delhi   Shanghai   Taipei   Toronto

With offices in

Argentina   Austria   Brazil   Chile   Czech Republic   France   Greece
Guatemala   Hungary   Italy   Japan   Poland   Portugal   Singapore
South Korea   Switzerland   Thailand   Turkey   Ukraine   Vietnam

Oxford is a registered trade mark of Oxford University Press
in the UK and in certain other countries

British Library Cataloguing in Publication Data

Data available

ISBN: 978-0-19-272622-3

1 3 5 7 9 10 8 6 4 2

Printed in China by Imago

FOR BARNABY AND MATILDA, YET AGAIN

Contents

THE SCHOOL TRIP

'*Wot?* You is doin' *WOT*?'

'I'm going on a school trip, Iggy.'

Iggy Niggle stared crossly at Measle. His round, fishy eyes were bright with suspicion and his pale lips were tight and pursed.

'Wot for?'

'What do you mean "what for"? It's a school trip. That means my class is going on a trip and it's been organized by my school—'

'Ssschool! Pooh!' muttered Iggy venomously.

Measle sighed. Sometimes Iggy was so difficult to deal with—and this was definitely one of those times. The moment he'd mentioned this outing, Measle realized there was going to be trouble. Iggy didn't like Measle going to school. As far as Iggy was concerned, Measle spent far too much time at school and not nearly enough time with him.

'Ssso . . . dis *ssschool trip*—wot is you goin' to do, eh? Fall over a lot? Eh? Cause it's a *trip*, innit? Ssso, you is goin' to *trip over*, sssee? And den you will hurt yoursssself and I will laugh! Ho, yesss! I will laugh my sssocks off!'

Measle decided—for the sake of peace—to try to find Iggy's joke a little bit funny. So he laughed and said, 'Good one, Iggy!' He looked expectantly into the little wrathmonk's face, hoping to see the trace of a smile there—but there wasn't one. Iggy remained resolutely cross and sulky.

''Ow long for, den?' said Iggy, haughtily.

'About a week, I think. Not long really.'

Iggy sniffed scornfully. 'A whole week! Dat is at least a sssquillion days!'

'Not quite, Iggy.'

Iggy had no idea about how numbers worked, but he knew that Measle *did*—so he didn't argue. Instead, he merely raised one eyebrow in a superior manner and twirled the handle of his umbrella, sending raindrops spattering against Measle's face.

The umbrella was brand new and very smart. Sam Stubbs, Measle's dad, had given it to Iggy— a good present for a wrathmonk, since all wrathmonks have small but permanent black rain clouds hanging over their heads. Without umbrellas, they get very wet. Since Iggy Niggle was a very pathetic and weak little wrathmonk, his rain cloud was tiny, no bigger than a man's fist, but, all the same, it did produce a constant fine drizzle down on Iggy's shoulders. The umbrella (or *humble-ella* as he called it) was Iggy's most treasured possession—although you'd never know it. Sam had given Iggy twelve umbrellas over the past year and Iggy had managed to either lose, or break, all of them. So Sam had made this latest umbrella something rather special. First, he'd magically strengthened the shaft and the ribs and the black material so that they were now almost indestructible. That took care of Iggy's rough handling. Sam had done something even cleverer about Iggy's carelessness with his possessions. He'd endowed the super-strong umbrella with a Return-to-Owner spell. All Iggy had to do—or indeed anybody who knew how—was whistle a special whistle that Sam had taught him. It started with a long *tweeeee*, then there were three short *twees*, and then another long one, all with special notes you had to get exactly right. It had taken Iggy a long time to learn it. But, once learned, all he had to do was whistle and the umbrella—wherever it happened to be at the time—would open up, lift off the ground, and fly back to Iggy's waiting hands.

So far, Iggy had whistled for his brand-new umbrella twelve times—and he'd only had it a week. To be fair to Iggy, on one of these occasions he hadn't really lost the umbrella at all. Measle had made quite sure that he, too, knew the special whistle. Unlike Iggy, who was a very slow learner, it had taken Measle all of a minute and a half to get it right. Then, just for a joke, Measle had summoned the umbrella, making it fly right across the grounds of Merlin Manor, with Iggy chasing it all the way. When, panting heavily, Iggy had reached Measle's side and seen Measle sitting there, on a tree stump, holding his precious umbrella, he'd got very cross and threatened Measle with all sorts of terrible magic spells, none of which he could do, of course.

'Iggy, you don't have to chase after it, you know,' Measle had said, in a calming voice.

Iggy had stopped shouting that he was going to turn Mumps into a rotten turnip and said, 'You wot?'

'Don't you remember? All you've got to do is whistle and it'll come straight back to you.'

Iggy's fishy eyes had swivelled uncertainly, while this novel concept found a corner for itself in his tiny brain. Then he'd grinned triumphantly and yelled, 'Hah! Well, look 'ere—I *won*, didn't I! Cos dere is no *point* you takin' my humble-ella, cos all I gotta do is *whissstle* for it, sssee!'

And now, in the middle of this awkwardness about the school outing, Measle and Iggy were standing by the kitchen door of Merlin Manor, right next to Iggy's little house. Iggy's house was actually a dog kennel. Tinker, Measle's little black and white terrier, had never used it, preferring the nice soft furniture *inside* Merlin Manor. Inside was where Iggy was not allowed, because of his small rain cloud.

'I don't care how tiny it is, I'm not having that thing dribbling all over my kitchen!' Nanny Flannel had exclaimed—so Iggy was forced to stay outside, which was why Tinker's kennel had become Iggy's house.

'Ssso . . . where is you goin' den—on dis *sssssschool trip*?'

On the word 'school', Iggy was hissing his esses even more than usual, in an attempt to put as much scorn as he could into the syllables. Measle realized he was going to have to make the trip sound awful, if only to please his wrathmonk friend.

'We're going to this horrible place. Way up

north. It's going to be cold and wet—and very boring, too.'

Iggy's expression brightened for a moment—and then fell back into its sulky profile.

'And wot is you goin' to be doin' in dis *'orrible* place?'

'We're going to be looking at all the things that live there.'

'Wot, like *jeeryfars* and *eggylumps* and rhiny—rhony—rossery ... er ... dose fings wiv pointy fings on deir noses?'

'No, Iggy. No *giraffes* or *elephants* or *rhinoceroses*. Nothing as exciting as that. Actually, I think we're mostly going to be looking at moss.'

'Moss? *Moss?* Wot is moss?'

'Green stuff. It grows where it's damp.'

Iggy stared blankly at Measle for several seconds. Then he said, 'Well, I is quite damp and it don't grow on *me*. Ssso dat is rubbish for a ssstart, innit? What else is you goin' to be *lookin'* at?'

'Er ... well, I think we're going to be looking at water, too.'

'Water?' squeaked Iggy. '*Water?* Coo—you know sssumfing, Mumps? You is tocally, *tocally* potty! And who is goin' on dis tocally potty *ssschool trip?*'

'I told you, Iggy. My whole class.'

'Huh! All your *friends*, are dey?'

Iggy hated Measle having friends other than himself. This wasn't fair because, although Measle did have quite a few friends in his class, he was never able to bring any of them home, so Iggy had never had any reason to feel that Measle preferred his school friends to him, since he'd never seen Measle in their company.

There were lots of reasons why Measle couldn't invite school friends to Merlin Manor. His little sister Matilda, the all-powerful Mallockee, was one of them. Tilly might easily take it into her head to turn them all green for a few minutes and the Stubbs family couldn't cope with trying to explain that. Then there was Iggy himself, who was quite *impossible* to explain— so Measle had concocted a fanciful story about how his parents were terribly allergic to anybody under the age of seventy-two, and how they became deathly ill within minutes of meeting anybody who wasn't really, really *old*— apart from himself and his sister, of course. It wasn't a very good story but it was the best he could come up with and, for the time being at least, it kept the curious at bay.

Iggy was busy replacing the scowling, sulky expression on his face with something new. This took quite a long time, because Iggy's face muscles seemed to have lives of their own. Measle watched as the small wrathmonk tried various combinations of bizarre expressions, finally settling on something that, to Measle, looked as if Iggy was about to be sick. From past experience, Measle knew that this particular face was supposed to mean that Iggy was going to be especially nice for a few moments—and that was never good. Iggy was only really nice when he wanted something.

'Can I come too, den?' Iggy's voice was sweet and wheedling.

Measle's heart sank. How to refuse without hurting Iggy's feelings too much? Perhaps there was a way out.

'No, Iggy, I'm sorry but you can't—'

Immediately, Iggy replaced the sick-looking expression with one of furious outrage.

'Can't? *Can't? CAN'T?*' he screamed, sticking his face close to Measle's.

'Wait, Iggy, I hadn't finished. You can't come because it's a school trip and you don't go to school—'

'Sssschool is ssstoopid! Ssschool is nasssty! Ssschool is 'orrible!'

'And you know why you don't go there, don't you?'

Iggy's eyes narrowed in sudden interest. The truth was, he had no idea why he didn't go to school.

'It's because you're far too clever for school!'

Iggy's face went through another wriggling transformation, ending up with an expression of self-satisfied delight.

'I *is* clever,' he admitted, earnestly. 'I is *'stremely* clever.'

'And that's why you don't go to a stupid, nasty,

horrible school. I have to go because I don't know anything. You don't have to go because you know *everything*!'

Iggy nodded smugly. His pale lips were stretched in such a wide smile now, Measle could see the tips of his two sets of pointed teeth, three on either side of his mouth.

'Ho, yesss, I do know everyfing, don't I? Every little tiny fing in de whole wide world! And dat, Mumps, dat is why I don't go to ssschool!'

Iggy ended his sentence on a note of high triumph and Measle heaved a sigh of relief. Iggy often adopted the last suggestion that somebody had just told him as his own idea and Measle knew it was a good sign. It meant that Iggy would give him no more trouble about the trip.

The expedition had been Mr Lockey's idea.

Mr Lockey was a substitute teacher, taking the place of the awful Miss Patterson, who was disliked by everybody. She was about fifty, with a sour, ugly face. She had frizzy grey hair, like a clump of wire wool. She wore thick tweed suits, bulky woollen stockings, and clumsy, clumpy shoes. The corners of her mouth were always downturned and her lips were pinched together in permanent disapproval of something or other, and an everlasting frown had put a deep vertical crease in the middle of her forehead.

So, when Miss Patterson had come down with a bad case of chicken pox, which meant she had to take at least a month off school, nobody—least of all Measle—was very sorry. Particularly since her replacement was Mr Lockey.

Mr Lockey was great. He told lots of jokes, he never lost his patience, he raised his voice only to hoot with laughter and, best of all, he managed to make school fun—and Measle thought that anybody who could do that must be some sort of genius.

Mr Lockey was like a big bear. He had an enormous chest, broad shoulders, and arms as thick as tree branches. A huge bushy beard covered the bottom half of his face, above which was a long horsey nose, and, above that, a pair of small, twinkling eyes that always seemed to be laughing at something. He reminded Measle a little of Toby Jugg—but only in looks and build. Mr Lockey's personality was nothing like Toby Jugg's. Toby Jugg was probably the most evil warlock Measle had ever met—and now that Toby had become a wrathmonk, and therefore unpleasantly insane, he was certainly the most dangerous wizard anybody was likely to meet.

The Wizards' Guild were out in force, looking for Toby Jugg. So far, they'd had no luck. Toby Jugg had disappeared and nobody had the faintest idea where he might be. There were a couple of other disappearances as well: the two officials from the Guild, Mr Needle and Mr Bland, had vanished at the same time and the hunters from the Wizards' Guild were searching for them, too.

The supply teacher was the exact opposite of the mad super-wrathmonk. Mr Lockey never said an unkind word to anybody (or about anybody, either). He had a smile for every person who crossed his path, he would listen attentively to (and sort out) any problem presented to him—and he was liked by the whole school within a few days of arriving there.

And, unlike Toby Jugg—and all the other wrathmonks Measle had encountered—there was no large and looming black rain cloud hovering over his head. In fact, it always seemed to be rather a sunny day whenever Mr Lockey was around.

He'd announced the trip that morning.

'Ladies and gentlemen!' he boomed, grinning cheerfully round the class. 'I have an announcement! I have managed to persuade our kind and splendid headmaster to let us go on a special excursion! This class—and this class only, because you're all such brilliant students—will be travelling to the wild and woolly foothills of Mount Spindrift! Who can tell me where Mount Spindrift is?'

Nobody could, so Mr Lockey pointed it out on the wall map.

'There—see! Way up north, where the wind blows so hard that the rain falls sideways! Where the snowflakes are as big as pancakes! Where the moss grows so thick that you can use it as your mattress! We shall be gone for a whole week! Oh, we shall have fun!'

Measle's parents, Sam and Lee, had done a little checking for themselves. Too many bad things had happened to Measle, and all because he was their son—so, without telling Measle, they had telephoned the headmaster. Mr Crusoe had reassured them.

'Mr Lockey comes to us with the most impeccable references,' he said. 'And this expedition—well, we have checked that he has done it before, with classes from different schools, and it's always been a great success. The children stay in a pleasant house, near a beautiful lake, and they'll be doing a good deal of interesting study of the local flora and fauna. And a week of fresh air never does anybody any harm, I always say!'

'Is anybody besides Mr Lockey going with the children?' asked Lee.

'Oh, indeed, yes!' said Mr Crusoe, enthusiastically. 'Two ladies will be accompanying the class. Mr Lockey's sisters. I have met them both and was most impressed! One is a qualified nurse, the other a retired teacher—and what could be better than that, eh?'

Lee said goodbye and put the phone down.

Then she and Sam had a discussion. They were a little uneasy about this trip, but the fact that the whole class was going on an expedition that had been mounted several times before, with a teacher who seemed to know what he was doing, put their minds sufficiently at rest.

'Measle can't always be left out of ordinary life,' said Lee. 'Just because he's involved in the magical world, that doesn't mean he has to cut himself off from the human one. After all, *he* is human, isn't he? Not a trace of magic in him, thank goodness!'

'Besides,' said Sam, tapping his front teeth with his fingers, 'with this nationwide hunt for Toby Jugg going on, I think I'd like Measle to be out of the way, in case anything unpleasant happens.'

Heading North!

The bus was shiny and very new. It had the words SPINDRIFT TOURS painted on the sides and it stood, huge and gleaming, right in the middle of the school car park.

'Right, everybody!' shouted Mr Lockey. 'Cases in the back and then all aboard!'

Mr Lockey stood by the bus door, his legs apart, his hands on his hips, beaming round at the assembled class. On either side of him stood his two sisters—and they were beaming, too, although not with quite the enthusiasm that Mr Lockey was showing. Measle detected a very slight look of tension in both women's eyes.

Well, he thought, *that's not really surprising. I wouldn't want to be in charge of us lot, either.*

The two Lockey ladies looked very similar, except that one had dark hair and the other was a blonde. The dark one, whose name was Agatha, was also quite slim and the blonde one, whose name was Annie, was a little heavier. They both seemed very nice.

Measle looked away from the two women and round at his noisy classmates. Charley Lucas and Michael Denny were, as usual, being the noisiest. They had decided to be in charge of loading the luggage space at the back of the bus and were yelling loudly for everybody to come and give them their cases—and, when everybody did, they were hurling the bags, with considerable force, into the dark hold. Charley was big and bulky, with a round friendly face and straight hair brushed flat to his head. Michael was the exact opposite—thin and weedy, with curly hair that flopped into his eyes.

Over to one side, several of the girls were in a huddle, their heads close together. Cheryl Tucker was there and so were Michelle Dunstable and Polly Williams. Measle watched as, quite suddenly, Cheryl threw her head back and shrieked with laughter. Immediately, Michelle did the same. Polly merely smiled.

'Oi!' yelled a voice, a little too close to his ear. Measle turned and saw it was his friend, Del Fisher. Del was grinning evilly.

'I saw you!' Del gurgled. 'I saw you staring at Polly Williams!' Then Del adopted a funny, sing-song voice

and, dancing round Measle like a mad witch doctor, he chanted, 'You want to be her *boyyyy*friend! You want to *kiiiiiss* her!'

'No, I don't,' said Measle, grinning back. In fact, Measle rather liked looking at Polly Williams and had vaguely thought of asking her if she'd like to go and see a film with him—but that was something he would never admit, particularly to Del Fisher. If Del ever thought that Measle was *really* interested in Polly, he would scream with laughter and immediately spread the news all over the school. Del had frizzy red hair, gangly arms and legs, and a face like a potato.

'Come along, come along!' roared Mr Lockey, boisterously. 'Let's all get a bally move on, shall we?'

Measle, Del, Michael, and Charley found seats right at the rear of the bus. A few minutes later, the door hissed shut, the engine rumbled to life, and they were off.

The journey seemed to take for ever. In fact, it took most of the rest of that day. They halted a couple of times at motorway service stations and stuffed their faces with bad motorway service station food. Later, after it got dark, Measle snoozed for half an hour. He was awakened when they finally lurched to a halt and Mr Lockey's booming voice filled the bus.

'Right! Wakey-wakey! We're here! Everybody out—collect your cases and meet us at the front door for room assignments!'

Measle and his friends found their cases and joined the crowd clustered around Mr Lockey and his sisters. It was dark outside the house, but Measle could see that it was a big place—almost as big as Merlin Manor. The walls looked massive, built as they were from large blocks of grey granite, and the front door was made of stout oak, blackened with age. There was an ornate lamp mounted to one side of the door and its yellow light spilled out over the heads of the small crowd gathered there.

Agatha and Annie stood under the light. Agatha held a clipboard and was consulting it.

'Girls will be in one side of the house, boys in the other!' she called out, glancing sharply over the top of the clipboard at everybody milling around her. 'Now, when I call out your names, I shall also call out a colour—and that will be the room you're assigned to. My sister Annie will show you the way! Quiet, please!'

'Yes, shut up, you horrible lot!' roared Mr Lockey, cheerfully.

Agatha Lockey read out names and, when she got to Measle, she said, 'Measle Stubbs—Orange!'

Measle grinned at his friends. Their names had been read out ahead of his and they were all in Orange too.

'Come along with me,' said Annie Lockey.

Measle, Del, Michael, and Charley followed Annie into the house. She led them along a passage, up a short flight of stairs, round several corners, up another, longer flight of stairs, along another corridor, down three steps, a sharp turn to the left, another sharp turn to the right—and then she threw open a door and said, 'Here you are! Del Fisher, Michael Denny, Charles Lucas, and Measle Stubbs—Orange!'

They all clustered into the room. There were two pairs of bunk beds along two of the walls. A large wardrobe filled the third wall and a chest of drawers occupied the remaining space. There was a tall window at the far end of the room, but it was too dark outside to see anything from it.

'We've put you down this end, because my brother tells me that you lot are inclined to be a bit noisy,' said Annie, smiling nervously down at them. 'Down here, you can be as noisy as you like! Now then, pick your beds and unpack your cases and dinner will be ready in half an hour. You'll hear a gong—just follow the sound all the way to the dining room—and don't be late, or there'll be nothing left to eat!'

Annie Lockey gave them a little wave and then left, closing the door behind her. Measle threw his case onto one of the top bunks, claiming it for himself. Del got the other and Michael and Charley settled for the bottom pair. They unpacked their bags, which pretty much meant just grabbing everything in one enormous armful and stuffing the whole crumpled heap into one of the drawers in the chest. Then, while the others were busy throwing pillows at each other, Measle went to the window. He cupped his hands round his eyes and pressed his face to the window and tried to see out.

'Any monsters out there, Measle?' called Charley.

'Can't see any,' said Measle, peering hard into the blackness. 'Can't see anything, actually. It's really dark—'

Something soft caught him on the back of his head. Measle turned round. He bent down, picked up the pillow lying at his feet—and then jumped straight into the fray of what was looking to be a very promising battle.

The gong sounded at the height of the combat. They all dropped their pillows and, panting slightly from the effort of the fight, they trooped out of the bedroom and followed the sounds, until they arrived at the dining room door. Everybody was there, some standing about, some already seated on either side of an enormous table, which stretched from one end of the long room to the other. The food was on the table—great pots of steaming stew, plates of mashed potatoes, bowls of peas and carrots.

Everybody was there—except for Mr Lockey and his sisters.

For a while, all the children simply waited for the three adults to make an appearance. After ten minutes, Del said, loudly, 'If we don't start, it's going to get cold!' Without wasting another moment, he sat down, spooned some stew into a bowl, picked up his knife and fork and started to shovel the food into his mouth. It was the signal for everybody to do the same. Cheryl tried to make a small protest about waiting for the grown-ups—but she was ignored. Measle, Charley, and Michael found seats next to Del and squashed in together, and everybody tucked in and helped themselves. Measle didn't think the food was very good. The stew was watery and tasteless and the vegetables were soggy and over-cooked. Measle was used to Nanny Flannel's food, which was always wonderful—but it seemed that many of his classmates didn't eat as well as he did, because they were piling their plates high.

Half an hour later, when everybody had finished eating, there was still no sign of the Lockeys. Some of the children got up and started to drift off into other parts of the house. Others gathered in small knots and held nervous, whispered conversations. Measle nudged Del, then jerked his head at Charley and Michael. When they had moved a little away from the noisy crowd, Charley said, 'What's up, Measle?'

'I think we should take a look around. See if we can find the Lockeys.'

They set off. It took them half an hour to explore every inch of the place, from the cavernous cellars to the small, cramped attic rooms under the eaves. They searched the big kitchen, the various living areas, the bedrooms and bathrooms; they covered every conceivable place and, when they were finished, they found themselves back in their own bedroom.

There were several minutes of thoughtful silence. Then Measle said, 'You know what this means, don't you?'

'What?' said Del.

'Until the Lockeys come back—*if* they come back—we're all alone.'

Del looked puzzled. 'No, we're not,' he said, picking up a pillow and throwing it at Measle. 'There's lots of us here.'

Measle ducked to one side and the pillow sailed past him. 'I mean, there are no grown-ups,' he said, his voice serious. 'If anything goes wrong—like, if anybody gets ill, or there's a fire or a flood or an earthquake—there's nobody here to take charge.'

'Earthquake?' said Michael, nervously brushing a lock of hair out of his eyes. 'They don't have earthquakes round here, do they?'

'No, of course not,' said Measle. 'At least, I don't think so. The point is—we're on our *own*.'

Michael nodded thoughtfully. Then he said, 'Do you think we ought to call our parents or something?'

'Good idea,' said Charley. He reached into his trouser pocket and pulled out a mobile phone. Del and Michael did the same and all three were in the middle of dialling when they noticed that Measle hadn't moved a muscle.

'Aren't you going to call yours?' said Del.

Measle shook his head. 'I haven't got a phone,' he muttered.

'Why not?'

Measle shrugged the question away. The fact was, mobile phones didn't work at Merlin Manor. There was far too much magic around, interfering with the connections, which rendered them useless. Even away from the Merlin Manor surroundings, mobile phones were still no use to the Stubbs family—Sam was a wizard, Lee was a Manafount and Matilda was a Mallockee, and the combination of their magic completely over-powered any signal the phones might be trying to receive.

Del, Charley, and Michael were stopped from asking any more questions by the fact that not one of their phones seemed to be working. Del shook his and tried again.

'I can't get through,' he said.

'I can't even get a signal,' said Michael.

'What about a land line?' said Charley, sticking his useless phone back into his pocket. 'We could use one of the phones in the house, couldn't we?'

Measle slowly shook his head. 'I'm pretty sure there aren't any,' he said, quietly.

His friends stared at him. Then Del said, 'How do you know?'

'I looked,' said Measle. 'While we were searching the house for grown-ups. I didn't see a single telephone anywhere.'

'That's ridiculous!' scoffed Charley. 'There's always telephones in houses!'

Without a word, Measle got up and walked out of the room. Del, Charley, and Michael followed. Over the next half hour, they re-examined every square foot of the house. Along the way, they met several little groups of classmates, all doing the same thing—it turned out that there wasn't a single working mobile phone among any of them.

At one point, they came across a weeping Cheryl Tucker, sitting forlornly on a window seat. Polly and Michelle were on either side of her. Michelle was patting one of Cheryl's hands.

'It's all right, Cheryl,' said Polly. 'Stop crying.'

'But what can we *do*?' wailed Cheryl. 'Whatever is going to become of us? We could all die and nobody would know! We could lie here—a house full of corpses—and they wouldn't find us for ages!'

24

Polly glanced up at Measle. She smiled faintly and rolled her eyes and Measle grinned back at her and rolled *his* eyes. Then he stopped doing that because he became aware that Cheryl was looking at him with irritation plastered all over her doll-like face.

'What are you staring at?' she demanded, angrily. 'Why don't you be useful for once and go and find a telephone!'

After nearly three quarters of an hour of more fruitless searching, some sort of instinct brought everybody together in the dining room, where the remains of dinner were still lying on the long table.

Cheryl had taken Mr Lockey's seat. With an air of noble bravery, she seemed to be in the process of electing herself the unofficial leader of the group.

'Not a phone in the house!' she declared loudly. 'And no internet connection, either! No grown-ups! Do you all understand what this means? Do you?'

'Yeah,' said Del, grinning hugely from ear to ear. 'I know what it means. It means we can do what we like! We can stay up all night! We can eat what we want! We can—we can—we can drown the girls!'

All the girls put on their *Aren't-Boys-Really-Stupid!* expressions—all except Polly Williams. Measle, who had been quietly observing her and thinking how much prettier she was than Cheryl, noticed that Polly's face didn't sneer at all. Polly's face had a look of deep concern written all over it.

A Conversation
in a Cupboard

Nobody got much sleep that night.

When thirty children are left alone for any length of time and with no authority figure anywhere in sight, one thing is bound to happen. They will split, usually quite evenly, into two sides. One group will try to keep some sort of control over everybody else and act, generally, like grown-ups. The other group will be determined to take full advantage of the situation and have as much fun as possible.

Cheryl was the leader of the *Let's-All-Be-Very-Responsible-And-Well-Behaved* group. The leader of the boisterous crowd was Del Fisher. It was Del who led a mob of howling kids through the house on a mad hunt for non-existent ghosts. It was Del who raided the refrigerator and produced a midnight feast fit for a whole dynasty of kings—and it was Del who organized a game that he invented on the spot, called 'Hide-And-Don't-Seek'. It involved everybody going off and hiding somewhere in the dark, while Del and Charley and Michael sat in the kitchen and tried to find out how much food they could eat in an hour and a half.

Measle was a little too worried to join in the fun. Besides, he couldn't see the point of charging about all night, yelling at the top of his voice and eating till he was sick. But, equally, the thought of doing what Cheryl was suggesting—sitting in his bedroom and occasionally having a good cry—was pretty stupid, too. What Measle really wanted to do was to find somewhere quiet and have a good think about what was happening here.

Which was why Measle decided to pretend to play Del's idiotic game of Hide-And-Don't-Seek. If there was a chance of being left alone with his thoughts for a few precious moments, he was going to take it. He remembered seeing a cupboard, full of what looked like blankets, somewhere up among the attic rooms. As a hiding place, it was perfect.

When he reached the top floor, Measle retraced his steps to where the cupboard was, at the end of a long passage. He opened the door. Somebody had got there before him.

'Hello,' said Polly Williams, in a puzzled voice. 'I thought the whole idea was *not* to find anybody?'

Polly was sitting on the floor of the cupboard, on a pile of blankets. She looked quite comfortable.

'Er . . . sorry,' said Measle. 'I wasn't actually *looking*—I mean, I *was* looking but not for people hiding . . . er . . . I was sort of looking for somewhere to hide *myself*. If you see what I mean? Sorry.'

That sounded really lame, he thought. He grinned apologetically and started to close the cupboard door.

'What are you doing?' said Polly.

'Er . . . well . . . I was going to . . . er . . . leave you alone.'

'Oh, don't do that,' sighed Polly. 'It's dead boring in here all by myself.'

'Oh,' said Measle.

Polly scooted over to one side and patted the floor next to her.

'Why don't you come and hide with me?' she said. 'Unless, of course, you won't be seen dead with a girl?'

Until quite recently, girls were exactly what Measle wouldn't be seen dead with—but lately he'd been coming round to the opinion that the odd girl wasn't too bad, as long as her name wasn't Cheryl Tucker who, while undeniably pretty, was just a bit too much to cope with. But Polly Williams was something else entirely.

'No, no. Er . . . I will be seen dead with girls. Well, I'd rather be seen *alive* with them, of course.'

'What are you talking about?'

'Er . . . well . . . it was a sort of joke.'

'Oh. One of those stupid ones, right?'

'Yes.'

There was an uncomfortable silence. Measle was about to start discussing the weather, when Polly said, with a distinct trace of irritation, 'Well, come on then. Don't just stand there like a turnip.'

Measle ducked his head, stepped into the cupboard and sat down next to Polly on the blankets. Then, in the semi-darkness, he leaned against the back wall and closed his eyes.

'You're not going to sleep, are you?' demanded Polly—and now she sounded a little cross. Measle's eyes flew open.

'Don't you want to talk about what's going on?' Polly hissed.

'Oh . . . er . . . sure.'

'Don't you think it's all really, *really* weird?'

'It is a bit,' he said.

'A bit? A *bit*?' yelped Polly. She shook her head so hard that her hair danced around her face. 'It's *totally* weird, Measle! What's *not* weird? Where are the Lockeys? And what's *with* the Lockeys? Mr Lockey is weird! His sisters are weird! This house is weird!'

Measle thought of all the weird things that had happened to him during the past couple of years and he decided that what was going on here wasn't really all *that* weird. But he didn't say

anything. Polly would ask too many questions, the
stories would take too long to explain—and Polly
would never believe a word of them. So instead he
simply nodded and kept his mouth shut.

'I'm glad you agree,' said Polly, severely. 'Well—
what are you going to do about it?'

'Me?' said Measle. 'What do you mean?'

Polly clucked her tongue impatiently. 'Oh, come
on, Measle,' she muttered. 'You're much cleverer
than the rest of them.'

'*What?*' said Measle, wondering if he could
possibly have heard that right. There had never,
ever, been any indication at school that anybody—
especially a girl—thought that he was anything
other than slightly peculiar.

'Well—' said Polly, 'you *think* about things
before you talk about them. And, when you *do*

talk about them, you usually make a bit of sense—and that's more than I can say for the other boys.'

'What about the girls?' said Measle, feeling his face going a little pink. He was glad it was quite dark in the cupboard.

'Well, of course girls are much more sensible than boys,' said Polly, firmly. 'Except for Cheryl. Cheryl's too much of an actress to be sensible.'

Measle felt mildly insulted. He muttered, 'Well, if the girls are so sensible—apart from Cheryl—why don't you get *them* to do something? Whatever it is you want doing.'

'They won't listen to me,' said Polly, a trace of irritation roughening her voice. 'They only listen to Cheryl.'

'So—not all *that* sensible, then?' blurted out Measle.

There was a long silence and Measle held his breath, waiting for an explosion of anger from Polly. But it never came. Instead, the girl simply sighed and said, 'No—not all that sensible, I suppose.'

Measle felt relieved enough to say, 'Well, what do you want me to do?'

'I don't know,' said Polly. 'Nothing. Well, perhaps—'

'What?'

'Perhaps—I think I want you to look at things the way *I* look at things.'

'How do you look at things?'

'Well, I think I'm more likely to believe that there really are some weird things in this world. Like the Lockeys—I think they're really weird. And I think you should think they're weird, too.'

'OK. I do,' said Measle—and he meant it too.

There was a short silence. To cover it, Measle reached into his pocket and pulled out a plastic bag of jelly beans.

'Want a jelly bean?'

'Thanks.'

Polly reached for the bag and Measle suddenly pulled it away.

'Oh, don't do that!' said Polly, crossly. 'That's such a stupid game!'

'No, look—sorry—I just want to know what's your least favourite? So you don't get one of those, you see.'

'Oh. Well, *pink*, I suppose. I don't like the pink ones much.'

Measle peered into the bag and saw a few pink jelly beans there. Carefully, he pushed them to one side and then offered the bag to Polly. She reached in, took a green one and popped it into her mouth.

'Thanks.'

Measle bit into a blue one. For him, the yellow beans were the special ones. Lemon was his least favourite flavour, which was why they were to be avoided, unless he needed thirty seconds of invisibility, in which case he'd crunch a lemon-flavoured bean between his teeth and then disappear for exactly half a minute. These magical beans had proved very useful in the past and had saved his life on more than one occasion—which was why Measle never went anywhere without a bag in his pocket.

Polly and Measle sat in silence for a while. The fact that they were sitting together and not talking—and, more importantly, that he didn't feel uncomfortable with the long silence—surprised Measle. He was just beginning to get used to the sensation, and also starting to enjoy it more and more, when Polly abruptly got to her feet.

'Well, I'm going to bed,' she announced. 'Thanks for the jelly bean.'

'Oh—right,' said Measle scrambling upright. 'Me too.'

'Remember what we talked about?'

'I *think* so,' said Measle, wondering how Polly could possibly think he could have forgotten, seeing that the conversation had only taken place a minute ago.

'Good. Well, let's get out of here.'

Measle was about to step out of the cupboard when Polly held up her hand, motioning him to stop.

'Wait a second,' she hissed. 'Just let me see if the coast is clear. The last thing I need right now is to be seen coming out of a cupboard with a boy.'

Knowing what Del Fisher would do if he ever discovered that he had spent any time in a cupboard with a girl, Measle nodded and backed into the shadows again. Polly stuck her head out, looked both ways, and then whispered, 'OK, but let me get well away before you come out.'

Polly stepped out into the corridor and Measle listened to the dwindling tap-tap-tap of her shoes as she hurried away. Twenty seconds later, Measle popped his head out. There was nobody there, so he left the cupboard and, a minute later, he rejoined the milling mob on the ground floor.

'Where have you been?' demanded Charley.

'Yeah,' said Del. 'We've been looking for you.'

'Where were you?' said Michael.

'Oh—nowhere,' said Measle, carelessly. 'You know, just wandering about.'

By now, everybody was tired. It had been a very long day. Children began to drift off to their respective bedrooms and Measle, Del, Charley, and Michael did the same.

There was a surprise for them.

On each pillow lay a small bar of chocolate.

'Now that,' said Charley, hastily unwrapping his bar, 'is *very* nice!!'

'Very nice indeed!' said Del, biting into his bar.

'Wickedly nice!' mumbled Michael, through a great mouthful of chocolate.

It was only after Measle had eaten every last piece that he wondered how, exactly, the chocolate bars had arrived on their pillows?

Who had put them there?

When?

Why?

But then a great wave of tiredness swept over him. Through drooping eyelids, he noticed that his friends were already asleep. None of them had even bothered to change into their pyjamas.

Well, then, I won't either, thought Measle, getting sleepier and sleepier by the second. He lay down on his bunk bed and, a moment later, a warm, velvety darkness washed over him.

WHERE IS EVERYBODY?

Measle woke to find sunlight streaming into his face. Obviously he and his room-mates had forgotten to close the curtains the night before. He lifted himself onto one elbow and peered, through bleary eyes, at the window. They had forgotten to close that too—it was wide open and a soft breeze brought the faint scent of cut grass into the room.

Measle bent over and looked down into the bunk below. Del wasn't there. He looked across the room at the other set of bunk beds. They too were empty.

Measle's head felt thick and stuffy. He climbed down from his bed. He couldn't help thinking that his friends were a bit mean—obviously they had gone off somewhere together and had left him behind.

Measle opened the bedroom door and set off towards the dining room. He met nobody on the way and, when he reached the dining room, there was nobody there either. Standing there, in the empty space, Measle listened carefully. There was a deep silence that seemed to lie heavily in the still air.

Feeling the first small pricklings of alarm, Measle left the dining room and made his way to the top of the house. Poking his head into every room, he slowly made his way back to the ground floor— and, when he got there, the prickling feeling had solidified into a small knot of real fear, lodged deep in his gut.

The house was completely empty.

I'm in big trouble, thought Measle.

Measle had had lots of experience with trouble—and all of it had come from his enemies in the magical world. And now he was as sure as it's possible to be that this occasion was no different. He searched his mind, trying to work out who could possibly be responsible this time?

All the wrathmonks who hated him were safely locked up in the Detention Centre, deep beneath the Wizards' Guild building. So there was little chance that his old enemies were the ones who had spirited away his entire class. So, who then?

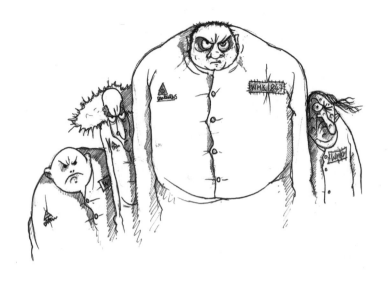

Reluctantly, Measle came to the only conclusion possible. Only Toby Jugg was still free to do what he wanted. Only Toby Jugg had the power to cause such a catastrophe. So logically it was Toby Jugg behind this latest misdeed. But where was he? And what did he want?

There was only one thing to do. Make another search—and this time, a more extensive one. First, to find out if he was truly alone; second, to find some clue as to the whereabouts of his classmates.

Measle's heart was thumping uncomfortably in his chest as he began the hunt. This time, he started on the ground floor. He examined every room and every cupboard and every chest of drawers—and the first thing he discovered was that all the clothes and the toothbrushes and the suitcases had gone as well.

Slowly—and making as little noise as possible—Measle worked his way up towards the top floor of the house. The deep silence was stretching his nerves taut, so every unexpected creak of a floorboard and every sudden squeal of a rusty hinge made him shiver with fright. At any minute, he expected some horror to jump out at him and he approached every dark doorway with caution.

At last, he reached the top floor. The corridor here stretched the length of the house and there were only two little windows, at either end. Most of the passage was dim and shadowy—particularly this door . . .

Measle opened the door slowly.

The door creaked a little.

The cupboard was very dark—

His foot touched against something soft on the floor—

'Ow! Watch where you're treading!'

Measle's heart jumped in his chest and he gasped and stammered, 'Who's there?'

'Me,' said Polly Williams, yawning and sitting up from her improvised bed of a heap of blankets piled on the cupboard floor.

Measle's heart settled down to a steady thumping. His eyes were becoming accustomed to the gloom and now he could see Polly clearly. She rubbed the sleep from her eyes and then looked up at Measle with a small, shamefaced expression.

'I expect you want to know what I'm doing in here again?' she muttered, lowering her eyes. 'Well, I couldn't sleep. I'm in with Cheryl and Michelle and they were snoring like walruses. So, I came up here.'

'Ah,' said Measle, wondering if walruses actually snored.

'It's nice and quiet in here,' explained Polly.

'Yes.'

There was an awkward pause. Then Polly said, 'Are they looking for me? Cheryl and Michelle, I mean. Did you guess where I was?'

'No,' said Measle, uncomfortably. 'I was just . . . er . . . searching—'

'What for?'

'Er . . . well . . . for everybody.'

Polly stared up at him for several seconds. Then she said, 'What do you mean?'

Measle wondered how Polly was going to take the news. He was glad it wasn't Cheryl sitting there in front of him. Cheryl would probably have hysterics. But Polly was different. Polly was unlikely to fall to pieces. All the same, it would be best to sound as calm and collected as possible.

So, using his most matter-of-fact voice, he told her what had happened.

When he finished, Polly had a look of incomprehension on her face. Abruptly, she got up and, without saying a word, she marched out of the cupboard and ran for the stairs. Measle followed.

Polly didn't bother searching every floor for herself. She simply flew down the staircases until she reached the ground floor. Then she ran to the dining room, with Measle at her heels. Together, they stood in the big, empty room. Then Polly said, 'Is it a joke, do you think?'

'A joke? What sort of joke?'

'Oh, you know—everybody goes off and hides and then they all jump out at you and shout "Surprise!" That sort of joke.'

Measle shook his head. 'I don't think it's a joke at all.'

'Well, where are they then?'

'Er . . . well, I think they've been taken away,' said Measle, quietly. 'I don't know where to.'

'Why?' said Polly, angrily. 'And who's taken them? And why are *we* still here?'

Measle couldn't answer the first question and was reluctant to offer a possible explanation for the second, but the third was something to think about—

Click, click, click, went Measle's agile brain.

'Well,' he said slowly, 'you weren't in your bed, were you? You were in that cupboard. Perhaps—perhaps whoever took them all away didn't know you were there and that's how you got missed out.'

'All right,' said Polly, 'but what about you? You weren't in a cupboard, were you? You slept in your room, didn't you? So why weren't you taken, along with Del and those other two?'

Measle didn't have an answer for that—at least, not one he could offer Polly. He couldn't possibly tell her his suspicions that he was being singled out for some sort of specially nasty fate at the hands of an especially nasty wrathmonk! Polly would never have heard of wrathmonks and would undoubtedly think he was mad. In the silence that followed, Measle thought back to the time he'd first met Toby Jugg.

That fast drive up the motorway in the dark—stopping at that café—Toby being so nice, getting him a fizzy drink—

'I think I know how it was done,' he said, suddenly.

'How *what* was done?'

'How whoever it was got everybody out of here without us waking up. And—and without *them* waking up, either.'

Polly's eyes were wide. 'You mean,' she whispered, 'you think they were taken away when they were still *asleep*?'

'Yes,' said Measle, firmly. 'Otherwise, they probably wouldn't have gone. I think—I think we were all drugged last night.'

'*What?*' squealed Polly, her mouth wide open in bewilderment.

Measle nodded. 'The chocolate.'

'What chocolate?'

'Didn't you have a bar of chocolate left on your pillow?'

'No. Did you?'

'Yes. We all did. Well, me and my friends had them in *our* room, anyway. I just assumed everybody got them.'

Polly frowned. There was a faraway look in her eyes, as if she was trying to remember something. Then her face cleared.

'So, that's what they were sniggering about!' she said.

'Who?'

'Cheryl and Michelle! When I got to our room, they were already there—and they were both chewing something! They looked at me and then they looked at each other and then they sniggered! They must have taken mine and shared it between them!'

'That's it!' Measle exclaimed, excitedly. 'You didn't eat the chocolate—but everybody else did!'

'Er . . . look, Measle, don't you think that's all a bit far-fetched?'

'No,' said Measle, firmly. 'I don't. And I'll tell you why. I've been drugged once before—'

'You *have*?' said Polly, sounding rather impressed for once.

'Yes, I have. And, when I woke up this morning, I had exactly the same feeling that I had when it was done to me before. I was all bleary and groggy and my eyes wouldn't focus—'

'And Cheryl's and Michelle's snoring!' yelped Polly. 'They *never* snored before! But last night, they were like—like—'

'Like walruses?' said Measle.

'*Absolutely* like walruses!'

'So—you think it's possible, then?'

Polly looked at him with serious eyes. 'I suppose I do, Measle,' she said, quietly. 'But—but why? What for? And why were *you* left? And what do we do now?'

Measle decided to avoid the first three questions and just deal with the last one. 'We could search outside,' he said. 'We could try and find some clues out there.'

'Come on then,' said Polly, her face brightening at the thought of some sort of action.

They left the dining room and walked across the hall to the front door. Polly went to a row of hooks that were screwed to the wall behind the door and selected a long woollen scarf. She wound it round her neck and said, 'Right. Ready when you are.'

Measle opened the front door.

Before they could take a step out onto the gravel drive, there was a sudden, blinding flash in the sky and, two seconds later, the loudest clap of thunder either he or Polly had ever heard. It seemed to come from directly overhead. Measle and Polly looked up and saw that a huge, rolling black cloud—stretching across most of the sky—was racing towards them. Hanging underneath the cloud was a veil of torrential rain and they could see the fat drops spattering down on the ground a hundred metres away.

The cloud was moving very fast and, a moment later, the first drops smacked down on their upturned faces.

'Come on,' said Measle and, together, they stepped back into the shelter of the house and closed the heavy front door with a bang. The pattering sound of the rain outside turned into a thunderous roar as the storm rolled overhead and there were several more flashes of lightning, followed almost instantly by the deafening crashing of thunder.

'I don't think we're going anywhere,' said Polly, morosely. 'Not until that's over, at least.'

'Maybe it won't last long,' said Measle.

They were down the hall, at the door to the living room, when there was a sudden, thunderous *crash!* from behind them.

Measle and Polly whirled round.

The front door was wide open.

A flash of lightning lit up the world outside—

Silhouetted in the open doorway was a hulking figure—

On either side of the dark shape stood two smaller ones.

With trembling fingers, Measle felt for the switch on the wall, the one by the living room door. It was a two-way switch, linked to one by the front door, and it turned on and off the big chandelier that hung from the hall ceiling.

Measle's fingers found the switch.

He flicked it down, and yellow light flooded the hallway.

'Ah—hello there, Measle, old son!'

The Return of the Enemy

The fact that Measle wasn't all that surprised to see Toby Jugg didn't decrease even a little bit the sudden, icy feeling of terror that flooded his body.

Toby sauntered into the hall. He carried an umbrella. Once inside, he closed it with a snap and then shook it hard, spattering drops of water on the stone floor. The two figures that had stood in silhouette on either side of Toby stepped into the light and Measle recognized them immediately.

Mr Needle and Mr Bland.

Unlike Toby, the two officials from the Wizards' Guild were soaking wet and trembling with cold. They seemed to be very small next to Toby, but then Measle saw that they were both hunched over, their knees bent, their heads sunk down on their breasts—almost as if they were *trying* to make themselves look smaller. Their faces were filled with fear and they stared up at Toby with a look that was partly terror and partly a strange sort of adoration.

Toby himself looked bigger and broader than Measle remembered him. His yellow eyes glittered in the light of the chandelier. His hair, which had been peppered with grey, was now pure white and hung in a great mane over his shoulders. He was dressed in a fine, dark-blue suit that fitted him like a glove and his red silk tie was held down by what looked to Measle like a very expensive diamond pin.

He grinned at Measle, exposing his two sets of pointed teeth. He was about to say something when he suddenly realized that Measle wasn't alone.

'Who is that, lurking behind you, Measle? Come out of the shadows, whoever you are!'

Polly stepped out from behind Measle, a friendly smile on her face. As far as she was concerned, here was an adult—well, *three* adults, actually— and they seemed to know Measle, and that meant that everything was going to be all right now.

Then Polly noticed Toby's glowing yellow eyes, and his pointed teeth, and the way he was grinning at Measle like a hungry wolf. She stopped walking forward and, instead, moved close to Measle's side, looking at Toby with apprehension.

Toby stared back, one eyebrow raised. Then he glanced down at Mr Needle and Mr Bland. Grasping their necks in his two massive hands, he curled his lip contemptuously and hissed, 'You *missed* one! You *imbeciles*!'

Mr Needle and Mr Bland shrank and trembled even harder than before. Mr Needle whispered, 'Forgive us, Master! We took every child from every room!'

'Indeed we did, Master!' bleated Mr Bland. 'That one must have been hiding somewhere!'

'Did you not count them?' snarled Toby, tightening his grip. Mr Bland winced with pain and Mr Needle screwed his eyes tight shut.

'C-c-count them, Master?'

'Yesss, cretins! *Count* them! In order to make sure you had got them all! Well—did you?'

Both men moaned and slowly swung their heads from side to side—and Toby lifted each one by the scruff of his neck and shook him like a dog.

'Fools! Morons! I give you a sssimple little task and you mess it up! I should tear you both limb from limb!'

Mr Needle and Mr Bland squealed like a pair of terrified pigs. Toby gave them one last violent shake and then dropped them, as if they were nothing more than two plastic bags of rubbish. The pair fell to the floor and cowered there, their heads buried in their arms. Toby turned his gaze onto Measle and Polly.

'Ssso, Measle—you've found a little friend, have you? Young Polly Williams, as I live and breathe!'

'How—how do you know my name?' said Polly, her voice trembling a little with uncertainty.

'My dear child,' said Toby pleasantly, 'we've all met before. Many times. On a daily basis, in fact.'

'I—I don't remember,' said Polly. 'Sorry.'

Measle was thinking furiously, his mind desperately searching for some way out of this danger. And then his thoughts latched on to Toby's last remark.

'*We've all met before ...*'

What on earth could he mean by that?

'*Many times ...*'

Whom had they met many times?

'*On a daily basis ...*'

Click, click, click, went Measle's agile brain.

Then a light bulb seemed to pop up in Measle's head and he understood.

'You were Mr Lockey,' he said slowly. Then he pointed at the cowering, shivering bodies of Mr Needle and Mr Bland. 'And those two—those two were Miss Agatha and Miss Annie, weren't they?'

'Oh, well *done*, Measle!' boomed Toby, his mouth splitting into a grin that was even wider than before. 'I always knew you were clever!'

Polly grabbed Measle's arm and blurted out, 'I don't understand. What are you two talking about? Who is this, Measle?'

'This is Toby Jugg, Polly,' said Measle. 'And you really—*really*—don't want to know him.'

'But—but what do you mean he was Mr Lockey?'

Measle shook his head grimly. 'You wouldn't believe it, Polly,' he muttered. 'Nobody would.'

'Try me!' said Polly, in a commanding voice.

'Yess, old ssson,' murmured Toby, grinning unpleasantly at Measle's predicament. 'Why don't you explain everything to Polly, eh?'

'Because it'll sound completely mad, that's why,' said Measle, glaring angrily at Toby. 'Wizards and warlocks and wrathmonks and magic and everything! She'll just think I'm a loony!'

Toby thought about this for a moment. Then he said, 'Perhaps a little demonssstration will help usss all out—yesss, I think sso. Come here, Polly. Come and ssstand next to me.'

Polly found herself moving forward without really wanting to. There was something about this strange man's voice that simply compelled the listener to obey. Four steps brought her to Toby's side.

Behind them, the torrential rain poured down, making a curtain of water in the rectangle of the open front door. Flashes of lightning lit up the sky and there was a constant muttering of thunder. Toby smiled pleasantly down at Polly. He took her arm and then turned—himself and her—to face the open doorway.

'Now then, Polly,' said Toby, lifting his voice a little against the roar of the downpour outside. 'Watch thisss.'

Toby took a deep breath. Then, blowing out slowly, he puffed the breath out through the open door.

Instantly, the fat raindrops transformed into big, fluffy snowflakes. The flakes drifted down, falling so thickly that, within a few seconds, a small snowdrift started to pile up on the threshold.

Polly stood rooted to the spot, her mouth open and her eyes wide. She could just about make out, through the curtain of snowflakes, that, a few yards further out, the heavy rain continued to cascade down, spattering the drive beyond—so Polly understood immediately that, whatever was happening, it certainly wasn't a *natural* event. She also understood that—whatever was happening— it was being *made* to happen by this weird and frightening man at her side.

'He's a wrathmonk, Polly,' said Measle.

Polly turned her head from the fascinating spectacle and stared uncomprehendingly at Measle.

'A *what?*'

Toby stopped blowing. 'A *wrathmonk*,' he said, gleefully. The moment he spoke, the snow turned back into slashing rain and the little pile of snowflakes on the threshold dissolved almost instantly into icy slush.

'But how—how did he do that?' gasped Polly, twisting her head round and staring at the rain cascading once again in the doorway.

'You're not going to believe it, Polly,' said Measle, 'but he's a sort of wizard and that was magic.'

'Sssort of a wizard? *Sssort* of a wizard?' snarled Toby, irritably. 'I am not a *sssort* of a wizard, boy! I am a wrathmonk—possibly the greatessst wrathmonk that has ever lived! And if, dear Polly, you want to sssee a further demonsssstration, I shall be more than happy to provide one! Now, why don't we go and make oursssselves comfortable, while these two ssservants of mine make usss sssomething to eat! Needle—Bland—food! And make it sssnappy!'

Mr Needle and Mr Bland rose hurriedly to their feet and scuttled away towards the kitchen, looking for all the world like a pair of panic-stricken black beetles. Toby extended both his arms and ushered Measle and Polly in the direction of the lodge's living room. Once inside, Toby closed the door and locked it, pocketing the key. Then he went and stood close to the fireplace. There were some logs in the grate, with a bundle of screwed-up newspaper underneath.

'*Calor callay carbonificus!*' he said, extending a finger and pointing down at the hearth. A blue-white spark zapped from the end of his finger and flashed into the newspaper. The paper burst into flames and, a minute later, there was a roaring fire in the grate.

Polly hadn't said a word. Now she sat down, quite calmly, in one of the big armchairs and folded her hands in her lap. Both Measle and Toby watched her, waiting for her reaction. When it came, it surprised them both.

'Is it because of you that there's that huge storm outside?'

Toby chuckled.

'Well, well. What an intelligent young lady you are, Polly. Yesss indeed, it's all because of me! That cloud follows me everywhere. All we wrathmonks are burdened by them. Sssince I am probably the mossst powerful wrathmonk ever to live, it is a great deal larger than mossst—but it's usually not quite thisss big! The explanation for its extraordinary sssize is sssimple. It has been artificially sssuppressed for a very long time. While I was being Mr Lockey, I was forced to use all my magic to cancel the thing—Measle would have been quick to ssspot that I was not who I pretended to be if I'd had a large black cloud permanently overhead!'

'So that's why it was always sunny when you were around,' said Measle quietly.

'Exactly, old ssson!' boomed Toby. 'But now I've let it go—and I mussst sssay, it impresses even me! Look at it out there! A tremendous ssstorm, isn't it? I sssuppose it has been getting bigger and bigger, accumulating energy, all the time I was keeping it at bay. I wonder how long it will lassst at this level, before returning to a more normal dimension?'

'It must have been very difficult,' said Measle, trying to inject a little admiration into his voice. *That's what I've got to do right now*, he thought quickly. *I've got to find out as much as possible—and keep him talking!*

'It wasn't *difficult*, Measle, old ssson,' said Toby, dismissively. 'Not for one of my powers! But it did use up a lot of mana. Not a problem, of course—not with the Doompit nearby.'

'Doompit?'

'Yes, Measle, the *Doompit*. Mana—*free* mana—flows out of it like a fountain. As you know, even the most powerful wizards such as me can only perform one major ssspell every twenty-four hours—but when I'm close by a Doompit, I can overcome that irritating limit!'

Whatever this Doompit is, thought Measle, *if it can supply Toby Jugg with limitless amounts of mana, it's the worst news in the world.* But he was careful to keep his expression neutral, without a trace of fear on his face. This was something Measle had learned in his dealings with wrathmonks—if you reacted to them in a way they didn't expect, it could sometimes confuse them—and a confused wrathmonk is less threatening than one that is sure of itself. Unfortunately, Toby didn't look in the least confused by Measle's apparent calmness. He gazed at Measle and Polly with a small smile hovering round the corners of his mouth.

'Ssso—any more quessstions, before we proceed?' he said, cheerfully.

'Proceed with what?' said Measle.

'Proceed with the expedition you are going to make,' said Toby.

'I want to go home,' announced Polly, firmly. Toby and Measle stared at her—Measle with the look of somebody who rather hoped he hadn't heard what he had, and Toby with a look of amused malice. Polly glared back at both of them and said, 'I don't care who you are, Mr Jugg—nor *what* you are—but you can't keep us here! You'll be in terrible trouble if you do! My father's a policeman and he'll—'

Toby interrupted her. 'Oh, no! A *policeman?*' he whispered, his voice suddenly trembling with terror. Measle shot him a surprised glance and saw immediately that Toby's terror was fake.

'Y-yes, he is,' said Polly, a little uncertainly. 'Quite a high-up one, too. He'll arrest you and you'll spend a very long time in prison, unless you let us go right away. And I mean *all* of us—where have you put the rest of the class?'

Toby threw back his head, his long white hair whipping about his face. He laughed and said, 'Ahah! That'sss for me to know—and you to find out!'

There was a timid knocking at the door and Toby went over, took the key from his pocket and unlocked it. He ushered in Mr Needle and Mr Bland. With eyes lowered fearfully, the two men scurried in. Mr Needle carried a large steaming bowl and Mr Bland had an armful of plates and cutlery. They set the dishes down on a table and, when they were done, Toby said, 'Come along, Polly and Measle—you must be hungry. Eat!'

Reluctantly, and moving slowly, Measle and Polly sat down at the table. It was the same old stew, just as tasteless as before.

'It's the only dish they ssseem to know how to make,' said Toby. 'Pathetic, aren't they?'

Neither Measle nor Polly were hungry, so they sat there, the food in front of them untouched. Toby ate a few mouthfuls, with obvious distaste. When he was finished, he leaned across the table, picked up the pot and dumped it on the floor next to his chair. Then he took up a couple of empty bowls and put them on the floor too. With a small gesture, he invited Mr Needle and Mr Bland to eat. The two men scrambled on all fours to the pot and, using their hands, scooped stew into their bowls. Then, like a pair of ravenous hyenas, they plunged their faces into their bowls and gobbled the food as fast as they could.

'What—what happens now?' said Measle, trying hard to keep the nervous tremor out of his voice.

Toby thought for a moment and then said, 'I shall lock you away until tomorrow—and then we shall have sssome fun! Needle! Bland! Get up, you lazy dogs and we'll take Master Ssstubbs and Miss Williams to their new quarters!'

Mr Needle and Mr Bland scrambled to their feet. Mr Needle took Polly's arm and Mr Bland took Measle's. Then they marched them both to the door. Toby sauntered after them.

'Where are we going?' said Measle.

Toby pointed a finger straight down at the floor.

'Down there, old ssson,' he said. 'Deep down there.'

Mr Needle and Mr Bland dragged Measle and Polly down the hall in the direction of the kitchen area. Toby followed. Just before they got to the kitchen door, the two men stopped dead. There didn't seem to be any reason for their halting—the corridor was quite empty here, apart from a dusty old tapestry that hung from ceiling to floor. The woven picture showed a group of hunters, with a pack of hounds, streaming across the countryside in pursuit of a distant fox.

Mr Needle pulled the tapestry to one side, revealing a stout wooden door. Polly and Measle glanced at each other and Polly raised her eyebrows, as if to say, *How come we never found this?*

Mr Bland took a bunch of keys from his pocket. He selected the biggest—a rusty iron thing with an ornate handle—and stuck it into the keyhole. He turned it. There was a squeal from the ancient lock, then the door swung open.

There were stone steps leading downwards, in a spiral. Mr Needle and Mr Bland pushed Polly and Measle ahead of them and they all tramped down the winding staircase, their shoes grating on the old stones. There were dim light bulbs set at regular intervals in rusty steel cages in the ceiling, and these gave just enough light so that they could see where they were going.

Where they were going, Measle reckoned, was just as Toby had said—deep underground. The spiral stairs wound round at least nine times before they reached the bottom. There was a small stone-lined area here, with a single door set in the far wall. Mr Bland selected a key from the bunch in his hand and opened the door. Then, without a word, Polly and Measle were pushed into the room beyond.

A single, weak bulb threw a little light into the circular space and it showed Measle what was in there: a narrow iron bed against the wall, with some dirty-looking blankets thrown over it.

Toby's booming laugh came from the open doorway.

'Not quite what you're used to, I sssuppose! But perhaps young Polly has ssseen sssomething like thisss before—her father being a policeman! A high-up policeman, no less, who arrests poor, unfortunate innocents and locks them up in facilities quite sssimilar to thisss one, I daresssay!'

'What's this all about?' said Measle. 'Why are you doing this?'

'Oh, Measle, old ssson,' said Toby, shaking his head with mock sorrow. 'Why am I doing thisss? Well, jussst think of all the terrible things *you've* done! Not jussst to me but to ssso many fine, upsssstanding wrathmonks and warlocks—and let's not forget that poor old Dragodon, too, nor his poor old dragon, either! Why, you've been an unending sssource of trouble, haven't you? And didn't I, and sssome of my friends, try to remedy that sssituation? And didn't you thwart usss at every turn? And is it not my turn to thwart *you*? And is it not *your* turn to sssuffer?'

'Well ... er ... what have you got in mind?'

Toby grinned and shook his head.

'No, no, Measle—not yet! I want this amusement to last a long time! You will find out—but not yet. Goodnight, my dears! Sssleep well, won't you!'

Toby motioned to Mr Needle and Mr Bland to close the door. Mr Needle scurried forward and started to swing the door shut, but just before it thudded home in its frame, Toby called out, 'Wait! Jussst one moment! Open it again, Needle!'

The door swung open and Toby strolled into the cell. He planted himself in front of Measle and held out his hand.

'I almossst forgot,' he murmured, amiably. 'Give them to me, old ssson,'

'G-give you what?'

'You know what, Measle.'

Measle thought he knew—but he wasn't going to give them up so easily.

'No, Toby—I don't know. Give you *what*?'

Toby sighed. 'That bag of sssweets you always carry in your pocket, Measle. The ones that have proved ssso useful to you in the past. I know you have them—kindly give them to me, before I have to resort to violence.'

Slowly, miserably, Measle reached down into his pocket, his fingertips touching the lumpy plastic bag of jelly beans. He could feel that the bag was open at the top and, in that moment, he had one of his ideas. Making as little movement as possible, he curled the ends of his fingers into a small scoop, and dipped them into the open bag. He managed to shovel a few jelly beans into his open palm. Then, in one fluid movement, he quickly pulled his fingers out of the bag and dropped the small number of beans from his palm into the bottom of his pocket.

'Come along, Measle!' barked Toby. 'Hurry up with it!'

Measle pulled the plastic bag out of his pocket and, with a defeated scowl on his face, he passed it to Toby.

'Excellent!' said Toby, holding the bag in front of his nose and staring contentedly at the multi-coloured contents. 'That's one less trick you'll be able to do!' He glanced at Polly and said, 'Remarkable things, these sssweets, Polly. Get the right one, and you turn invisible! Not for long—perhaps thirty ssseconds—but our young friend here has found them absolute life sssavers in the past! Haven't you, old ssson?'

Measle didn't reply. Instead, he simply gazed, with no expression at all, into Toby's piercing eyes. Toby smiled unpleasantly. Then he tipped the plastic bag upside down and poured the jelly beans into his open palm.

'Minor magic,' he sneered. 'Very minor magic indeed!'

Toby opened his mouth, bent his head, and wrapped his lips around the heap of jelly beans.

Then he made a slurping noise, raised his head—and his hand was empty. Measle watched as Toby chewed a few times, a thoughtful expression on his face. Then, in one convulsive movement of his throat, he swallowed.

'Why you human kids like those things is beyond me,' he said. 'I now feel ssslightly sssick. But never mind. At leassst we won't be bothered with any of that disappearing nonsssense any more.'

Casually, he held out the empty plastic bag to Measle, as if expecting him to get rid of the rubbish. Measle took it without a word and stuffed it back into his pocket.

'Now,' said Toby, 'both Needle and Bland will be ssstationed outside the door—all night. They will remain awake—neither needs any sssleep. And do try to get sssome rest. You will need all your ssstrength for what lies ahead!'

'What, Toby?' said Measle. 'What lies ahead?'

'Many things, old ssson. Many wonders. And all of them *extremely* dangerousss!'

Toby nodded at Mr Needle and the wet and frightened man swung the door shut with a solid thump. There was the sound of a key turning in a lock.

Silence.

And then Polly said, 'All right, Measle. You'd better tell me all about it.'

A Revelation

One look at Polly's determined face convinced Measle that now was the moment to tell her everything. Polly had seen more magic in the last few minutes than most people saw in their entire lifetimes—and that alone would make the whole bizarre story he was about to tell her that much more believable.

So Measle told her all about Basil Tramplebone and the train set; he told her the story of the Dragodon, his dragon Arcturion, and his squad of murderous wrathmonks; he told her about how his father was the President of the Wizards' Guild and he explained about his mother, the Manafount. He told her about how he'd met Toby Jugg—and how he'd thought at first that he was his friend and how later, at Caltrop Castle, he'd discovered that he wasn't. Lastly, he related the story of the ghastly Slitherghoul and its attack on Merlin Manor—and Polly screwed up her face in disgust at his description of the huge, slimy horror.

When Measle finished, there was a long silence. He looked at Polly, who was sitting on the narrow bed, with her back resting against the stone wall. She was staring at nothing in particular and there was no expression of any sort on her face.

Measle said, 'You don't believe a word of it, do you?'

Polly glanced at Measle.

'Yes, I do,' she said, very quietly.

Then, without warning, the door to the cell crashed open. Toby Jugg loomed large in the opening.

'Sssplendid, Measle!' he roared, cheerfully. 'You told all those wicked lies mossst convincingly!'

'Lies?' said Polly, her eyes widening.

'Well, the bits about how terrible wrathmonks are, Polly! All lies! We are the mossst *perfect* of all creatures! It's all the *other* wretched creatures who are evil! Humans and wizards and warlocks— *they're* the ones that cause all the trouble! We wrathmonks merely want to make the world a finer place, that's all!'

'Oh. But—but apart from *that*, is it all true?' said Polly.

'Oh yesss, my dear! Quite true! And I have ssso

enjoyed lissstening to it all. Measle is an excellent ssstory-teller!' Toby stepped into the cell and Measle saw that Mr Needle and Mr Bland were close behind him.

Toby extended a hand towards Polly. 'Come along, Polly,' he said. 'I have other plans for you.'

Polly pressed herself harder against the wall, shrinking away from Toby's outstretched hand.

'Where are you taking me?' she whispered.

'Why, to join the ressst of your classmates, of courssse!' boomed Toby. 'Surely you didn't think that you would be left out? No, no, my dear child! I only left you in Measle's care while I made sssome suitable preparations for you. And now those preparations are quite ready—ssso come along!'

Polly edged herself to the furthest end of the bed and shook her head.

'I want to stay here.'

Toby frowned with irritation. 'Well, you can't,' he growled, taking another step into the cell.

There was a moment when nobody moved and not a word was said. Then Polly did something utterly unexpected.

She pointed her finger at Toby and said, loudly, '*Pugilis Crestor Sejetto!*'

A crimson spark spat from the end of her finger and zipped across the room, directly towards Toby's nose. As it sped across the small space, it changed—in the blink of an eye—from a tiny red spark into a large, bright red, leather boxing glove.

Toby was so surprised, he didn't have time to duck. The boxing glove, accelerating all the way, whistled across the room and didn't stop until it hit him square in the face. There was an audible *thump!* as it landed on Toby's nose—and a gasp of pain as Toby was knocked backwards on his heels. The moment the boxing glove made contact, it disappeared in a puff of scarlet smoke. Toby staggered for a second, both his hands pressed to his nose. Then he lost his balance and fell heavily onto the stone floor.

Mr Needle and Mr Bland hurried forward to their master's side. They bent over him solicitously, but Toby waved them away. He was gazing at Polly with astonishment. Slowly he got to his feet. He took his hands away from his nose and Measle saw that a small trickle of blood was seeping from each

nostril. He watched as Toby's look of astonishment was replaced with one of anger and pain.

'Well, well,' said Toby slowly. He took the silk handkerchief from his pocket and dabbed at his bleeding nose. 'Well, well,' he repeated, more quietly this time.

Polly stared back at Toby, a look of defiance—mixed with fear—on her pretty face.

'Ssso—young Polly is a wizard, is she?' continued Toby. 'That comes as sssomething of a sssurprise! To me at leassst!' He swung his yellow eyes to Measle and said, 'How about you, Measle? Were you aware of our young friend's magical abilities?'

Measle didn't answer. He was so astonished, all he could do was stand and stare at Polly, his mouth gaping.

'Yesss, well,' murmured Toby. 'From that vacant look on your face, Measle, old ssson, I gather it comes as much of a sssurprise to you at it does to me!'

Toby turned back to Polly and said, 'That, I imagine, is all you have to offer me? At leassst for twenty-four hours—unless, of course, you're another Mallockee? Sssomething I would find hard to believe, sssince Mallockees are hardly thick on the ground these days!'

'I don't know what a Mallockee is,' muttered Polly, grimly. 'I don't even know what *I* am.'

Toby laughed—a quick bark of a laugh, like a sea lion. 'What you are, my dear,' he said, 'is sssomething

I shall have to invesstigate. But not in here! Ssso, if you have no more violence to offer me, please oblige me by accompanying me immediately!'

Polly shook her head again and stayed huddled at the far end of the bed. Toby clucked his tongue and gestured to Mr Needle and Mr Bland. The two men marched into the cell, grabbed Polly by her arms and yanked her to her feet. Then they dragged her out of the cell. Measle stepped forward, his fists bunched—and Toby laughed again and said, 'Now, now, Measle! No fisssticuffs, I beg of you! I've had quite enough of that for one night!'

'Where are you taking her?' said Measle, glaring furiously at Toby.

'Don't worry, she won't be harmed. I jussst want to talk to her, that's all.'

'What for?' said Measle.

'What for? Why, to find out all about her, Measle! A little wizard in our midst! Wouldn't you like to know too?'

'If you hurt her—'

'I won't hurt her,' said Toby. 'I don't *need* to hurt her. I can find out anything I want, from anybody, at any time. It's quite a sssimple spell, the Veritas Enchantment. And quite harmless to the one being enchanted. And then, tomorrow, we'll all depart on our little expedition. I, of coursse, will only be with you in an *observational* sort of way.'

'Where are we going?'

'Well, among other adventures, you will, of course, be ssseeking your lossst classmates. Polly will be among them. And, even if you don't care about the ressst of them, I'm sure you will exert every effort to find *her*, eh?'

'Yes—but where—'

'Measle, if I tell you that, then there's no expedition of *discovery*, is there? "*They're all in the secret cave, Measle!*" Where's the fun in that? No, no—it'll be up to you to ssseek them out, and I shall be watching with enormousss enjoyment as you fail to find them! I shall alssso enjoy the interesssting way you will manage to get yoursssself killed! And killed you most probably will be, Measle!'

Toby started to pull the door closed. Then he paused, a thoughtful look on his face.

'I'll tell you *sssomething* about where they are, Measle, because it won't mean anything to you, and therefore won't be of any help. But I can't sssee the harm in giving you a name. A name to sssleep on. *Dystopia*. That's where they are. They're all in *Dystopia*. Goodnight!'

The door swung again and then shut with a bang. There was the sound of a key in a lock.

Dystopia. The name meant nothing to Measle. Toby was right—it was no help at all.

Miserably, Measle went and sat on the edge of the iron bed. The rusty springs creaked under his weight. Apart from that small noise, and the faint sound of his own breathing, there was a heavy silence.

Measle could feel the despair beginning to take control of his mind and, quickly, he shook it off. There had been many times in the past when he'd felt this way and he knew, from experience, that it was all too easy to let the feeling of helplessness overwhelm all the other emotions, until quite soon one was unable to do anything but sit there, staring hopelessly at the floor. Staring hopelessly at the floor was something Measle never did—not when there was something useful he could be doing.

He stared round the walls and ceiling of the cell, examining every inch of the stonework for any signs of devices like video cameras or microphones. There didn't appear to be anything of the sort but Measle wasn't finished yet. He bent down and peered under the bed. There was nothing there either—other than a pair of sturdy iron brackets, screwed to the stonework, that were attached to the pair of bed legs that were closest to the wall.

That's a bit odd, thought Measle. *If you want to stop a piece of furniture from moving, you usually bolt the legs to the floor, not the wall . . .*

There didn't appear to be anything in the cell that could eavesdrop on him or watch him, so Measle felt safe enough to stuff his hand in his pocket and pull out the few jelly beans he'd managed to extract from the bag.

There were so few! And—and only *two* yellow beans among them!

Measle lay down on the narrow bed and stared up at the weak light bulb and started to think. There was one thought that dominated—

Polly. Polly is a wizard. But she doesn't seem to understand anything much about it—and yet, she knows at least one spell! A pretty peculiar spell, too. I wonder how many others she knows—let's hope they're more effective than a red boxing glove.

And then exhaustion swept over Measle and, quite without meaning to, he fell fast asleep.

THE HOLE

It was a sound that woke Measle.

A strange, grating sound, like large flat stones being dragged across one another.

Measle's eyes flew open. Above him, the bare light bulb still glimmered dimly. The grating sounds were getting louder and louder—and they seemed to be coming from somewhere next to his bed.

Cautiously, Measle leaned sideways and looked down at the stone floor.

In the dead centre of the floor, there was a small, dark, round hole. As Measle watched, it grew bigger. At first sight, it looked a little like a stain of spilled ink that was seeping steadily over a dirty cloth. But, as Measle's eyes grew more accustomed to the dim light in the cell, he saw that it was indeed a hole—and, somehow, the hole was steadily enlarging. He peered closer and saw that the stones of the floor were formed in a series of overlapping triangular plates—and these plates were moving wider and wider apart.

The edges were getting dangerously close to the legs of Measle's bed. Measle tried to peer down into the hole, hoping to see that the bottom was not too far away—but there was an inky blackness that seemed to extend forever. The walls of the hole were very smooth. They looked like polished rock.

The grating was louder now, as the movement of the triangular stone plates brought the edge of the hole closer and closer. Measle could do nothing but huddle fearfully on the bed, his back pressed hard against the cold stone wall.

Then the hole reached the outer legs of the bed and Measle felt the bed give a little lurch as the floor disappeared beneath it. But the bed didn't slide into the yawning chasm—it was held fast by the brackets that screwed its other two legs tightly to the wall and Measle, through his fear, understood why the bed had been fastened the way it was.

The grating sound continued for a few more seconds and then stopped—because there was no more floor to remove. Measle and the iron bed hung, suspended, over a huge, circular pit, which appeared to be bottomless. Very carefully, Measle eased his back away from the comforting solidity of the stone wall. Holding tightly to the frame of the bed, he lay down on his stomach and peered over the edge.

A black nothingness.

The bed creaked ominously and Measle thought he felt a tiny shifting movement of the frame—*downwards*! He thought of the screws that held the bed to the wall—*they hadn't looked all that strong* . . .

Trembling with fear, Measle slowly pulled himself back from the edge and pressed his whole body as close to the wall as he could.

There was a sound from outside. Measle turned his head and watched as the door to the cell swung open. The burly figure of Toby Jugg filled the gap.

'Hello, Measle, old ssson! Sssleep well, did you?'

Measle didn't answer. What was the point of even *trying* to be polite—particularly towards a wrathmonk!

Toby glanced down at the enormous hole that yawned at his feet.

'Jolly interesssting, don't you think?' he said, lightly. 'That's the Doompit. I wonder how deep it is?' Toby reached into his pocket and took out a coin. Then, holding tightly to the door frame, he leaned out over the hole, stretched out his arm as far as he could—then let the coin drop into the abyss.

It fell silently. Measle strained his ears to hear it fall against something—but he listened in vain.

'Hmm,' said Toby. 'Mussst be *extremely* deep, mussstn't it? Let's try again—with sssomething a bit bigger!'

Toby stepped to one side, reached behind him—and pulled Polly into the open door frame. Polly's eyes were rimmed with red and she looked very tired and frightened. When she saw the great black hole yawning at her feet, she gasped and tried to step back away from it, but Toby's grip on her arm was like steel.

'Shall we drop our little wizard friend down into the Doompit, Measle?' said Toby, grinning wolfishly.

Measle didn't reply. Toby was going to do what he wanted to do and nothing Measle could say was going to stop him.

'We've had a very nice chat, young Polly and I,' said Toby. 'It ssseems she's not much of a wizard at all. She found an old book that had belonged to her great-grandmother and learned a few sssimple ssspells from it. The sssurprise is, of courssse, that Polly didn't know of her abilities, until she tried them out. Her great-grandmother had died long ago and her parents hadn't told her anything about the old lady—ssso it came as sssomething of a shock to Polly when she managed to make all the clocks in the house run backwards! Luckily for all of usss, the boxing glove ssspell was the only attack enchantment she managed to learn! All the ressst are fairly pointless ssspells—like turning a lemon into an orange, and rubbish like that. Ssso, really, we have no further use for her, do we?'

Toby's smile broadened. Then, without any warning at all, he simply pushed Polly over the edge of the hole and released his grip on her arm.

Polly gave out one long, wailing scream and then she plummeted down into the darkness.

For a moment, Measle was too shocked to say, or do, anything. He stared, wide-eyed, at Toby, who had cocked his head to one side and put a hand behind his ear. Seconds ticked by. Then Toby straightened his head, took his hand away from his ear and said, 'Not a bump, nor a thump—not a sssound, in fact! It really must go on for ever, thisss Doompit!'

'You—you—you killed her!' blurted out Measle.

Toby frowned. 'What?' he said, in a puzzled voice.

'You've murdered her!' yelled Measle, shaking with the shock of it all.

Toby shook his head and grinned. 'No, I haven't, old ssson. Well, not *directly*. Sssomething *else* might harm her—but I haven't killed her at all.'

'But—when she hits the bottom—'

'Ah—but there *is* no bottom to a Doompit, you sssee.'

Measle gaped at Toby. What he'd just said made no sense.

'There *has* to be a bottom!'

Toby nodded thoughtfully. 'Well, yesss—if we were talking about a sssimple hole, I would agree with you, Measle. But a Doompit *isn't* a sssimple hole, you sssee. In fact, it isn't really a hole at all.'

'What is it, then?'

'It's a portal.'

'A portal? What's a portal?'

'An opening. A gateway. A sssort of *door*, if you like.'

'A *door*? Where to?'

'Why—to Dystopia, of courssse.'

That word again. Dystopia.

'I know what you're going to ask me, old ssson,' said Toby, smiling even more widely. 'But, the fact is, I don't entirely know *what* Dystopia is. Nobody does. It's a sssubject generally avoided by the Wizards' Guild, because nobody in that ridiculousss organization wants to appear ignorant. Of courssse, the *reality* of Dystopia is known and has been known sssince the first Doompit was discovered. They've all been lost for centuries, you understand. It took a genius like me to find thisss one! Having discovered it, my subsequent research led me to believe that Dystopia is a kind of alternative world, which exists in a parallel universe to our own. I *do* know that it's extremely magical— surely you can feel the mana pouring out of there?'

Toby was pointing down into the hole and looking at Measle enquiringly. Measle shook his head.

'Ah, yesss,' sighed Toby. 'That's right—you claim to be non-magical, don't you? Well, if that is really true, then let me assure you that thisss is the richest sssource of natural mana I've ever come across. All I have to do is ssstand here, close to the portal, and let the mana flow into me—and what a wonderful sssensssation it is, to be sure!'

Measle thought for a moment. Then he said, 'How did you find it?'

Toby threw back his head and laughed. 'What a good quesstion!' he boomed. 'It deserves a truthful answer. I found it, Measle, because I *looked* for it! There's a good reason why the locations of the Doompits were lossst. The mana that floods out of them has a ssstrange, unnatural tinge to it, which mossst wizards find extremely unpleasant and even a little frightening. Ssso, rather than make use of it, they tended to avoid these places. Humans also dissslike areas where a Doompit exists—and so do animals and birds and, in fact, all living creatures—I daresssay you noticed outssside, that nothing was flying through the air, or trotting or ssslithering across the ground and that there wasn't another house to be ssseen? All indications that a Doompit is nearby.'

'But—somebody had built this house, right on top of it—'

'Ah,' grinned Toby, looking very pleased with himself. 'Well, that was me, you sssee.'

'*You* built this house?'

Toby nodded delightedly. 'Easily done, with all the mana that flows out of there. The whole thing only took about ten minutes! I know it looks old, but the place has only existed for a month!'

'But—what about the other trips—with other schools? They've all been here, haven't they?'

Toby snorted, derisively. 'No, they haven't. There *weren't* any other ssschool trips, Measle. With my magical genius, it wasn't hard to plant false memories in the various ssschool principals involved. They all *believed* that the trips had happened but of course they hadn't. Thisss one is the first. And, I'm afraid, it'll be the last, as well!'

Then Toby did a strange thing. He pointed his right forefinger towards Measle. At first, Measle thought the finger was aimed directly at himself but, on closer examination, he saw that in fact the finger was directed at a point that was rather lower than his head, or even his body. Toby seemed to be aiming his finger at somewhere on the bed or, even, perhaps *beneath* it—

'*Dessspiralicos antempi cobendo!*'

A line of black light sped and lengthened from Toby's finger and disappeared under Measle's bed. There was a faint sound of metal twisting against stone.

'What are you doing?' said Measle, uneasily.

'Not really *doing* anything, old ssson!' said Toby with a throaty chuckle. 'I'm actually *un*doing, if you sssee what I mean?'

'Undoing? Undoing what?'

'Why, the screws that hold that bed to the wall, Measle—ah, there's one out! Only ssseven more to go—'

Measle's heart gave a little lurch. So, to his horror, did the bed beneath him. *I've got to stop him doing that!* he thought, wildly. *But how? I know—I've got to keep him talking! Distract him somehow!*

'Er . . . um . . . have you been down the Doompit yourself, Toby?'

Toby shook his head and went on concentrating on his unscrewing spell. There was a tiny clinking sound as the second screw dropped and clattered against the iron leg of the bed, before falling away into the black abyss.

'Well, how do you know it's—what was that word you said?'

This time, Toby looked up—and he dropped his hand and the black light faded away. 'How do I know it leads to Dystopia?' he said.

'Yes! Dystopia! How do you know that it goes there? It could just be a hole in the ground, like—like an old mine or something!'

'Old mines don't spew mana, Measle.'

'Well, the Dragodon's cave did and that started out as a hole in the ground, didn't it? Maybe that's not Dystopia down there at all. Maybe there's just another dragon down there?'

Toby laughed. '*Just* another dragon?' he said, wonderingly. Then he frowned thoughtfully and said, 'Well, actually, there probably is another dragon down there—or, at least, something quite like a dragon. I would imagine there might be several, in fact. Along with a whole horde of other equally outlandish creatures, I have no doubt. No, no—that's definitely Dystopia down there, as you'll find out in a minute or so.'

Toby switched his gaze from Measle's face back to the spot beneath the iron bed. He pointed his finger once again and muttered, '*Dessspiralicos antempi cobendo!*' and, once again, Measle heard the small grating sound of metal twisting in stone.

'Look, Toby—' he began, in an effort to distract the wrathmonk from his task—but Toby simply held up his free hand and shook his head and went on with the spell.

Clink!
Another screw had gone!
Grind ... grind ... grind ...
Clink!
And another!

And then there was a more solid sort of sound as the entire steel bracket fell away from the wall. It clonked heavily against the bed leg and then dropped away into the darkness.

At exactly the same moment, there was a sudden squeal of protesting metal and Measle's bed—with one of its legs no longer fastened to the wall—sagged sideways, tilting the foot end down at a steep angle. Terrified, Measle clung to the top rail at the head end, like a man clinging to a life-raft in rough seas. He could feel the vibrations of the iron frame, as the entire weight of the bed—with him on top of it—was now straining against the single bracket that held the last leg to the wall.

'Gosh,' drawled Toby. 'That looks jolly danger-ousss! There's a ssstrong possibility that that remaining bracket could break! And what would happen then, I wonder?'

Measle, clinging for dear life to the bed rail, gritted his teeth and said nothing.

Toby smiled sympathetically—and then moved the end of his finger an inch to the left. The long, wavering beam of black light shifted too, moving from a spot beneath the foot of the bed to a place somewhere under the head of the bed.

Grind ... grind ... grind ...

Clink!

Grind ... grind ... grind ...

Clink!

The iron bed frame groaned and tilted to a slightly steeper angle. Now, Measle was lying full length on the bed, both hands gripped round the head rail, his head turned sideways so that he could see what Toby was doing.

Grind ... grind ... grind ...

Clink!

'Jussst one more screw to go, Measle!' called Toby, cheerfully. Then he paused, his forehead furrowed with a sudden thought. 'Now then,' he muttered, 'there was sssomething else, surely? What have I forgotten? Ummmmm ... oh, yes! of course!'

The black beam winked and then disappeared

from the end of Toby's finger and Measle felt a small surge of relief. *Perhaps he's changed his mind!* But the hope didn't last long.

'Watch thisss, Measle!' called Toby. 'It's absolutely *disssgusssting*, so you should quite enjoy it!'

Toby raised his hand. He put the ends of his fingers together and moved them slowly towards his face. Then, with a sudden darting movement, he jabbed all five digits directly into his eye socket! There was a faint, squelching sound—then a pop!

Toby pulled his hand away from his face and Measle saw, to his horror and disgust, that Toby's right eye was held delicately between the ends of his fingers. Toby turned the horrible thing, so that it appeared to be looking directly at Measle.

'That was really rather painful,' said Toby. 'But it had to be done. How could I appreciate all your coming adventures, if I couldn't see what was happening, eh?'

Toby brought the eye close to his mouth and

Measle watched as Toby's lips moved. He seemed to be muttering something to the eye itself, but Measle couldn't hear the words. As far as Measle could see, there was no blood from the empty eye socket—just Toby's eyelid, now closed, over an obviously empty cavity.

So, he used magic to do that! Obvious, really— there was no way a person could do that to himself in any ordinary *way!*

'Right!' said Toby. 'Let's just get to that last screw, shall we?'

Measle thought of all the things he could say. He could beg. He could say he was sorry. He could offer Toby money . . .

He didn't say anything.

'*Dessspiralicos antempi cobendo!*'

Out shot the black beam.

Grind . . . grind . . . grind . . .

Clink!

And, with a scraping sound of metal on stone, the iron bed fell away from the wall and, with Measle clutching tightly to its frame, dropped like a stone into the inky blackness.

Measle threw one despairing glance upwards and saw, above him, the fast-diminishing figure of Toby, leaning out over the hole. Toby had his arm outstretched and, even though the distance between them was increasing with every second, Measle could see that he was clutching something in his hand.

A something that, with a quick flick of his wrist, Toby dropped down the hole. At this distance, it was a mere speck against the dim light of the cell ceiling—but Measle guessed what it was and, a moment later, he was proved right. By actually throwing it downwards, Toby had managed to give the object a little extra speed and, within a few seconds it had caught up with Measle and his falling bed. Then it hung there, just out of reach, and falling at exactly the same speed—

Toby's eye.

DYSTOPia

Even in the clutches of the most paralysing terror he'd ever felt, Measle still found himself able to think.

What if the bed turns upside down? Not that it would make any difference—he and the bed were now falling at such a rate that, whichever way up or down they were, hitting anything at this speed was going to mean certain death.

He was dropping through a black void—and yet, there was really no sensation of falling, and that was weird. There was no whistling, blasting wind; there was no feeling of your insides floating about in places they didn't belong; there were no black walls flashing by—just this silent, soft, inky blackness. But there was no question about it—he and the bed were still unsupported by anything solid beneath them, because every tiny movement of his body caused the iron frame to tilt alarmingly this way or that.

There was nothing Measle could do, other than hang on grimly to the rail and try to keep as still as he possibly could.

But how much longer could this go on?

Only five seconds after he'd had this thought, everything changed.

There was a sudden lightening of the velvety blackness that surrounded him—and Measle dared to risk a careful peek over the side of the bed.

There was a hole below—a round hole filled with light. It was getting bigger quite gradually, which could mean only one of two things: either the hole was vast but still a very long way away— or it was the same size as the hole he had fallen into, which would mean that he and the bed were now *actually* floating gently down towards it at a speed that was unlikely to hurt him very much if he bumped into anything—like the ground, for instance.

The bed was tilting a little, so Measle stopped peering over the edge, pulled himself back onto the centre of the thin mattress and waited.

It grew brighter and brighter, the blackness turning to a smoky grey. Then he was through and into daylight—and, the moment he and the bed dropped slowly past the lower lip of the hole, the bed lurched suddenly and it fell, at normal speed, the last few metres. It landed a moment later. There was a bone-shaking crash and Measle felt the whole bed frame shake and shudder beneath him. The ancient rusty springs twanged, the mattress sagged, and Measle was bounced up off the bed almost high enough to throw him over the side. He landed with a thump back on the mattress, but on his back this time, so he was able to see, through dazed eyes, the black hole hovering above him. Then, a second later, the hole disappeared. This time, there were no stone plates grinding over each other. The hole simply squeezed itself smaller and smaller until it closed shut, with a sound of a slamming door.

But half a second before the hole squeezed itself out of existence, a small round object dropped out of the now tiny circle of blackness. Once clear, it didn't fall to the ground, like Measle and the bed had done. It slowed its fall and then stopped, hovering just high enough over Measle's head to be out of reach.

Toby's eye swivelled and stared down at Measle. Being only an eye, without any face around it, it had no expression at all—and that made Measle feel deeply uneasy. It was like being watched by a remote camera that followed you everywhere.

Then the rain began.

It fell onto Measle's upturned face—a rain so cold that it was almost sleet. It wasn't a downpour but it was a steady, icy drizzle, falling from grey, lowering clouds which didn't seem to be going anywhere.

Feeling a little sick with the shock and fear he'd been through, Measle rolled off the bed and stood on solid ground. He turned in a circle, staring out at the landscape around him. It was a dreary sight. He could only see for about fifty metres—a damp grey curtain of mist all around made sure of that. The ground looked almost featureless. Short, coarse grass, lumpy in places, with an occasional dark rock, shiny with moisture, sticking up through it.

Measle took a couple of unsteady steps away from the bed, then he thought better of that idea and went back and sat down on the edge of the mattress. *There could be anything out there!*

Including Polly . . .

'Polly!'

Measle's voice was swallowed up in the mist.

He peered about him, trying to see through the curtain of grey fog that hung all around him. He strained his ears too, listening intently for any sound other than the soft hiss of the falling rain. There was nothing to see in this dull grey landscape, nothing to disturb this unnerving silence.

Measle shivered. He was getting very cold. If only there was somewhere he could take refuge from the rain! He leaned forward and looked under the bed, but it wasn't much of a shelter and, besides, the grass was soaking wet.

What I need is an umbrella, he thought gloomily.

Then he thought of which umbrella he'd like.

Iggy's umbrella.

All you had to do was whistle.

It probably wouldn't work. But there was no harm in trying.

Measle pursed his lips and whistled the special whistle.

Tweeee—tweetweetwee—tweeeee!

Measle waited for something to happen. The seconds ticked by . . .

Measle heaved a hopeless sigh. Obviously, it was too far for the whistle to work. Or, perhaps, the umbrella couldn't travel from one dimension to another.

And then, off in the distance somewhere, from a spot shrouded from Measle's view by the mist, there came a long, wailing cry. The cry was one of terror at first—then, abruptly, it turned into a faint thump, followed immediately by a squeak of pain. A moment later, there was another distant sound. It was the noise of a dog, barking furiously.

A small dog.

A very familiar-sounding small dog.

Measle stood up and peered into the mist. *It's not possible*, he said to himself. *But then again, perhaps it is! And there's only one way to find out ...*

'Tinker! Tink! Here, boy! Over here! Come on, Tinker!'

The barking stopped. There was a moment when nothing happened. And then, out of the mist galloped a small, fuzzy, black and white object. It tore across the short grass, bounding over the rocks, its ears streaming behind it, its short legs a blur of speed—and, when it reached Measle's feet, it didn't stop there—it took a single bounding leap and hurled itself against Measle's chest.

The impact knocked Measle back and he sat with a thump on the bed. Tinker's tongue was lapping all over Measle's face and his whole small, wiry body was wriggling with happiness. Tinker was soaking wet, which made it difficult for Measle to hold on to him. With one more convulsive wriggle, and one final lap of Measle's face, Tinker slipped free. The moment he was on the ground, he turned and started to bark into the surrounding mist. And then Measle saw something emerging out of the mist—

An umbrella was bumping quite slowly across the ground towards him. Measle could only see the top of the open black canopy—the shaft was hidden from sight beneath it—but the umbrella was dragging itself along on its side, as though there was somebody—or something—holding tightly to the handle. A moment later, this was confirmed when the umbrella bounced over a protruding rock and there was a sharp yelp of pain from directly behind it.

The umbrella rolled and dragged and bounced its way up to Measle's feet. Then it stopped. It was a big umbrella, so whoever was on the other side of the canopy was still out of sight. Measle got up and peered cautiously over the top.

Two furious, red-rimmed, fishy eyes stared back up at him.

'Dis is not *your* humble-ella, Mumps! It's not, it's not, it's *NOT*! You is a very bad persssson, ssstealin' uvver people's fings! Dis is *my* humble-ella! You dad give it to me, it's mine, mine, *MINE*—and you is not goin' to get it off of me, not never! Not no how!'

IGGY'S TRIP

Iggy Niggle was lying on his back, both bony hands
locked fast round the umbrella's handle. He
seemed rather bruised and battered. Like Tinker, he
too was soaking wet. Little puddles of water were
forming under him. His greasy hair was standing
up all over his head, as if he'd been dragged
backwards through several hedges. His eyes were
narrowed with fury and he was breathing hard
through his big beaky nose.

'Hello, Iggy. What are you doing here?'

Iggy's mouth opened and closed several times,
like a goldfish in its bowl. Then he squeaked, 'Wot
is I doin' 'ere? *Wot is I doin' 'ere?* I'll *tell* you wot
I is doin' 'ere! I is ssstoppin' you ssstealin' my
humble-ella, dat is wot I is doin' 'ere!'

'I'm not stealing your umbrella, Iggy—'

'Well den—wot is it doin' lyin' at your feet, Mumps? Eh? Ansssswer me *dat*, if you can!'

It was no use arguing with Iggy. Once he'd got an idea into his head, nothing was able to dislodge it. So Measle started to ask Iggy what had happened to him and how, exactly, he and Tinker had arrived in this desolate place. Iggy wasn't good at telling stories and Measle had to get all the events that had happened out of Iggy one by one, by asking a series of questions—until eventually the whole weird tale came out.

Iggy and Tinker had a strange relationship. Neither liked the other one very much—but they both loved Measle a lot, so they were forced to do their best to get along with each other. If Iggy wanted to be with Measle, then he would have to put up with Tinker being with them as well; and if Tinker wanted to spend his day with Measle, then he'd have to try and not growl and show his teeth every time Iggy came along too.

With Measle away on a school trip, things had changed. Iggy and Tinker were left to their own devices and there was no Measle around to tell them what to do.

At first, Iggy had tried to think up ways of being nasty to Tinker. But then—before he could put any of these unpleasant plans into action—Iggy had got hold of a rather strange idea. It had come to him in a flash: instead of being horrible to Tinker, he was going to try to teach Tinker some tricks. If he could teach Tinker some good tricks while Measle was away, surely when Measle came home, he'd be pretty impressed by what Iggy had managed to do and therefore he'd spend a lot more time with Iggy and a lot less time with Tinker . . .

The first trick Iggy decided to teach Tinker was to make the little dog follow him wherever he went. Iggy had spent long hours saying, in an oily, wheedling voice, 'Come on, den, doggie! Come on, den! Follow nice Iggy, doggie! Follow de nice wraffmonk! Come on, doggie!'

Tinker hadn't co-operated at all. He'd stared stonily up at Iggy and then simply turned his back on him and walked calmly in the opposite direction. This behaviour had made Iggy furious and he'd ruined any chance of Tinker obeying him by screaming at the top of his voice, 'YOU IS A NAUGHTY DOGGY! YOU IS A NAUGHTY, WICKED, *EVIL* DOGGIE! I HATE YOU, YOU 'ORRIBLE DOGGIE, YOU!'

When Iggy's temper tantrum had subsided, he tried to think of another plan to get Tinker to follow him. He racked his tiny brain for an idea and, slowly, a little germ of a thought began to sprout in his feeble mind.

I like jelly beans . . . I like jelly beans lots and lots and lots . . . I will do anyfing to get jelly beans . . . de nasssty doggie likes bacon . . . it likes bacon lots and lots and lots—it will do anyfing to get bacon ...

Iggy hung about the kitchen door for a whole day, waiting for Nanny Flannel to go somewhere else. When she finally did, Iggy sneaked into the kitchen, pulled open the refrigerator door and snatched out a packet of bacon. Then he ran and hid behind the garage.

Iggy unwrapped the bacon and sniffed at it. Then he wrinkled his nose in disgust. Iggy only liked the smell of meat when it was rotten.

Carefully, Iggy pulled the bacon strips apart and then he knelt down and stuffed them into the turn-ups of his trousers. He was delighted to see that the turn-ups were exactly the right size and shape for bacon strips and he felt enormously pleased with himself for thinking the scheme up. 'Ho, yesss—you is ssso clever, Missster Ignatius Niggle!' he muttered to himself, tucking the last stray end of bacon into the turn-up. 'You is a tocal *geniusss*, you is!'

Iggy stood up and wiped his greasy fingers down the front of his jacket. Then he went in search of Tinker.

He found the little dog sitting by the side of the magnificent swimming pool, which he and Measle had built, with the magical help of Lord Octavo, of course. Tinker was gazing at his reflection in the dark water. Tinker was quite vain and spent a lot of time doing this, thinking thoughts like, *Hah! No doubt about it—you are a handsome devil of a dog!*

And now these thoughts of Tinker's were being interrupted by a variety of very interesting smells. The main smell—and one he didn't care for much—was that which belonged to the nasty, damp little person who hung around with the smelly kid all the time and generally got in the way when a smelly kid and a small dog ought, by rights, to be having fun on their own. Beneath the familiar wrathmonk pong, there was also the not-so-unpleasant odour of red jelly beans. And, beneath that, another scent as well—

A *glorious* scent!

A *heavenly* scent!

Tinker's all-time favourite scent in the entire *world*!

BACON!

The smell seemed to be coming from the bottom of the nasty damp thing's legs. Tinker got up, trotted over and sniffed at Iggy's turn-ups.

Yes! Definitely bacon!

Iggy was grinning triumphantly down at Tinker. This was the very first time the nasty little dog had *ever*, by his own choosing, come anywhere near him!

'Good doggie!' crooned Iggy. 'Clever doggie. Now—come along wid me, den.'

Iggy started to walk away quite slowly, and naturally Tinker followed, trying to keep his nose as close as possible to that wonderful, glorious smell.

It began to rain. Iggy looked up at the sky and saw that it wasn't going to be one of those short, sharp showers, which pass over quickly. No, this one was going to be there for the rest of the afternoon—the grey clouds stretched to the horizon.

Iggy pursed his lips and whistled the special whistle.

Tweeee—twee-twee-twee—tweeeee!

Tinker didn't even look up. He'd heard that whistle several times and he knew it wasn't for him. Besides, he thought he could see a small corner of bacon, poking out from the bottom of Iggy's left trouser leg—and *seeing* bacon is even better than *smelling* bacon . . .

A few moments later, the big black umbrella came flying towards them. It flew about ten metres off the ground and looked exactly as if it was being blown along by a stiff wind. A second later its curved handle smacked into Iggy's waiting hand.

Tinker, standing very close to the little wrathmonk, felt the rain suddenly stop falling on his back. *Ah, that's better*, he thought. *A chap can concentrate so much more when there ain't no rain fallin' on his poor little body and makin' him all cold and wet. Now to see about this bit of bacon—*

Then, two things happened, one immediately after the other. First, Tinker managed to get his muzzle down into the tuck of Iggy's turn-up and make contact—with the tip of his nose—with a single strip of bacon. He pushed a little harder and carefully opened his jaws about a centimetre. Just as he was about to close his teeth over the elusive bacon, the second thing happened.

The umbrella in Iggy's hand gave a sudden, powerful jerk and it was only Iggy's extraordinarily strong grip that stopped it flying away again. Iggy looked up and frowned and then, when the umbrella made another straining jerk to get away, he raised his other hand and wrapped it over the one grasping the handle.

'Wot is goin' on?' he muttered to himself.

The umbrella heaved upwards again, this time lifting Iggy off his feet and then dropping him back down onto the grass with a small thump.

The idea that somebody might be trying to steal his umbrella came to Iggy quicker than most ideas came to him, simply because it had happened before—although not quite like this. He'd never been *holding* the umbrella when somebody tried to steal it! He tightened his grip and shouted as loudly as he could into the driving rain, 'Now, you ssstop dat, Mumps! I'm tellin' you, you jussst ssstop dat! Dis is *my* humble-ella and you is not havin' it!'

The umbrella took no notice and continued to try to pull itself out of Iggy's grasp. Meanwhile, down at the other end, Tinker was having problems of his own. Every time he got his teeth within range, the bacon hiding place kept bobbing up and down.

Tinker was getting irritated. When small terriers get irritated, sometimes they bite. That's what Tinker did.

He growled and then leaned forward and snapped at the flapping, bobbing trouser bottoms. Then he clamped his jaws together with all the strength of a very strong dog and began to tug, furiously, at the thick material.

Iggy was now being pulled both at the top and at the bottom—and he didn't like it one bit.

'Oi—ssstop dat, you bad doggie! Ssstop dat dis *inssstant*!'

Tinker ignored him. There was bacon in there—it was *his* bacon, because he'd found it and no amount of bobbing and flapping was going to make him let go.

The umbrella relaxed its upward pull for a moment, like somebody taking a breather in the middle of a tiring exercise. It did this to allow whoever was holding on to its handle one last chance to let go. Sam had obviously given some thought to this spell—he'd realized that there was a possibility that somebody might be clinging to the handle at the precise moment when it was being summoned by the special whistle—and that could be dangerous.

Iggy had been told all about this, but of course he'd forgotten it. The only thing that occupied his mind at this moment was the thought that Mumps was once again trying to steal his precious umbrella.

Down at the other end, the only thing that occupied Tinker's mind at this moment was the thought that the nasty damp thing was trying to steal his precious bacon.

So Iggy and Tinker held on with all their strength—one with his extraordinarily strong hands, the other with his extraordinarily strong teeth.

And then, with an enormous jerk, they were

yanked up off the ground and rose rapidly, soaring high into the falling rain.

'But—but how did you get here so fast?' said Measle, his eyes wide with wonder. 'It's miles and miles from home and I know how fast that umbrella flies! Not that fast!'

Iggy frowned and squinted his eyes and tilted his head sideways and looked up at the mist—and, having done that for several minutes (in an attempt to make his brain work) he finally shrugged. 'I dunno. We jussst did. De nasssty part was when we went in de water—'

'What water? Where?'

'De water at home.'

'You mean the swimming pool?'

Iggy shook his head dismissively. 'No, no—not de ssswimmin' pool. No, de uvver water—you know, de big black water.'

'You mean Limbo Lake?'

'Yusss—de lake. It was nasssty when we went in dere. Very *wet*, you sssee, Mumps.'

Measle screwed up his face into an expression of extreme puzzlement. He said, 'Now, wait a minute, Iggy. Are you saying that the umbrella flew up, with you hanging on to the handle and Tinker hanging on to your trousers—up out of the rose garden, then over the house and across the fields, all the way to Limbo Lake?'

Iggy nodded earnestly.

'Well, then what happened?'

'Oh,' said Iggy, 'well, den de humble-ella flew down! And den it went in de water and we got all wet!'

'And then what happened?'

Iggy put on a very solemn, serious face and then he pointed one long, bony finger down at the ground.

'It went down and down and down and down and down and down and down—'

Measle held up both hands. It was the only way to stop Iggy once he'd started on one of his word-repeating routines.

'You mean, it went to the bottom of the lake?'

Iggy's face went blank for a moment—and then started twisting and grimacing, so that it looked as though all his face muscles were trying to put themselves somewhere else. Measle waited patiently until Iggy's face had stopped wriggling and had settled down to a small frown across his pale forehead.

'No,' said Iggy, a little uncertainly.

'No?' said Measle. 'You mean—it didn't go all the way down to the bottom of the lake?'

'Well, it *sssort* of did—but den again, it *sssort* of didn't,' said Iggy. Then he grinned, apparently rather pleased with his explanation.

'I don't understand.'

'No, well—I don't undersssstand, neither, do I? Wot 'appened was—we was goin' down and down and down and down and down and down—'

'And *then* what?' interrupted Measle.

'And den we *ssstopped* goin' down and down and down and down and d—'

'Iggy!'

'And den we was goin' sssort of *sssideways*—and dere was no more water, ssso I could breave again—and it was ever ssso dark and I couldn't sssee nuffink—and den there was a sort of light—and den dere was a sort of pop—and den I fell down on de ground and my humble-ella ssstarted to pull me along and de nasssty little doggie let go of my trousis and ssstarted making dat nasssty noise he does when he's bein' naughty—'

'Barking?'

'Yusss, dat. And den you was dere. And dat's dat.'

By this time, Iggy and Measle had made themselves as comfortable as possible, seated together on the iron bed. They huddled under the umbrella, with Tinker at their feet and, when Iggy came to the end of the story, Measle pondered for a moment and then said, thoughtfully, 'There must be a Doompit down at the bottom of Limbo Lake, I suppose.'

'Doompit? Wot's a Doompit, Mumps?'

'It's a sort of doorway—a doorway into another world, Iggy. A place called Dystopia. And now we're all in Dystopia and I don't know how to get back.'

Measle fell silent, his mind buzzing with the thought that there was a Doompit only a couple of

miles from his own doorstep. But that would explain so much about the place. Limbo Lake was a dark, brooding stretch of water, smooth as glass, surrounded by a thick forest of pine trees. Sam and Lee had always discouraged Measle from going anywhere near it. Sam had said, 'There's something about the place I don't like—and I'd rather you didn't go there, all right?'

Measle had learned that when his dad said things like that, it was a good idea to listen, so he'd avoided going anywhere near Limbo Lake ever since.

'Wot do we do now, Mumps?' said Iggy, plaintively. Measle pushed his thoughts of home out of his mind and looked around him. The landscape—at least, as much of it as they could see—was cold and barren and wet. Measle had no idea which way was north or south or east or west and, even if he had known, the knowledge would not have helped him. The grey mist that hung in a wide circle round them blocked any view there might have been, so no way looked any more inviting than another.

'I don't know what we do, Iggy,' said Measle.

Iggy shivered. 'I wanna go 'ome,' he muttered, miserably.

'So do I.'

Iggy's red-rimmed eyes wandered gloomily around the barren landscape. Then he made the mistake of shifting the umbrella to one side to look up at the heavy grey sky.

Iggy squealed and jumped to his feet. He extended one bony finger and pointed it upwards.

'Wot . . . wot . . . wot is dat fing?'

'That's Toby's eye, Iggy.'

'His eye? His *eye*? Wot is his eye doin' up in de sssky?'

'It's following us about, I think.'

Iggy's face went through a number of contortions, while his tiny brain tried to absorb this information. Then his face cleared and he whispered, in an awe-struck voice, 'You mean, Missster Jugg can sssee us, Mumps?'

'I suppose so, yes.'

A wide, humble, and sickeningly ingratiating smile spread across Iggy's face and he bowed low to the eye and said, 'Wot an *'onor*, Missster Jugg! Always ready to *ssserve* you, Missster Jugg! Jussst sssay de *word*, Missster Jugg, and I, Ignatius Niggle, is at your *ssservice*, Missster Jugg!'

'Stop it, Iggy,' muttered Measle in a disgusted voice. 'You don't work for him any more, remember? And, he's our enemy, not our friend—remember that too?'

Iggy stared doubtfully up at the hovering eye—which stared glassily back. Then, because it didn't do anything more interesting than that, Iggy seemed to lose interest in it. He sat down again on the edge of the bed and sighed heavily.

'I is cold, Mumps,' he whimpered.

Tinker sensed the misery around him and he whined, a small, unhappy sound.

The three of them sat, huddled under the umbrella, on the edge of the iron bed—a small, depressed, and damp group, waiting for something to happen.

And then it did.

Shapes started to emerge from the mist.

They came slowly at first, hovering at the edge of the grey fog, so that it was impossible to see clearly what they were. They moved through the mist, the dark shapes criss-crossing past each other, never venturing completely out into the clear air but staying just within the safety of the edge of the concealing mist.

Tinker was on his feet, standing as still as a statue, staring out at the dark, shifting shapes. Measle glanced down at him. Tinker usually had a pretty good idea whether creatures were friends or enemies and reacted accordingly—and Measle had learned to trust the signs that the little dog made with his body. Tinker's tail wasn't moving— but it wasn't tucked down between his back legs, either. It stood straight up, like a furry finger. The hair on his neck wasn't raised either—so, whatever was out there, at least Tinker didn't regard them as enemies.

Well, not yet.

'Wot is dey, Mumps?' whispered Iggy, fearfully.

'I don't know.'

Then, a single shape apparently decided to come a little closer, because it moved out of the mist and, for the first time, Measle and Iggy and Tinker could see the thing clearly.

It was a wolf.

A very big wolf, its fur as grey as the mist from which it had emerged. Its head hung low and it stared at them from gleaming yellow eyes. Slowly, silently, more wolves drifted out of the mist and ranged themselves on either side of the leader. Then, the leading wolf, which was about twice the size of the others, stepped forward, followed by the wolves on either side of him. The pack took another slow careful step—then another—and another.

The gap was narrowing.

'Er . . . ' said Iggy, with a little panicky catch in his voice. 'Mumps—I do not like dese fings, Mumps—'

Measle reached over and gripped Iggy's arm firmly. Measle didn't know anything much about wolves, but he knew that most predators will chase after an animal that runs away from them. The last thing he needed right now was a terror-stricken wrathmonk screaming his head off and running all over the place. Another thing he didn't need was a brave and fierce little dog, who might suddenly decide that these approaching creatures needed to be taught a lesson about who's boss around here . . .

Measle reached down and curled the fingers of his free hand around Tinker's collar.

Measle's small movements had been seen by the leading wolf and, for a moment, it stopped dead. All the other wolves stopped too, the whole pack frozen like statues. Measle noticed that they were all very thin. Their ribcages could be seen clearly through the shaggy fur. Slowly, the leading wolf moved a single grey paw forward—and the rest of the pack did the same. They were slinking along now, their emaciated bodies held low, moving towards Measle and Iggy and Tinker in a stealthy, hunting manner—and, all the time, in utter silence.

THE WOLVES

Tinker didn't like other dogs much, particularly strange dogs. One was bad enough, but a whole pack of them, creeping low towards him, their eyes glowing hungrily, their long noses twitching, their teeth beginning to be bared in the shaggy grey muzzles—under normal circumstances, these threats would send Tinker into a frenzy of furious barking and a whole lot of teeth-baring of his own.

But these were not normal circumstances.

These were very peculiar circumstances indeed, particularly for a small dog who knew that he was *staring* at a bunch of very large, very mean-looking (and probably horribly dangerous) wild dogs—but who also knew that he was *smelling* something entirely different. He was *smelling* a group of rough, tough, and seriously unwashed men—and Tinker hardly ever had a problem with men (or women, come to that). He liked people, which was why he was standing still and quiet, his nose twitching and his stubby tail upright.

The leading wolf was now just five metres away. It suddenly stopped and the rest of the pack stopped too. Then the leader lowered its haunches to the ground and sat still, staring at Measle through its gleaming yellow eyes. The rest of the pack sat down as well—almost as if they were a squad of soldiers, obeying the command of their senior officer.

There was a long, tense silence.

Measle found his hands being slowly pulled in opposite directions. The one gripping Tinker's collar was inching forward, the one on Iggy's arm slipping sideways and backwards. Tinker was beginning to strain a little towards the wolves, his nose twitching—but Iggy had started to edge away along the bed, putting as much distance between himself and the animals as he could.

Measle tightened his grip on both of them and the opposite movements stopped, which was a good thing, because he needed all his concentration at this moment. There was something a little odd about these wolves—particularly now that they were so close—and he was having difficulty working out what it was. Something about their appearance . . .

Ah—

Their ears were too small.

Wolves' ears are long and pointed. These ears—especially the ones on the head of the great leading wolf—were much shorter and rounded, more like a bear's ears, in fact. And its eyes—they were yellow, but the wrong shape for a wild dog. They looked—

They looked—

Well, almost human.

The lead wolf's almost-human eyes suddenly switched from staring at Measle and moved upwards, so that the creature seemed to be looking at something above Measle's head. Then its grey jaws opened.

'What, in . . . the name . . . of whiskers, is that . . . thing?'

The voice was a throaty growl and the words came slowly, as if each one was an effort to produce. At the unexpected sound of a wolf speaking real words, Iggy gave a small squeal of terror and tried to drag himself out of Measle's grip. Tinker let out a single yelp and, with a tremendous jerk, actually managed where Iggy had failed. Tinker's collar slipped out of Measle's grasp. Tinker ran forward and then reared up right in front of the leading wolf, planting his two front paws flat on the broad shaggy chest and sniffing hard. The wolf ignored him.

'That thing up there . . . that thing looks like . . . an eye . . . what is it?'

'Er . . . well . . . um—' stammered Measle, 'it's . . . um . . . well, it *is* an eye, actually.'

'A flying . . . eye,' observed the wolf, cocking its head to one side. 'You don't . . . see . . . too many of . . . those.'

'It belongs to Toby Jugg,' said Measle. 'He's a wrathmonk.'

The wolf's eyes shifted back to Measle's face. It said, 'A wrathmonk, eh? Unpleasant . . . creatures, I understand.'

'Very,' said Measle. Then, aware that Iggy was at his side, he added, 'Well, most of them.'

'And us?' said the wolf. 'What do you make . . . of us, eh? What . . . do you suppose . . . *I* am?'

'Um . . . a wolf?' said Measle, with all the politeness he could muster.

'Almost. Not quite. There's still . . . a little of the human . . . left in us. Mostly in me—the others can't . . . speak any more. My name . . . was Lucian, once. We're lycanthropes.'

'Lycan—*whats*?' said Measle.

'Lycanthrope is . . . the scientific name. You're a little young . . . for science. How about . . . *werewolves*?'

It felt as if somebody was trickling a stream of icy water down Measle's spine. *Werewolves!*

'What . . . are you doing . . . here?' growled the creature.

'Er . . . the wrathmonk dropped me in here. What . . . er . . . what are *you* doing here?'

Lucian lifted the corner of one lip. It might have been an attempt at a smile—or perhaps it was just a sneer. Measle couldn't tell.

'We've been here for a long time,' said Lucian. 'A very long time. Since the legends began. That's what *here* is, if you're still wondering.'

Measle nodded. 'I am, yes.'

'It's where the *unreal* creatures—the ones created by the minds of men—live. Often creatures from your nightmares. Like us. We werewolves have been around for centuries. Others have been here longer than that.'

'Oth-others?' stammered Measle.

'Certainly,' said Lucian. 'You might meet a few.' Then he muttered, 'If you get that far. How far . . . do you want . . . to go?'

'Well, I'm—I'm supposed to find my school friends—'

'You mean . . . there's more of you?' said the werewolf—and a sudden glint of interest gleamed in its eyes.

Tinker was having a very unsettling experience. He still had his paws against the werewolf's chest and had just finished his close-up investigation of the creature. While it certainly smelt like a man, there was something about it that hinted of danger—*extreme* danger, in fact, which the man-scent had masked at first, but which now was changing rapidly from a hint to a real possibility.

Tinker hurriedly dropped his paws from the

werewolf's chest and backed away, his tail drooping. Lucian glanced down at him and then ran a long red tongue across his lips.

'Do you have . . . any food?' he said, suddenly.

Measle shook his head slowly. He sensed that the atmosphere had changed—a little for the worse. He felt Iggy's arm shift beneath his grip.

'We're hungry,' said Lucian. 'Very hungry. No food . . . for days.'

'I don't got no food, neither,' said Iggy, his voice squeaky with fear. 'I got nuffink in my pockets! Nuffink! No red jelly beans—nuffink!'

The werewolf glared at Iggy for a moment and then growled, 'What . . . are you?'

Iggy's mouth gaped open and shut several times, then he stammered, 'I is Missster Ignatius Niggle.'

Lucian curled his upper lip, showing several long canine teeth. 'I didn't . . . ask . . . your name. I asked . . . *what* you are? You're not . . . *human*. That much I know.'

Iggy's eyes were wide with fear. He went on opening and closing his mouth, but this time, no words came out. Measle decided he'd better speak for him. He also decided to come clean. When dealing with a hungry werewolf, it seemed the sensible thing to do.

'He's a wrathmonk. But he's a nice one. And he's my friend.'

The werewolf switched his gaze down to Tinker, who was now standing very close to Measle. His

stubby tail was tucked down between his back
legs and there was a look of extreme nervousness
in his eyes.

'And . . . this?' said Lucian.

'That's Tinker. He's my dog.'

'He's quite . . . *fat*,' said the werewolf, and out
came the long tongue again, swiping across the
lips. Then the yellow eyes flicked up, switching
back and forth between Measle and Iggy. 'You
two . . . on the other hand . . . are rather skinny.
But . . . when you're as hungry . . . as we are . . .'

Slowly, Lucian rose to his feet and, behind him,
the rest of the pack did the same. The werewolf
stretched lazily and the pack followed suit. Then
the werewolf stepped a pace closer to Measle,
baring his teeth in a silent snarl.

Measle was about to back away when a sudden change came over Lucian's face. His eyes glazed over for a moment and his back legs sagged, dropping his haunches to the ground. Without a word, he leaned his head back and to one side, lifted a rear paw, and started to scratch vigorously at a spot on his neck, just behind his right ear. For the rest of the pack, it seemed to be a signal that they could do the same because the whole mob of werewolves sat down and they too started to scratch at various parts of their shaggy bodies.

'Stinking . . . fleas,' muttered Lucian, his back leg becoming a blur.

And that was when Measle had one of his ideas.

'Will you help us, please?' he said, trying hard to make his voice sound calm and collected.

The werewolf paused his scratching and said, 'Help you? *Help* you? When we've . . . finished doing this . . . we're going to . . . *eat* you.' Then, in a matter-of-fact sort of way, he went back to trying to dislodge the flea from behind his ear.

Iggy started whimpering in terror and Measle had to clamp his hand down hard on the bony wrist to stop him running away into the mist.

'Yes,' said Measle, carefully, 'I understand that— but, if we help you, could you change your mind about that?'

Lucian's back leg stopped its frantic motion.

126

Lazily, he gazed at Measle for a moment. Then he said, 'All right. I'm . . . interested. Go on.'

'You have to promise first.'

'I . . . promise . . . I'll *think* about it,' grunted the werewolf. His back leg was starting to twitch again and the creature was obviously longing to get back to his scratching.

Measle took a deep breath and said, 'If we get rid of all your fleas, will you not eat us and help us instead?'

The leg stopped twitching. It froze, the paw hanging motionless in mid-air and looking—to Measle's eyes—just a little comical.

'Get rid . . . of the fleas?' said the werewolf, in the sort of voice people use when they don't believe such a thing is possible.

'*Completely,*' said Measle.

'How long will . . . it take?'

Ah, thought Measle, *I've got his attention now.* 'Just a few minutes.'

The werewolf narrowed his yellow eyes. 'How?' he growled.

Measle shook his head. 'You have to promise— no eating. Not me and not my friends.'

'I already promised . . . to *think* about it,' snarled Lucian.

'And now I want you to promise not to do it at all,' said Measle, firmly. 'That's the condition—if you want your fleas gone.'

The werewolf seemed to consider this for a few

moments. Then he rose stiffly to his feet, gave his great grey body a vigorous shake and said, 'All . . . right. I . . . promise.'

That, thought Measle, *is about all I'm likely to get out of this creature.* He turned to Iggy, who was still straining his whole skinny body in the opposite direction from the wolves and said, 'Breathe on them, Iggy.'

'You wot?' said Iggy, so astonished at the suggestion that his body, still as rigid as a poker, stopped trying to pull itself out of Measle's firm grasp.

'Breathe on them, Iggy. Fleas are bugs. Your breath kills bugs, Iggy. So, you can kill their fleas, can't you?'

Iggy's face muscles started doing their usual contortions, indicating that he was trying to use his tiny brain to its utmost. Five seconds later, Iggy managed to come to the conclusion that his best friend, Mumps, wanted him to go right up and breathe all over the huge, nasty, dangerous, and horribly ferocious wild doggies.

'I'm not doin' dat, Mumps!' he hissed, into Measle's ear. 'Dose fings is *ssstremely* dangerousss! Dey is goin' to eat usss!'

'Not if you breathe on them, Iggy. They promised!'

Iggy shook his head and started to pull away from Measle's grasp again.

'Iggy, listen!' whispered Measle. 'They won't hurt you! And you can show them how brilliant you are, can't you? And then they'll think you're brilliant and you know what?'

'Wot?'

'Werewolves never eat brilliant people, Iggy! *Never!* They only eat stupid people and you're not stupid, are you?'

Iggy's body relaxed again and he drew himself up to his full height and looked down his bony, hooked nose and said, 'I mossst certainly *isn't* ssstupid! I is tocally, *tocally* brilliant, Mumps! You know dat, don't you?'

Measle nodded enthusiastically. 'Yes, Iggy—*I* know it, and *you* know it and almost *everybody* in the whole world knows it—' (and here Measle pointed to the group of werewolves, who were standing in a semicircle, regarding them curiously, with their heads cocked to one side) 'but *they* don't, do they? Why don't you show them how brilliant you are, Iggy?'

Flattery always worked with Iggy. He nodded importantly and then gently disengaged his arm from Measle's grip. Ceremoniously, he handed Measle the umbrella. Then he walked, with all the confidence that a small and frightened wrathmonk can manage, towards the great hulk of the werewolf called Lucian. When he got to within a metre of the creature, Iggy stopped and said, in a squeaky little voice, 'Now den, doggie, *nice* doggie, *good* doggie, dis will not hurt, okey-dokey?'

Lucian curled his lip and looked at Measle and said, 'What's he going . . . to do?'

'He's going to breathe on you,' said Measle.

'Breathe?' said the werewolf, disbelievingly. 'That's all?'

'That's all.'

Lucian glared at Iggy from under his shaggy brows and then muttered, 'All right. Get . . . on with it.'

Iggy took another nervous step towards the werewolf and then bent over, took a deep lungful of air and started to blow his wrathmonk breath into the werewolf's face.

Lucian wrinkled his long nose and let out a short, barking cough. 'Hmm,' he murmured to himself, 'dead fish . . . old mattresses . . . the insides of some sort of . . . rotten shoes . . . this is *disgusting!*'

Iggy nodded delightedly. As far as he was concerned, the more disgusting his breath smelt, the better class of wrathmonk he was. With growing confidence, he went on breathing, moving away from Lucian's face now and starting the process along the werewolf's painfully thin body. The steady blowing out went on and on and on, without Iggy ever seeming to need to take any air back in, and only when he reached the tip of Lucian's tail did he give one last puff and finally stop. Then, just a little red in the face, he stepped back and looked expectantly at the werewolf.

'Well, den?' he said. 'Is I brilliant or wot?'

'What do you . . . mean?' growled Lucian.

'All de bugs is dead! Dead as . . . dead as . . . *dead as*—' Iggy couldn't think of anything dead at this exact moment, so he said, lamely, 'dead as dead fings!'

The werewolf tilted his great head to one side and gazed into the distance, keeping his body very still as if he was waiting to experience some sort of sensation somewhere under his wet fur. Then, starting at his neck and moving steadily down his spine and continuing all down the length of his bushy tail, Lucian started a long, violent shaking. Raindrops from his drenched fur flew in all directions and Iggy stepped back, shielding his face from the spray with his hands.

Unseen among the millions of drops of water flying off the werewolf were the tiny bodies of several hundred dead fleas. They landed, scattered far and wide, some falling among the short blades of rough grass, others onto the few low rocks that protruded from the ground—but they were all too small to be noticed by anyone.

At last, the shaking stopped. Once again Lucian froze—then, five seconds later, he appeared to relax. He looked at Iggy and said, 'All right. Something ... has happened. Not ... sure what. But I don't feel ... the need ... to scratch any more.'

'Courssse you don't!' squealed Iggy, triumphantly. 'Courssse you don't! De bugs is all dead, ain't dey? Dead as ... dead as ... *dead as* ... dead as lots and lots of *dead bugs*!'

The werewolf nodded thoughtfully. Then he turned his huge head and looked back at his companions. He selected one and then jerked his head, gesturing for the creature to come forward. The second werewolf obeyed, advancing and standing next to Lucian.

'Do her next.'

It took Iggy ten minutes to do his breathing act on the rest of the werewolves. By the time he was finished, he was a little out of breath. One by one, at the end of their treatment, the breathed-on creatures had shaken themselves free of their now-dead parasites and then had lain down on the wet ground, waiting for it all to be over. And now it was.

'Can we go now?' said Measle. 'And—and, will you help us?'

Slowly, the werewolf raised his head and stared, without expression, at Measle. Then he looked down at Tinker and then to Iggy. Iggy had returned to Measle's side, taken the umbrella firmly back into his possession and was now perched on the edge of the bed, shivering under its canopy.

'Well, now,' said Lucian, pleasantly, 'there's still . . . one small problem . . . to be resolved.'

'Wh-what's that?' said Measle.

'We may be flea-less,' said the werewolf, 'but we're still . . . extremely hungry. Starving, in fact. Not much . . . game in these . . . parts, and what there is . . . is hard . . . to catch. But I think . . . you three would be . . . pretty easy to catch.'

The tingle of fear solidified into a great lump of terror, lodged just under Measle's heart.

'But—but you promised!' he blurted out—and, at the same moment, he grabbed tightly on to Tinker's collar and, with his other hand, gripped down hard on Iggy's thin wrist.

'I promised . . . yes,' said Lucian. 'But . . . *they* didn't.'

The moment the werewolf stopped speaking, he sat down and, at the same instant, the rest of the werewolves rose to their feet. The group stepped forward, passing by their leader, who seemed to have lost interest in the proceedings and had started to lick his damp and muddy paws. The group walked slowly, and very deliberately, towards the iron bed and, as they got nearer to Measle and Tinker and Iggy, their jaws began to part, revealing rows of long yellow teeth and red, lolling tongues. Their small ears flattened to their heads, their round yellow eyes became slits and a thin line of rough fur rose in a crest all along their backbones.

'But—but we *helped* you!' yelled Measle, his voice quivering with a mixture of fear and anger.

There was no reply from the mob of advancing werewolves—just a slight lowering of their bodies and a small gathering of muscles in their rear legs, as if they were all going to pounce together in one savage group.

'That's not *fair*!' shouted Measle. Tinker obviously felt the same, because he was growling deep in his throat, and Iggy, in the desperate hope that a little more wrathmonk breathing might somehow make the problem simply go away, was puffing out his smelly breath as hard as he could in the general direction of the advancing creatures.

But neither Measle's cry of outrage, nor Tinker's growls, nor Iggy's pointless puffing, did anything useful at all.

The werewolves ignored them all and came nearer and nearer and nearer.

Feast or Famine

It was at times like these when Measle's mind worked best.

Right now, it was working as fast and as efficiently as it ever had, but no brilliant idea seemed to be popping into his head, the way it usually did—and, all the time, the werewolves were advancing.

Iggy decided that the whole experience was too much for him and, with a helpless squeal, he suddenly fell back onto the damp mattress and curled himself into a tight ball. He pulled the umbrella close down over his trembling body, so that he looked a little like a turtle hiding under its shell—and, as he did so, a few small red objects spilled out of his trouser pocket.

Click click click, went Measle's brain.

It's not much—but it might hold them for a minute or two . . .

'Wait!' shouted Measle, jumping to his feet and holding out his hands, palms outwards, to the werewolves. 'Food! We've got some food! Really nice food! You don't need to eat us!'

There was a short, sharp bark from behind the mob of werewolves and the whole group stopped dead in their tracks. Lucian stopped licking his paws. He rose to his feet and walked forward and the rest of the werewolves parted silently, to let him through.

'Food?' he growled, softly. 'Where? I don't . . . see any food. Well—I *do*—it's . . . right in front of me. But that's not . . . what you mean . . . is it?'

'No,' said Measle. 'This is different food. There isn't very much—but it's quite . . . er . . . quite *filling*.'

'Filling, eh? Well . . . that's what we . . . need. We need . . . *filling*.'

Measle nodded, smiling in as friendly a way as he could manage. Then he looked down at Iggy. Nothing much of Iggy was visible under the umbrella, apart from the top of his head, the soles of his shoes and a little bit of his backside, which the umbrella couldn't quite cover. His trouser pocket was exposed and gaping wide. Ignoring the whimpering noises coming from under the umbrella, Measle reached out and plunged his hand deep into Iggy's pocket. His fist closed round a big handful of red jelly beans and he pulled them out.

The reaction was immediate.

The umbrella was pushed to one side and Iggy's face, purple with fury, emerged, his fishy eyes glaring furiously up at Measle.

'You is a *feef*, Mumps! A nasssty, rotten *feef*!'

'Iggy—'

'Firssst you sssteal my humble-ella, now you nick my jelly beans! I fort you was my friend, Mumps!'

'Iggy—'

'But *no*. No, no, no, no, *NO*! You is nuffink but a sssneaky, beassstly, feevin' feef!'

Measle thought this was a bit much, coming from Iggy, who had started out in life as a professional burglar—but there was no point reminding Iggy of that now, because the werewolves seemed to be getting restless again.

'Iggy, shut up! We'll get you some more jelly beans later but, right now, we have to give them to the werewolves, or else THEY WILL EAT US! Do you understand, Iggy?'

'We might . . . eat you anyway,' murmured Lucian, 'unless you can come up . . . with something pretty quick!'

The very real threat of becoming dinner for a bunch of starving werewolves slowly dawned on Iggy and his face lost its angry purple colour and faded quickly to the colour of old candles. Hastily, he fumbled in his pocket and pulled out the few red jelly beans that Measle's fingers had failed to grasp. His other hand plunged into his other trouser pocket and came out with another, bigger, handful of jelly beans—but these weren't red. These were all different colours and Measle knew immediately that Iggy had, once again, managed to sneak inside Merlin Manor, to the big jar in the dining room, and help himself to some extra sweets. The red ones were made for him by Nanny Flannel every morning and they were what Iggy lived on—but he was a greedy wrathmonk, who took every opportunity to get a few extra, even if it meant risking a great whack on his backside from Nanny Flannel's mop.

Iggy held his two heaps of jelly beans out to the werewolves. Measle did the same with his single handful.

'What are these?' said Lucian, staring doubtfully down at Measle's hand.

'Er . . . they're jelly beans,' said Measle. 'They're really nice. And good for you. And very, *very* filling. You won't feel a bit hungry once you've eaten a few.'

Measle, of course, didn't believe a word of any of that. He was just playing for time.

Lucian lowered his head and sniffed. Then his long crimson tongue slid from between his lips and the tip was run experimentally over the topmost jelly bean. Lucian sniffed again—and then his jaws opened and, bending his head sideways, he snapped every single red jelly bean out of Measle's open hand.

There was an angry growling from the pack behind him and they started forward—whether to attack their leader for his greed, or to attack Measle and Iggy for not sharing equally with them, Measle didn't know. Neither did he care—this was not the moment to analyse a situation.

'Throw them, Iggy!' Measle shouted. 'Throw your red jelly beans! But not the—' He was about to shout, 'But not the *other* ones!' because he'd noticed, to his excitement, that there were several yellow ones, a few green, and even an odd pink one in the pile in Iggy's hand—but he was too late.

Iggy had learned that, when Measle yelled at him to do something—using that particular sort of voice—it was best just to do it and ask questions later. So Iggy drew back both his arms and then tossed both handfuls of jelly beans high in the air. They landed, scattering in a wide circle, right in the middle of the pack of werewolves. The effect was instantaneous. The pack bent their heads and started to gulp down every jelly bean they could find.

Lucian, his mouth full, turned to watch. There was a lot of snapping and snarling and teeth baring among the crowd, as each one laid claim to a particular jelly bean, but no serious fight broke out.

Not until one werewolf, at the edge of the mob, suddenly gave a yelp of pain and jumped sideways, twisting his rear quarters away from—from *something* that appeared to have bitten him.

But there was nothing there. The hurt werewolf looked around in puzzlement then he returned to the single jelly bean he'd spotted, nestling in the shadow of a low rock. He put his nose down—

Again, he gave a sudden yelp and jerked his nose away from the rock, and now Measle could see that there was a definite puncture wound on the creature's muzzle and blood was oozing from the small hole.

Something was attacking this particular werewolf.

Something . . . invisible.

The bitten werewolf snarled in fury and then launched himself at what looked like thin air. Logically, he should have landed back on solid ground on all four feet but, instead, he crashed down on top of an unseen shape, his legs straddling an unseen back, his jaws clamping down onto an unseen neck. To those watching, it looked as if the werewolf was suspended somehow by invisible wires, and those wires were jerking him about in a wild and uncontrolled manner.

'What . . . is going on?' growled Lucian.

Measle knew. A werewolf had eaten a jelly bean, and it hadn't liked the taste.

Lucian turned and thrust his shaggy jaws close to Measle's face and snarled, 'Tell me what is going . . . on—or I shall . . . kill you . . . here and now!'

'The—the beans,' blurted out Measle. 'Some of them are a little magical—'

Lucian gave a great roar and leapt, in a single huge bound, right into the middle of the pack. He whirled in a circle, his teeth bared, daring any of the other werewolves to attack him. Respectfully, they backed away, their ears flattened, their tails down, and their hackles raised. Then Lucian swung his head to Measle and said, 'Come here! Pick them up! Pick them . . . all . . . up!'

Hurriedly, Measle and Iggy ran to the circle and started to gather up the few remaining jelly beans. Most of them were the red ones, but there were a few of the other coloured ones still uneaten. Measle concentrated on picking up these, leaving the strawberry ones for Iggy to find. All the while, he kept an eye on the snapping, snarling, tumbling (and what seemed to be oddly one-sided) fight that was still going on at the edge of the crowd, between a werewolf and a—well—a nothing at all.

Thirty seconds after the first bite on the werewolf's flank, a second, wolf-shaped form began to swirl, in an eddy of grey smoke, in the air beside him. The bitten werewolf was so surprised that he stopped attacking his invisible enemy and stood back to watch what was going on. A few seconds later, the other werewolf materialized fully and Measle saw that it was smaller than most of the others, a female, with a dark blaze of black fur on her forehead, a black tail, and four jet black paws. She also had two thin streams of blood trickling down on either side of her neck.

'Blackfoot!' said Lucian, sharply. 'Where did you appear from?'

Blackfoot seemed to be as surprised as her leader at what had just happened to her and didn't reply. She just stood there, blinking foolishly and staring at her front paws. Lucian turned to Measle.

'What magic . . . was that?'

'Well . . . er . . . if you eat one you don't like, you turn invisible for thirty seconds,' said Measle.

'Why . . . did no others . . . become invisible too?'

Measle wasn't sure but he had an idea. In the past—and as part of a Measle experiment—Tinker had eaten lots of the magical jelly beans and he had *never* disappeared. Measle's theory about that was that Tinker basically liked *all* the flavours and didn't have a particular one he disliked enough to avoid eating it. And, since these creatures were partial wolves, a species which were the ancestors of all domestic dogs, perhaps the same theory could apply to them—with the exception of the one called Blackfoot, whose taste buds must be somehow a little different from the rest of the pack.

Measle quickly explained this to Lucian.

'You mean . . . to say,' said Lucian, wrinkling his

furry brow, 'that if Blackfoot eats . . . another of those things . . . she'll turn invisible?'

'Well . . . yes,' said Measle. 'Of course, it has to be the right colour—and she'll only be invisible for half a minute.'

Lucian swung his head away from Measle and went and stood in front of Blackfoot, who was looking rather frightened. Her bushy black tail was tucked between her legs, her ears drooped, and she was staring submissively at the ground.

'Which one is it, Blackfoot?' growled Lucian. 'Which one . . . do you like the least?'

Blackfoot didn't move. Impatiently, Lucian called back over his shoulder:

'Boy! And you . . . other creature! Bring the beans here!'

Measle and Iggy joined Lucian and Blackfoot. Iggy was trying, in as unobtrusive a way as possible, to stuff his red jelly beans back into his pockets and Measle was about to stop him when he realized that it couldn't possibly have been one of Iggy's sweets that had done the trick, since Nanny Flannel was careful not to put any magic in them at all.

Lucian said, 'Hold them out . . . for her to smell.'

Measle did as he was told, holding both hands out in front of him, the few remaining beans nestling in his cupped hands. He saw that there wasn't a single yellow one there . . .

Blackfoot lowered her nose and sniffed at the jelly beans.

'Well?' snapped Lucian.

Without looking at her leader, Blackfoot raised a paw and touched an orange bean with a single muddy claw.

'What colour . . . is that?' said Lucian.

'It's orange,' said Measle. 'Can't you see it's orange?'

'No!' snapped Lucian. 'Our colour sense . . . isn't up to much. Mostly we see . . . in shades of black and white. How many orange ones . . . are there?'

Measle counted quickly. It didn't take long.

'Four.'

'Give them to me.'

Measle picked out the four orange jelly beans and held them out to Lucian. Lucian raised a paw and turned it over, and Measle saw that Lucian's paw wasn't very doglike—it looked nothing like Tinker's, for example. It was broader and flatter and, apart from the great curving claws, looked a little bit like the palm of his own hand. He dropped the beans into Lucian's paw/hand.

'What are you going to do with them?' he asked.

Lucian's eyes glittered with excitement. 'Don't you see?' he muttered. 'If our prey . . . can't see us, it'll be that much easier . . . to catch! Blackfoot is fast . . . and a good hunter . . . but even she succeeds . . . only five times out of a hundred! But invisible . . . she'll catch every time!'

'But—but you've only got four,' said Measle.

'Indeed,' said Lucian, and there was a touch of

sly menace in his voice. 'Well, then—you'll have to . . . get us some more, won't you?'

'Right,' said Measle thoughtfully. 'But . . . um . . . that could be a bit difficult, if you've eaten us.'

Lucian let out a short sharp bark, which sounded to Measle a little like a laugh.

'We won't eat you,' he said. 'Not now you've given . . . us the means to hunt so efficiently. We shall let you go. But first . . . you must promise . . . that you will send us some more . . . of the orange beans.'

'OK,' said Measle, beginning to relax with relief. 'But—but how can I get them to you? We might not be able to find this place again.'

'Things . . . that fall through the portals . . . tend to find themselves . . . where they are *supposed* to be,' said Lucian. 'Don't ask me how . . . it works. It just . . . does.'

Unexpectedly, Lucian held out his right paw and Measle took it in his right hand. It was a curious feeling—the limb felt more like a human hand than a dog's paw, and yet the long, curving claws dug gently into Measle's palm, and that was definitely not at all human . . .

'Good luck, boy,' said Lucian. 'Wish us . . . Good Hunting.'

'Good—good hunting,' said Measle.

'Don't forget . . . your promise.'

For a moment, Measle was tempted to say something about Lucian's own promise and how he'd twisted it to his own convenience—but there were too many lean and hungry creatures staring at them with starving eyes.

'I won't.'

'Be very . . . careful . . . out there. Things are sometimes . . . not what they . . . seem. Or what . . . they *should* be. We, for instance. Werewolves are supposed . . . to be mindless brutes. And yet . . . we're not entirely, are we? That is the nature . . . of legends, you see. Legends are stories. Stories are . . . lies. Remember that, boy.'

'I will.'

Measle turned in a full circle, staring out at the mist that still surrounded them.

'Er . . . which way should we go?' he asked.

Lucian shook his shaggy head.

'It makes . . . no difference here,' he said, sadly. 'No difference at all.'

'What do you mean?'

Lucian sighed and fixed his eyes on Measle's face. 'Where you end up . . . is chance, boy. Pure chance. Besides, you can't . . . get out. Once you're in Dystopia . . . you stay for ever.'

Measle and Tinker turned to go. Reluctantly, Iggy pushed himself up off the bed and followed them, casting nervous glances over his shoulder, back at the group of werewolves.

Measle was about to step into the mist when something made him stop and look back. Tinker stopped too and whirled round, showing his teeth. Iggy, who was carrying the umbrella rather low, didn't see that they had both halted and simply went plodding on, his scuffed old shoes shuffling over the wet grass.

It was a sound that had drawn Measle's and Tinker's attention. But not the slow, shuffling sound of Iggy's feet. It was the sound of bare, pattering paws, moving fast towards them.

It was Blackfoot. She was racing across the ground, running in a dead straight line towards them. Tinker growled low and Measle stepped forward to warn Iggy that something was coming up fast behind him—

But there was no time. Blackfoot put on a burst of astonishing speed, jumped over a rock that was in her path and then, when she was three metres away from the unaware little wrathmonk, she bunched her powerful rear legs and leapt—straight onto Iggy's back.

THE FOREST

Iggy screamed and started to turn around but the weight of the wolf pushed him forward at the same time and he lost his balance, staggered, and began to fall. The umbrella flew from his grasp and, with both hands now free, he reached round to protect the back of his neck.

But Blackfoot wasn't interested in the back of Iggy's neck. Blackfoot was interested in something else entirely, and was only using Iggy's body as a sort of ladder in order to reach the thing she was after. Her fluid movements had all been upwards and now her hind legs were on Iggy's shoulders, and she flexed them again and jumped high in the air, twisting her slim body in an attempt to get even higher.

Blackfoot's jaws snapped in the air. Then, with extraordinary grace, she fell back to the ground, landing like a cat on all four paws.

Iggy finished off falling to his knees on the wet grass and it was from that position that he started to wail.

'Oooh! De nasssty fing jumped on me! It is goin' to eat me up! Sssave me, Mumps! Sssave me from de 'orrible gobblin' monster! Oooh! An' now my kneeses is all wet an' muddy!'

Blackfoot ignored Iggy. She took no notice of Tinker either, who had stopped growling and now was looking rather impressed—that had been some jump, and one that he could never have managed. He'd specially liked the bit when the wolf had run up the nasty damp thingy's back . . .

Blackfoot stepped gracefully up to Measle and then nudged his hand with her nose. Measle opened his fingers and held his palm flat and Blackfoot opened her jaws and dropped something onto it.

It was round and damp and slimy—and surprisingly heavy. At first glance, Measle didn't understand what it was. Then he looked a little closer.

It was Toby Jugg's eye.

'A small token . . . of our favour!' called Lucian. 'Do with it . . . what you will, but I advise you to . . . imprison it somewhere . . . before it flies out of your grasp!'

A moment after Lucian had finished speaking, Measle felt the eye shift in his hand. Quickly he closed his fingers over the horrible thing. It was like holding a cold, slimy, rubbery marble—and one with a life of its own, because now it was rolling around inside his closed fist, obviously looking for a way out.

Measle reached into his pocket. His fingers touched a plastic bag.

He pulled the bag out. It was empty—

Of course! It was the one I gave to Toby—and he ate all the beans out of it and then he gave the bag back and I just stuffed it in my pocket, without thinking about it.

Measle fumbled the bag open and, shuddering with disgust, he managed to slip the eye into the opening. The eye slithered down to the bottom of the bag, making a slimy smear on the inside of the plastic. Quickly, Measle squeezed the fastening seams together, then held the bag up at eye level.

Measle could see, clearly, Toby's eye and Toby's eye, presumably, could see him clearly too.

Measle made a face at the eye. He squinted his eyes, wrinkled his nose, and stuck out his tongue—and the eye did nothing but stare, expressionlessly, through the worn plastic. It didn't even try to move any more. It just lay there, at the bottom of the bag, a slimy lump of white jelly, with a circle of yellow on one side, and a big black dot in the middle.

It was just too disgusting to look at any more, so Measle put the bag back into his pocket, being very careful not to squash it. Then he turned and waved at Lucian.

'Thank you!' he called, although he wasn't sure quite what he was being thankful for, other than the fact that Toby wasn't going to be able to see what they were doing, not from the inside of a dark pocket—and, perhaps, that was a good thing.

'Don't forget . . . your promise! Orange jelly beans!' shouted Lucian, lifting a paw in farewell.

Measle nodded. Then he bent down, grabbed Iggy by the arm, and pulled him to his feet. The mist closed around them and now Measle could see only a couple of metres in front of him. They walked slowly forward for several metres and then, quite suddenly, there was a change in the air around them. It was no longer cold and damp. Now, there was a definite warmth to it, and it smelt, not of a cold grey mist, but of sunlight and old trees and fallen leaves.

A moment later, Measle became aware that his feet were no longer treading on short, coarse, wet grass and slippery rocks—now they were shuffling through a thick layer of dry, dead leaves. Their shoes made a *shush-shush-shush* sound as they moved through the leaves and Iggy stopped dead and stared down at the ground.

'Where did all dis ssstuff come from, den?' he demanded, crossly.

'I don't know, Iggy,' said Measle, his eyes trying to pierce the mist that surrounded them. 'But I think we're in a different place now.'

'Well, of *courssse* we is in a different place, Mumps,' said Iggy, patiently. 'Because, you sssee, we 'ave been walkin', 'aven't we? And, when you walk, den you get to a different place, don't you?'

'Yes, but—'

'You 'ave to fink dese fings frough, Mumps,' explained Iggy, kindly, as if he was talking to somebody whose brain didn't work very well. 'Walky, walky—different place! Walky, walky—different place! Dat's how it works, sssee?'

Measle was about to point out that they really hadn't walked far enough to explain such a dramatic change in their environment, when, without warning, there was a puff of warm air and the mist that surrounded them blew away.

They were in a forest. A very old forest. The trees

were enormous. Their great greyish-brown trunks were gnarled and lumpy. Huge exposed roots snaked across the leafy ground, before disappearing back underground. The air was still and warm. It was very quiet.

Sunlight filtered down from the high canopy far above their heads. It had a greenish tinge to it and it dappled the ground in spots of light and shade. The rain seemed to have vanished, apart from the small droplets from Iggy's tiny rain cloud that drizzled a little dampness from over his head down onto his umbrella.

Other than the great trees, there were no living things in sight. No birds or insects—not even a bush, or a flower, or a blade of grass. The trees had the place entirely to themselves, each one having a large, clear space around it, so that no tree was too close to its neighbour.

It was very beautiful, in a strange sort of way.

Iggy found the sudden transition very unsettling. ''Ere!' he exclaimed, loudly. 'Where did dis place come from?'

'I think it's another part of Dystopia,' said Measle, looking around with pleasure. The surroundings were certainly more comfortable than the wet, cold, and misty moor.

Iggy didn't like it at all. 'Dis place sssmells funny!' he announced, his big beaky nose twitching with disgust.

Measle sniffed. The air smelt exactly the way you

would expect the air in a forest to smell—of fallen leaves, of growing wood, of clean earth—but there was no point telling Iggy that, because the only smells Iggy really liked were the sort that would make the rest of us hold our noses so we wouldn't have to suffer them.

Tinker was busy shuffling around in the deep leaf litter, *his* nose close to the ground, discovering all the odours that dogs can detect and humans can't.

'I is 'ungry, Mumps,' said Iggy, mournfully. 'And you made me frow away all my loverly jelly beans!'

'Where are the ones you picked up, Iggy?'

'I eated some already. Wot is we goin' to do now? We is goin' to ssstarve to deaf, dat is what we is goin' to do!'

Measle had heard this whine before, when he'd first met Iggy. The trouble was that, this time, Iggy could be right.

True, the forest seemed to be a living, growing thing. But the trees didn't appear to be the sort that had fruit on them and, with nobody around to ask the way to a larder, or to a supermarket, or even to a packet of cornflakes, there was a possibility that Iggy's prediction might come true.

The thing to do, Measle decided, was to walk through the forest and see what was on the other side. Always assuming the forest *had* another side . . .

'Come on, you two,' said Measle, in what he hoped was an encouraging voice. 'At least it isn't raining any more and it's nice and warm and the sun is shining—'

'Huh!' muttered Iggy, moodily. 'De sssun! Ssstoopid fing!'

'Let's go that way,' said Measle, ignoring Iggy's sulks and pointing straight ahead—and, with a heavy sigh from Iggy, they set off through the forest.

They walked a long way, for several hours. They saw nothing different from their first sight of the forest: the ancient trees all looked identical, the fallen leaves were all the same colour and consistency, and the stillness that hung over the woods never varied for a moment. Everything looked similar—so much so, that, at one point, Measle wondered if perhaps they were walking in circles, not really going anywhere, but passing the same spot over and over again.

Measle also had the vague feeling that they were being watched. He didn't say anything to Iggy about it, because Iggy would probably have panicked and gone running off through the woods, squealing his head off. But Measle kept his eyes darting around, searching the forest for any sign of life. He saw none. He was a little reassured by Tinker's behaviour. As far as Tinker was concerned, they were all going for a nice walk through the woods—just the three of them—and he gave no indication of feeling the faint unease that Measle was experiencing. Tinker's tail was up, his ears were pricked forward and he trotted along, his nose to the ground, apparently enjoying every moment of the outing.

Iggy, on the other hand, was sulking. He trailed ten metres behind Measle and Tinker, occasionally heaving great, heavy, dramatic sighs of misery—and getting crosser and crosser because neither Measle nor Tinker was taking any notice of them. The sighs were supposed to let them know that he was not very happy, that he hated walking through this awful, depressing, smelly forest, that wading through the stupid dead leaves, with the stupid sun beating down on him, was making him all hot, and that the huge stupid trees were getting in his way all the time.

Tinker felt a sudden urge. He trotted up to the nearest tree and had a good sniff of the rough bark. Usually, with trees, there was the smelly evidence that another dog had done its business up against it—but this tree gave off no such scents. Like all dogs, Tinker liked to leave his mark by doing his business over the spot where another dog had done *his*, and it was a little unsettling for him that there appeared to be no such spot. But the urge was still there, so—out of habit—Tinker lifted his leg and did what he'd come over here to do.

High up above him, almost invisible among the topmost leaves of the huge tree, a tiny figure turned its bright, emerald-green eyes and glared down at the forest floor. The emerald eyes narrowed. Then the tiny creature raised its head, pursed its lips and whistled—and, far below, Tinker stared upwards, his ears twitching.

Only Tinker caught the whistle. It was at a very high frequency—too high for Measle or Iggy to hear it—but dogs have ears that can pick up sounds inaudible to humans and Tinker had heard the whistle loud and strong.

'What is it, Tink?' said Measle, who had noticed the sudden change in Tinker's attitude.

At the sound of his name, Tinker flipped his tail twice then he went on staring intently up at the distant canopy of leaves.

Iggy shuffled up and stopped. He looked at Tinker, then sniffed irritably.

'Wot is de ssstoopid doggie doin'? Why is he ssstarin' at de ssstoopid sssky?'

'I don't know, Iggy,' said Measle. 'I think there may be something up there.'

Iggy looked up and squinted his eyes against the dappled sunlight.

'Sssumfink up dere? Wot? I can't sssee nuffink. Except for ssstoopid leaves.'

'Neither can I.'

'Well den, let's keep doin' dis ssstoopid walkin'—and find sssumfink to EAT!'

'All right, Iggy.' Measle clicked his fingers at Tinker and was about to say, 'Come on, Tink, there's nothing there—' when the buzzing began.

At first, it was quite faint and distant—but it grew louder very quickly. It seemed to be coming from somewhere up ahead and Measle, Iggy, and Tinker all stared in that direction, trying to see what was making the noise.

BzzzzzzzzzzzzzzzzzzzzzzzzzzzzzzzzZZZZZ . . .

Then a dark, swirling cloud appeared about a hundred metres away. It was flying towards them fast, its shape constantly shifting as it raced along. As it came nearer, Measle saw that it was made up of hundreds of tiny flying creatures that looked, from this distance, like dragonflies.

Iggy grabbed Measle's hand.

'Wot is dose fings, Mumps?'

'I don't know, Iggy.'

'I don't fink I like dem, Mumps.'

'I don't think I do either.'

Measle and Iggy took a step backwards—and then another and another. The buzzing noise had dragged Tinker's attention away from the top of the tree and he, too, was staring at the advancing cloud, his head to one side and his ears pricked forward.

When the cloud got to a few metres away, it stopped. The buzzing sound continued, because the wings of the creatures were still working at keeping them in the air, but all forward motion halted and the mass of tiny things just hung there.

For the first time, Measle could see what they were.

And he couldn't believe his eyes.

Fairies?

Matilda had a book—a picture book—filled with images of fairies. To Measle's astonished, disbelieving eyes, it was as if those images had lifted themselves off the pages of Matilda's book and were now hovering in front of him. All the usual elements that artists have used when they draw pictures of fairies were there. The lacy, dragonfly wings; the tiny, perfectly-proportioned bodies— and all dressed in the usual fairy costumes. The females wore tunics made out of petals, some with bluebell flowers for hats. The males had the kind of clothes that Peter Pan wears, in shades of brown or green, all ragged at the bottom—and several had caps made from the cups of acorns. All of them, male and female, had attractive, heart-shaped faces, with brilliant, emerald-green eyes that slanted upwards at the outer corners; all of them had over-sized, pointed ears; all of them had tiny, uptilted snub noses; all of them had—

With a jolt, Measle saw that all of them possessed something that no fairy had ever possessed—or, at any rate, not in any picture that he'd ever seen. Certainly, the fairies in Matilda's book didn't have them and, if they had, then Sam and Lee would never have bought the book for her in the first place.

They all had tails.

And not nice, friendly, furry tails, either.

These were horrible.

They looked exactly like scorpion tails. They were huge—at least, in proportion to the rest of the fairies' bodies. Like Arabian swords, the tails curved up and over their heads. They were divided into shining brown and green seg-ments, which became progressively smaller as the segments got closer to the tip. And the tips were the worst part of the tails. They hung over each fairy's head, massive and menacing. They were shaped a little like a light bulb, and sticking out of the forward facing end was a long, thin spike. Hanging from the point of the spike—and quivering with every movement the fairies made (if, indeed, they *were* fairies)—was a fat drop of greenish, yellowish liquid.

'Ooh, Mumps,' whispered Iggy, in a hoarse voice that was quite loud enough for the fairies to hear, 'dose tails look really nasssty! And—look, Mumps!—all de tails is *leakin'*!'

'Ssshhh, Iggy,' muttered Measle into Iggy's ear. 'And I don't think their tails are leaking. I think that's—*poison*.'

Iggy gave a little squeak of terror and tried to hide behind Measle. Tinker, at their feet, was growling, very quietly but very steadily, as if daring the hovering mob to come any closer.

Lucian was right, thought Measle. *Things here in Dystopia are not quite what you expect them to be . . .*

The cloud of creatures split suddenly, making a sort of narrow corridor in the air, and a figure that was just a little larger than the rest advanced through this passage, its wings a blur. It flew slowly forward, until it was just a couple of metres from Measle. Then it stopped, and Measle could see it clearly.

This was a fairy with a difference. Instead of petals—or rags—for clothes, it wore a long, silver gown, tied around the waist with a gold cord. On its tiny head was a polished silver helmet, which covered all its head and neck, and half its face, so that only the lower section of the creature's nose, and its mouth, were visible. Its oversized, pointed ears stuck out from holes on either side of the helmet, like a pair of wings, making it look a little like the head covering of the Viking god Thor. There were two slits in the front of the helmet and Measle could see the glint of a pair of emerald-green eyes deep inside them.

The silver fairy hovered in the air for a few moments, turning its head this way and that as if surveying the three creatures in front of it. Then, it spoke—and its voice was small and tinny, and sounded as if it was coming from far, far away.

'One of you has marked a tree. Which one?'

Iggy popped his head out from behind Measle and pointed excitedly back in the direction they'd come from. 'It was a great big brown one,' he said, 'about a sssquillion miles back dat way!'

'It doesn't mean which *tree*, Iggy!' said Measle. 'It means which one of us did it?'

Iggy immediately pointed down at Tinker and said, 'It was *'im*! De nasssty little *doggie*! It wasn't me! I didn't widdle on no tree! It was *'im*!'

'Shut up, Iggy,' said Measle, out of the corner of his mouth.

'To mark a tree in any way is an insult to our persons,' said the fairy.

'An insult?' said Measle. 'Oh—well, we're very sorry. And Tinker didn't mean it. Honestly—it—it—it was an accident.'

The fairy didn't reply for several seconds. It hovered in the still air, its wings vibrating. Sunlight glittered from its robe and helmet—and its head was bent and its eyes were glued to Tinker.

'We are waiting,' it said, at last.

'What for?' said Measle, carefully.

'For the creature who gave the insult to apologize for its discourtesy.'

Measle glanced down at Tinker, who was glaring up at the hovering fairy with just as much intensity as the fairy was glaring at him.

'He's a dog, sir,' said Measle. 'He can't apologize.'

'*Can't?*' said the fairy. 'Or won't? We have severe penalties for those who touch our trees!' And, on the word 'trees', the fairy's scorpion tail arched higher over its head and seemed to swell—making it look more menacing than ever.

Hurriedly, Measle looked up, meeting the fairy's gaze. 'It's not "*won't*", sir. He just can't.'

'Why?'

'Because he can't speak, sir.'

A drop of poison was swelling at the tip of the tail. The fairy bent its head in the direction of Tinker, its large ears twitching. Tinker growled a little louder.

'It makes a sound,' said the fairy, sternly. 'Therefore, it has a voice. A voice with which to make the apology.'

'Wot's it talkin' about, Mumps?' whispered Iggy, nervously.

'It wants Tinker to say sorry,' muttered Measle. 'But he can't, of course.'

Iggy stepped out from behind Measle, smiled a big smarmy smile at the fairy, and then aimed a kick at Tinker's backside.

'Go on, you naughty doggie!' hissed Iggy. 'Sssay you is sssorry!'

Tinker, who was used to these occasional clumsy attempts of Iggy's to give him a good kick, slipped neatly out of the way of Iggy's foot and then showed the wrathmonk his best teeth, which usually did the trick of making Iggy back away. But this time Iggy had an audience and he had to pretend he wasn't in the least bit frightened by a few little teeth.

'Bad doggie! Wicked doggie! *Evil* doggie!' shouted Iggy, sidling sideways in order to get another kick in.

'Stop it, Iggy,' whispered Measle.

Iggy took no notice. He scowled down at Tinker and wagged one bony finger at him. 'You didn't sssay you is sssorry to de nice—de nice—de nice flyin' fing, wiv de wings and de shiny dress, so now you is goin' to get such a kickin' from me! Me—de *nice* persssson who didn't widdle on *nobody's* trees!'

Iggy drew back his foot again and aimed another wild kick in Tinker's general direction— and Tinker skipped out of the way, pulled back his lips in a full-blown snarl, and growled a lot more ferociously.

Iggy looked a little sick and took a step away, moving closer to Measle. He'd never seen the nasty little doggie looking quite this fierce . . .

'The apology is long overdue,' announced the fairy. 'So, the penalty will be exacted.'

'Er . . . what's the penalty?' said Measle.

'The penalty—'And now the fairy raised both its head and its voice, bellowing out the next few words as if it were addressing the spectators in a football stadium, 'the penalty is Death By Six And Sixty Stings.'

Every fairy in the hovering mob suddenly darted forward by half a metre, and their tails arched higher and the thin, cruel spikes at their tips grew just a little longer—

'You're not going to sting my dog,' said Measle, trying to sound very calm.

'Your *dog*?' sneered the fairy. 'Ah—is that what it is? And what makes you think that the penalty applies only to your dog? No, no—Death By Six And Sixty Stings is meted out to all who accompany the criminal! All three of you are guilty!'

Iggy only understood the simplest of sentences and certainly had not got a word of what the fairy had said, so he muttered, 'Wot's it talkin' about, Mumps?'

'It says we're all going to be stung to death, Iggy.'

Iggy's face wriggled in thought. He shook his

head violently, pointed at Tinker and squealed, 'But—but it was 'im! 'E did it! Not *me*!'

The chief fairy took no notice. It raised one arm high over its head and shouted over its shoulder, in its tiny, faraway voice, 'On my command of one, two, three, you will all advance and carry out the sentence! One . . . two—'

'Non**onononono**!' screamed Iggy, wildly. He pointed at Tinker again and yelled, 'Look! I will kick 'im for you! Sssee? Sssee me kickin' 'im?'

Iggy lashed out with his foot, and Tinker sidestepped again. But now Tinker was getting very angry. *Oi! That's enough of that, you nasty, damp thingy! Try kickin' me once, and I'll show you me teeth! Try kickin' me twice, and I'll add a snarl or two! Try kickin' me three times and I'll be after you, matey!*

Tinker bared his teeth, snarled—and then made a sudden dash at Iggy's feet. Iggy squeaked with fear and jumped out of the way—and that was when Tinker started barking.

Sometimes, when a small dog starts barking for a really good reason, it's hard to stop him. And Tinker had a really good reason—he was furious, and determined to teach the nasty damp thingy a serious lesson. So, the barking was very loud, and shrill, and almost continuous and, all the while, Tinker was dashing about, trying to get a good bite out of Iggy's ankles and Iggy, of course, was leaping about trying to avoid the little dog's snapping jaws.

The effect on the fairies was immediate. Every single one of the tiny creatures threw up their hands and covered their large pointed ears. Several uttered faint, high-pitched screams of fear and distress—and all of them flew backwards across several metres, as though the sound of Tinker's barking acted like a powerful wind that blew them out of the way. Even the chief fairy had put his hands over his ears and was pressing them hard against the sides of his helmet—and Measle could see, from the twisting, contorted lips of the creature, that it too was as deeply affected by the ear-splitting noise as all the rest of them.

A thought flashed through Measle's mind. *It's so quiet in the forest—maybe the things aren't used to loud noises, maybe their ears are too sensitive and Tink's barking is actually hurting them.*

The hovering mob of fairies had now retreated a good thirty metres, but they went no further and Measle saw that, at that distance, the volume of Tinker's barking was diminished enough to let them take their hands away from their ears and cluster together in what looked like an urgent discussion. And Tinker wouldn't bark for ever—

'Come on!' yelled Measle, starting to run. 'Iggy! Tink! Run!'

Iggy didn't need any more urging than that. Running away was as good a method as any of avoiding Tinker's teeth, so he gave one last little leap in the air and then set off in a shambling trot behind Measle.

Tinker, sensing a whole new mood, started to gallop in their wake.

And—he stopped barking.

Measle threw a quick glance over his shoulder. The grey cloud that was the hovering fairies was on the move again—it was zooming through the air in hot pursuit, and catching up fast.

'Kick him again, Iggy!' yelled Measle.

'You—you—wot?' panted Iggy.

'*Kick Tinker!*'

Measle had never encouraged Iggy to be mean to Tinker and always stopped him the moment Iggy showed any sign of spitefulness towards the dog, so this order came as something of a surprise.

Iggy gasped, '*Me*—kick—'im? I tried dat, didn't I? Now, 'e's tryin' to—*bite* me! If—you want 'im kicked—why don't—*you*—kick 'im?'

Measle threw another quick look over his shoulder. The fairies were gaining ground and were now so close that Measle could see that the stingers at the tips of the horrible, segmented tails were twice the length as before—now they looked like polished steel needles, poised to stab.

Measle knew that there was no point in *him* trying to kick Tinker, because—coming from Measle—Tinker would just think it was some sort of game and wouldn't be angry at all—no, it *had* to be Iggy!

By this time, the little wrathmonk had fallen behind by a couple of metres. His narrow chest was heaving for air and his skinny legs were trembling with the effort to keep up. Measle saw the chief fairy suddenly wave his tiny arm and a small, fairy-shaped object darted at high speed out of the flying cloud of the creatures and made a beeline for Iggy.

That was when Iggy decided that all this rushing about was too much for him and that he absolutely had to have a breather. He halted, put his hands on his knees and bent double, gasping for breath.

The tiny fairy, which was obviously built for speed, zoomed forward, its scorpion tail arched high, the gleaming stinger projecting as far as it would go. It smacked hard into Iggy's taut trousers, burying its stinger deep into his backside—then, instantly, it flew backwards, turned, and rejoined the flying crowd.

Iggy screamed, dropped his umbrella, and jumped a good metre and a half into the air, both hands clutching the spot. All thoughts of tiredness left him and he started to try to outrun the awful pain. His knees pumping like pistons, and with tears streaming down his face, he galloped level with Tinker. At the sight of the little dog, whose responsibility it was that he was in so much pain, he screamed, 'Ow! Ow! Ow! You 'orrible doggie, you! Ow! Ow! Ow! Dis—dis—dis is all your fault! Take dat! And dat! And DAT!'

And, on each 'dat!'—and while still running for all he was worth—Iggy swung a foot and tried to kick Tinker as hard as he could.

Tinker dodged the kicks easily and, to Measle's relief, started his furious barking once again. Measle looked back.

Yes! It was working! The fairies were no longer racing after them. Now, the whirling cloud of the creatures seemed to have stopped dead and, with every stumbling, panting step that Measle and Iggy and Tinker took, the distance from their pursuers became greater and greater.

'Come on!' shouted Measle, who was running in the lead. 'Faster! And keep kicking, Iggy!'

Now there were a good two hundred metres between them and the fairies but Measle began to wonder where, exactly, could they run to? The forest had looked the same for a long time now—just the great trees in their own clearings, mile after mile of them, and that was no good, there was nowhere to hide.

But they had no choice. Measle knew that they had to keep running, because sooner or later Tinker or Iggy would give up their battle, the barking would stop, and then the fairies would be upon them and, judging from the way Iggy was behaving from just *one* sting from those terrible scorpion tails, then sixty-six of them would certainly kill them all.

And that was when he saw the cave.

THE CAVE

They were running towards a small rocky hill that rose out of the forest floor and in the face of the hill was a small black hole.

'Come on!' yelled Measle, pointing ahead. 'We've got to get in there!'

He was tired now, but he managed to put on a final burst of speed. Tinker, bored with the kicking war, stopped barking and raced along by Measle's side—and Iggy, the pain in his backside still very bad, ran as fast as his skinny legs would let him, simply trying to get away from the awful stinging.

They only just made it and, even as they raced into the shadows of the cave, Measle wondered if, perhaps, this wasn't such a good idea after all? This could be nothing but a trap—a dead end.

The cave was narrow at the entrance, its rocky wall little more than a slit, through which Measle, Tinker, and Iggy had to pass in single file. But, a few metres further inside, it opened up to a space that was easily the size of the great hall back home at Merlin Manor. At first, their eyes were so unaccustomed to the darkness that they could hardly see a thing, but Measle noticed that the ceiling of the cave was a good ten metres above their heads and the floor was soft and sandy. Further back, there seemed to be another tunnel of some sort, leading deeper into the hillside. Measle wanted to go and investigate it, because the cloud of fairies couldn't be too far behind them and the creatures had undoubtedly seen them enter the cave.

'Come on, you two!' gasped Measle. 'We can't stop now!'

Iggy was walking in small circles, both hands rubbing his bottom. The stinging seemed to be dying down a little, but it was still painful enough to make the tears dribble down his cheeks and for him to mutter, 'Ow! Ow! Ow!' under his breath. He glared at Tinker through tear-filled eyes and sniffed hard to stop his nose from running.

'All your fault!' he hissed. 'Nasssty doggie! 'Orrible doggie!'

Tinker stood there, watching Iggy cautiously, panting heavily, with his tongue lolling out of his mouth. Neither of them seemed particularly anxious to go any further.

Measle tried again. 'Come on! We've got to keep going!'

There was a sudden buzzing sound and a shadow fell over the narrow entrance. A single fairy—perhaps the one that had stung Iggy—flew slowly forward, its tiny head turning from side to side, the emerald eyes peering. It too was having difficulty seeing in this gloom and it was advancing very slowly and cautiously.

Tinker saw the single fairy—and decided that it was an intruder.

'Wowwowwowwow!' he barked, furiously, glowering aggressively up at the tiny figure.

The fairy uttered a high-pitched shriek, clamped both hands over its pointed ears, and put its dragonfly wings into reverse. It flew backwards at such a speed that it crashed into the curving rock wall by the entrance. The fairy fell towards the sandy floor, then it recovered, its wings blurring and lifting it back into the air again. It turned in an instant and zoomed out into the sunlight.

There was a moan from Iggy. Tears were still running down his cheeks, making his eyes even more red-rimmed than usual.

'Does it hurt very much, Iggy?' said Measle, sympathetically.

'Yesss, it does!' sobbed Iggy. 'An' it's all de nasssty doggie's fault!'

'Iggy, if it wasn't for Tinker, we'd all be dead right now. Remember that.'

Iggy sniffed loudly and went on rubbing his backside. Measle decided that the best way to take Iggy's mind off his pain was to get him interested in something else.

'Come on, Iggy, let's go and see where that tunnel leads to, shall we?'

Reluctantly, Iggy allowed himself to be pulled to the back of the cave. Tinker followed, keeping one watchful eye on the narrow opening.

The tunnel was small and so low that Measle and Iggy had to duck to peer inside. It was also very dark.

'Come on, then,' said Measle, trying to sound cheerful. 'Let's see where this goes.'

He dropped onto all fours and, very slowly, started to crawl into the tunnel. Iggy, moaning and muttering to himself, did the same. Tinker gave one last, loud, warning bark in the direction of the sunlit opening and then followed close on Iggy's heels.

After the first two metres, Measle had to feel his way. It was so dark, he might as well have had his eyes shut.

'Hold on to my foot, Iggy!' he said, over his shoulder.

They crawled slowly through the pitch blackness. Every few metres, Measle would stop and put one hand up over his head, feeling for the ceiling of the tunnel. It was always there, so low that it forced them to remain on all fours.

'Where is we goin', Mumps?' snivelled Iggy. He was no longer crying, because the stinging wasn't nearly so bad now, but all this crawling through inky darkness was a bit boring, not to mention just a little scary, even for a wrathmonk who shouldn't be even a *little* bit afraid of the dark.

'Somewhere really interesting, Iggy,' said Measle over his shoulder. *I just hope it isn't too interesting, though* ...

Measle stopped again, and put his hand up to feel for the ceiling. This time, it wasn't there. Cautiously, he got to his feet, his hand still reaching up in case there was a low rock roof somewhere above, but his hand met nothing but the dry cave air.

'You can stand up, Iggy.'

Measle sensed Iggy rising slowly to his feet beside him. Then Iggy said, 'You can ssstand up too, you 'orrible little doggie.'

Measle smiled to himself in the darkness. Tinker was too low to bump his head in the tunnel, let alone here.

But where *was* here? There was still no speck of light anywhere. He felt around for rock walls, but there was nothing. Only the soft, sandy floor beneath his feet. There could be anything up ahead—for all they knew, they could be standing right on the very edge of a precipice ...

Measle reached behind him, his hand groping for Iggy.

'Hold my hand.'

'Wot for? Dat is sssissy, holdin' hands.'

'I don't want us to lose each other.'

The idea of losing Mumps was awful, so Iggy reached out and fumbled for Measle's hand.

At the precise moment when their fingers touched, they heard the faint clatter of falling stones.

The sound seemed to come from somewhere almost directly above them.

Measle held tightly to Iggy. He could hear Tinker growling softly in the darkness.

'Ssshhh!' he whispered.

There were the sounds of more pebbles bouncing off rock walls and then a rather human grunting noise, from high above their heads. Measle took a step backwards, treading heavily on Iggy's toes.

'Ow!' squealed Iggy.

'Ssshhh!'

'I won't sssshhh!' said Iggy, crossly, his voice getting steadily louder and louder. 'It's not enough dat I have got a great big ssstingin' sssting in my bum! Ho no! I 'ave to 'ave a sssquashing sssquish on my tootsies, too!'

Measle turned round in the blackness, used his

free hand to feel its way to Iggy's face, and then clamped his palm across the little wrathmonk's mouth.

'Mmmmmf!' mumbled Iggy.

A distant gleam of light—which seemed to be swinging erratically from side to side—appeared in the darkness high above their heads. Measle pulled Iggy backwards, until his back bumped into a rocky wall. Iggy saw the light as well and immediately stopped trying to protest, so Measle slowly took his hand away from Iggy's mouth and whispered in his ear, 'Let's be really quiet, Iggy. We don't know what that light is.'

Iggy nodded. Pebbles and dust still fell from up there somewhere and the grunting sounds became louder and louder.

Then, suddenly, the spot of light turned into the beam from a powerful torch. The beam swept over the sandy floor in wild, uncontrolled arcs—*as if it's hanging from the end of a rope, perhaps?* thought Measle, huddling back against the cave wall.

The light went on sweeping backwards and forwards, revealing a little more of where they were on each swing. They were in another cave, but much bigger than the first one. This cave obviously had some kind of hole in its roof, because the light was still slowly descending and, in one sudden jerky movement, its beam revealed that it was suspended from a thick rope that disappeared upwards into the gloom—and that this rope was slowly being lowered from somewhere far above.

It was impossible to see who was holding the torch. The light swung in another great arc and, this time, it swept over the huddled figures of Measle, Iggy, and Tinker. It moved on past them, the pool of white light ranging across the uneven floor for several metres. Then suddenly it stopped and moved backwards, finding the three figures again.

'Well, well,' came a distant voice. 'Measle Ssstubbs, as I live and breathe. Ssso, there you are.'

It was the booming, cheerful voice of Toby Jugg.

TOBY ON a ROPE

It was a horrible shock for Measle. While Dystopia was, undoubtedly, a very dangerous place, at least it seemed to be a long way away from Toby and, with the evil wrathmonk's eye tucked away in his pocket, Measle had felt at least safe from any dangers that *he* might threaten.

But now, here he was, Toby Jugg—dangling at the end of a long rope, only a few metres over their heads!

To give himself time to think, Measle decided to pretend he didn't know who it was.

'Who's there?' he called.

The beam of light left them for a moment, moving like a flash across the floor of the cave, then up a distant wall, before finally settling on Toby Jugg himself.

'It's me,' said Toby, grinning cheerfully. 'Your old buddy Toby.'

'Hello, Toby,' said Measle, carefully.

'And there's Missster Ignatius Niggle, too. And that impressive little dog. Well, well—I'm ssso glad to have found you at lassst!'

Measle could see Toby clearly now, because the wrathmonk was holding the torch at waist level, pointing it upwards towards his head. The upper part of his face was in shadow, but Measle could just about see that, where his right eye should be, there was just an eyelid closed over an obviously empty eye socket. Measle saw that the rope was tied around Toby's waist, in a series of complicated-looking knots. In his right hand, Toby held the powerful torch. His left hand clung tightly to both the rope and to a length of plain white string, which hung parallel to the rope and disappeared (like the rope) into the gloom far above.

Toby swung gently to and fro. Then he said, 'You've no idea what a time I've had, trying to locate you! Poor Needle and Bland—they mussst have lowered me on thisss rope half a dozen times! I expect they're getting rather tired, poor fellows! But the things I've *ssseen*! What a truly *fascinating* place this is! And now here we are, in sssome sssort of cave, I think. Yesss, definitely, a cave. Why don't I come down there and join you, eh?'

Toby looked upwards, along the length of the rope. Then, carefully, he twitched at the white string, giving two sharp little tugs. Nothing happened, so he did it again. Still nothing.

'Ah,' said Toby, thoughtfully. 'I imagine the rope is not long enough. Perhaps thisss time I have reached—quite literally—the end of my tether! Ha ha! But let me try jussst once more!'

Toby tugged at his string again. The rope suddenly dropped down half a metre and then was jerked up again, sending Toby swinging once again.

'Yesss, yesss—all right!' shouted Toby, glaring upwards into the darkness. 'I get the message! No more rope!'

Toby waited for the swinging to die down a little. Then he tilted the torch back down towards the floor and the pool of light found Measle, Iggy, and Tinker again.

'Ssso sssorry!' he called out of the darkness. 'It ssseems I'm unable to get down there thisss time!

I shall jussst have to conduct my business from up here—I do hope you don't mind, Measle, old ssson?'

'What do you want, Toby?' said Measle, shading his eyes from the powerful beam.

'My eye, of courssse! What did you *think* I wanted?'

Measle felt in his pocket and the tip of his forefinger made contact with the squishy, slimy eyeball. It occurred to Measle, quite suddenly, that—for the first time—he had something to bargain with.

'I think I'm going to keep it in my pocket, Toby,' he said, firmly. 'I don't like being watched all the time.'

Toby laughed—but it was that fake kind of laugh that was tinged with anxiety.

'No, no, old ssson,' he boomed. 'You're going to give it to me—or else I shall have to cassst a particularly nasssty ssspell on you, won't I? Let me ssee, which one will it be, eh? I've got ssso many!'

Measle closed his hand around the plastic bag.

'Well, you'd better not try that, Toby. Because the moment I see you even starting any magic then I shall just have to squeeze this bag in my pocket really, really hard—and then you'll have no eye at all, will you?'

'Oh, Measle, Measle—you really are sssomething ssspecial!'

Measle didn't answer. There was a short silence—and it was in that silence that Measle realized that this was one round in his long battle with Toby Jugg that he might have won.

Then Toby said, 'What do you want?'

Measle thought quickly. 'I want my school friends back—every single one of them. And I want us all to get out of here, safely.'

'And then you'll give me back my eye?'

'Yes.'

Toby thought about this for a few moments, relaxing his hold on the torch just a bit, so that the beam drifted away from Measle. A little of its light spilled across the floor and then wandered over the expanse of the huge cave, revealing a small part of the opposite wall. Measle saw that there was another opening over there—an almost perfect circle of darkness in the rock face. It offered another way out of this huge cave and Measle wondered if, perhaps, it was a way to the other side of the hill? He was still clutching Iggy's hand and, giving it a small tug, he started to move very slowly across the floor of the cave, towards the distant tunnel. Iggy followed meekly, and Tinker did the same. The three of them shuffled along, with Measle trying to make it look as if he was just idly strolling about, not going anywhere in particular, while giving Toby time to think about the proposition.

'I'm afraid I can't help you with your school friends, old ssson,' said Toby suddenly. Measle stopped walking.

'Why not?'

'Well, because they're not here. They're all back home, in their little beds, sssafe and sssound with their mummies and daddies.'

'Wh-what?' spluttered Measle. '*Why*—and *how*?'

'*Why?* Because I have no interessst in ssstirring up trouble for the magical world by eliminating a bunch of human ssschoolchildren, Measle! I may be a wrathmonk, but even I underssstand the concept of keeping a low profile! The sssudden disssappearance of thirty brats would cause usss all no end of trouble. As to *how*, why, that was perfectly sssimple, Measle! Sssome lovely memories planted in their little ssskulls, about all the wonderful things we'd done on our trip—then fassst asleep on the busss, all the way back to ssschool! Once there, the headmassster was informed that the outing had been cut short because of a mysssterious illness that ssseems to have laid low one of the pupils—none other than Massster Measle Ssstubbs! Poor Measle, he had to be taken home to Merlin Manor in a sssspecial ambulance! And, for the health and sssafety of the ressst of the children, the ssschool trip had to be abandoned!'

'But—what about my mum and dad—?'

'They know nothing of this, Measle! They don't expect you home for another four days! That should be time enough! In four long days, I believe you will meet your match down here!'

Measle glared up at Toby. Then, a thought occurred to him:

If there's nobody down here for me to try and rescue, why don't we just stay in this safe cave until Mum and Dad discover I'm missing? They'll be sure to get us out of here somehow ...

'Jussst in case you think there's no point in going on, Measle,' said Toby—and, for a moment, Measle wondered if the wrathmonk was powerful enough to read his mind—'I mussst remind you that there is just *one* classmate of yours here. You sssaw me push her in, didn't you?'

'Polly is still down here?'

'Oh yesss! And you'll certainly want to ressscue *her*, won't you? Of courssse, I have no more idea about where she is than you have. Her location all depends, you sssee, on what ssstories she knows.'

Measle nodded, as if he understood what Toby was saying. *What does he mean, 'what stories she knows'?* Nonchalantly, he started his slow, meandering stroll again, gently pulling Iggy along with him. Iggy was strangely quiet. The fact was, he was mortally afraid of Toby Jugg, and the sight of his former master dangling on a rope, several metres above the ground, was so beyond anything he could understand, that he'd been stunned into silence and was allowing Measle to pull him this way and that without making any of his usual complaints.

'Where are you going, Measle?' barked Toby, suddenly suspicious.

'Uh . . . nowhere, Toby. Just . . . *thinking*. You know.'

By now, they were about halfway to the circular mouth of the tunnel—but it was still a long way off. Measle slowly came to a halt, in a careless sort of way, and started to draw patterns in the sand with the toe of his shoe. The last thing he needed right now was Toby thinking that they were about to make a run for it. Even with the threat of losing his eye, there was no guarantee that Toby wouldn't hurl a horrible spell down at them if they made a sudden, unexpected move . . .

'What do you suppose inhabits these holes in the ground, Measle?' said Toby, flashing the torch beam around the huge space.

'Nothing. They're just some empty caves—'

'No, no, old ssson!' shouted Toby, boisterously. 'They're not empty! This is one of Dystopia's little worlds—there's always *sssomething* in them! And that *sssomething* is already in your head, Measle! Don't you undersssstand?'

'No, I don't.'

Toby sighed, like a teacher faced with a slow learner. 'And I thought you were ssso clever, Measle. Thisss place—Dystopia—is whatever *you* make it. The legends that exissst here can only be the ones you know about. Obviously you knew all about werewolves. And what has happened to you sssince then, eh? What have you ssseen while my eye has been hidden away in your pocket?'

'Uh . . . well . . . um . . . there were these fairies—'

'*Fairies?*' shouted Toby, gleefully. 'Hah! I would have thought that was more your little sssissster's area than yours!'

'She's got this picture book—'

'Well, there you are! You underssstand now?'

Measle thought for a moment and then he said, 'You only meet the things you know about?'

'Exactly!'

'So . . . Polly is going to meet—well—things she's read about, or seen pictures of?'

'Got it in one, old ssson!'

'What did *you* see, Toby?'

Toby rolled his one eye dramatically and said, 'Have you ever heard of the Hydra?'

Measle shook his head.

'Then you won't sssee it, Measle! But I knew of the Hydra—and I sssaw it! A monstrous dragon creature of the marshes, with nine great heads, each one full of razor-sharp teeth—and, if you cut one of the heads off, two more grow in its place! Needle and Bland only jussst got me out of there in time! And what about the Golem?'

Measle shook his head again. There seemed to be an awful lot he didn't know.

'The Golem! A great giant man, a sort of robot, made out of clay! He was set loose by his master years ago! He wanders the deserted old city, stamping to death anything that he sees. He was reaching for me when I managed to tug my string! I felt his rough, knobbly fingers brush against my foot as Needle and Bland lifted me away! Worst of all was the Lindorm Worm—a great white ssslithering thing! It was ssso horrible, I ssstayed as far away as possible and the thing never even knew I was near!'

Toby paused, then he said, 'You've never heard of these things, Measle, ssso you won't sssee them. They're all legends, of courssse. Ancient ssstories, from different countries. The Hydra is from Greece, the Golem is a famous Jewish story—and the Lindorm Worm is part of the beliefs of the Norsemen of olden days. But what about you and the ssstories and legends *you* know? Because, you sssee, there is sssomethng in these tunnels and caves that you know about—otherwise, you wouldn't be here! I wonder what it could be?'

Measle peered round the great cave, suddenly a little fearful. He hadn't been aware that they might have crossed from one magical space to another—there'd been no grey mist to pass through, just dark tunnels—but perhaps you didn't need a grey mist, perhaps the pitch darkness they'd crawled through had actually been the division between one bizarre place and another. As for the creatures he'd met so far—well, everything Toby had said about that made a mad sort of sense in this mad sort of world.

Even as Measle was thinking about all this, and getting increasingly nervous with every passing second, he saw that Tinker had turned round and was standing facing the direction from which they had just come. The little dog seemed to be staring intently back at the entrance to the low tunnel, his ears pricked forward, his head cocked to one side. Tinker's nose was twitching—and suddenly he sneezed, violently, three times. A moment later, Measle felt a strange, tickling sensation in his nostrils. There was a sharp smell in the air, one he'd never smelt before, and now there was a sound too, a clicking noise, like the tapping of a thousand keys on a computer keyboard. Both the smell and the sound were definitely coming from the tunnel they'd just crawled through. Not only that, but the smell was getting stronger and the sound was getting louder—

'What's up, old ssson?' said Toby, flashing his torch beam around.

'There's—there's something coming through that tunnel, Toby,' said Measle.

'Ah, sssplendid! That'll be one of *your* legends, Measle. I shall be ssso interesssted to sssee what it is!'

Measle was backing away from the tunnel and Iggy and Tinker were coming with him. Measle no longer tried to pretend he wasn't going anywhere in particular—now, moving backwards, away from the dark hole in the wall, was the obvious thing to do. But he threw a quick glance over his shoulder to make sure that they were still heading in the direction of the other tunnel in the opposite wall.

Toby suddenly sniffed loudly. Then he said, 'Hmm. I think I recognize that sssmell, Measle. Yesss—I'm almossst sure I do!'

'Wh-what is it?'

'That, old ssson, is the sssmell of formic acid.'

'Wh-what's formic acid, Toby?'

'Well, it's an acid, obviously. And it's made by— well, you'll *sssee* what it's made by any sssecond now, won't you?'

FORMICIDAE
FORMIDABLE!

The beam from Toby's torch was now fixed firmly on the tunnel's entrance. Measle, Iggy, and Tinker moved as quickly as possible towards the opposite tunnel and they were almost there when the first of the creatures emerged from the dark cavity.

At first, Measle couldn't understand what he was seeing. A pair of slim brown sticks, that waved to and fro in the torchlight. The sticks were bent in the middle. They seemed to be attached to a big, roundish sort of structure, also brown, with a pair of darker brown dots set on either side.

More of the thing emerged into the beam of the torchlight. The round section thinned down at the back to a narrow stalk and the end of this stalk was joined to a much bigger object. This part of the creature seemed to be covered by a sparse layer of coarse hair.

'Why, Measle, old ssson!' shouted Toby. 'I do believe that it's sssome sssort of *ant*! Well, that would explain the formic acid—it's sssomething ants make. But—good heavens!—it's the sssize of a tiger! What sssort of ssstory does a monsssster like *that* come from?'

Measle knew at once which story they'd come from. An old film he'd seen recently on television, about a nest of giant ants. The ants in the film weren't very convincing—they looked as if they were made of foam rubber. Now here was one of the creatures emerging fully from the tunnel, and this one didn't look at all as if it was made of foam rubber—this ant looked horribly real, particularly the huge, curving, pincer-like jaws that clicked and clattered beneath its massive head.

The ant moved a little way into the cave, its antennae twitching. A moment later, another head was thrust through the tunnel opening, quickly followed by the body of a second ant—and then a third and a fourth—

'It looks as though we might have ssstirred up the whole nessst, Measle!' called Toby, playing his flashlight over the growing crowd of ants. 'Of courssse, I'm quite sssafe up here, aren't I! And what a sssplendid view I have! I shall be ssso interesssted to sssee what happens next!'

Iggy whimpered with terror. Measle threw a quick glance over his shoulder. The round opening of the tunnel was right behind him. Quickly, he pushed Iggy into it and then he scooped up Tinker in his arms and ducked into it himself. It was very dark in there, and Measle realized, with a sick feeling of horror, that they simply couldn't feel their way blind—not this time. Not with the knowledge that what they were crawling through was actually a nest of giant ants . . .

If only we had some light! thought Measle. He paused just inside the entrance of the tunnel and looked back towards the crowd of ants that were milling about at the far side of the cave. They didn't seem to be doing anything much. Toby was still playing the beam of his torch over their enormous bodies.

That's what we need—Toby's torch. But—how to get it?

Quite suddenly, the ants started to move. At first, Measle thought they were headed directly towards him and Iggy and Tinker, but, a moment later, he saw that they were scuttling to a point in the middle of the cave floor, directly beneath the dangling figure of Toby Jugg. Once there, six of the leading ants stopped dead and five of the ants that were right behind them crawled up onto their backs. These five also then halted all movement, while four of their followers climbed up onto *their* backs—

They were after Toby.

Toby himself realized this almost immediately. Measle watched as he tugged urgently on his piece of string—presumably the signal to Mr Needle and Mr Bland to pull him up and out of there.

But nothing happened. Toby looked up sharply and then tugged the string again, a little harder this time.

Still he hung there, slowly turning in the still air. He looked down and saw that the top of the mound of living ants was getting closer and closer to his dangling feet. Measle saw Toby swing himself sideways, so that his body was now horizontal, and Measle wondered what he was going to do? A moment later, the question was answered.

Toby took a deep breath and blew out hard, aiming his wrathmonk breath directly down at the top of the crawling heap of ants. Measle watched, with fearful fascination, as the two topmost layers of giant ants froze solid in an instant. Their bodies were enveloped in a thin layer of ice, which turned their colour from a dusky brown to a frosty blue.

On this occasion, it was a mistake—a big mistake—for Toby to use his freezing wrathmonk breath. The *solidifying* effect of the spell only seemed to make the growing tower of ants firmer and more stable, thereby allowing more and more ants to climb up the sides of the tower to form yet another layer on the top, bringing their clicking, clattering jaws closer and closer to Toby's feet. Desperately, Toby tried his breathing spell again, and another five ants froze into a connected block of ice—which brought six more scurrying up the tower towards him.

Toby frantically bent his knees, pulling his feet up and away from the approaching ants. Again, he tugged wildly at his length of string, and this time, the rope started to move. But it was too slow—

Mr Needle and Mr Bland must be very tired, thought Measle, watching as Toby started to rise— slowly, so slowly!—*or else, they're doing it on purpose . . .*

'Faster, you idiots!' screamed Toby, staring upwards, his big face twisted with an ugly mixture of fear and fury. 'Pull me up *faster*!'

Measle saw that, unless something changed, the race was going to be won by the ants. Already, the top layer of ants was scuttling into position, ready to take on their backs at least three more—and Measle reckoned that those three should, by reaching up far enough, be able to seize Toby's dangling feet quite easily with their scythe-like jaws.

The beam of light from Toby's torch was flashing all over the cave walls now as he struggled to pull his legs up out of the way—and it was then that Measle had one of his ideas. He let go of Iggy's trembling hand, put Tinker down by Iggy's side and then slipped out of the low tunnel and stood upright in the cave.

'TOBY!' he yelled, at the top of his voice. 'It's your *torch*! They're attracted to the light! Get rid of it! Throw it away!'

Measle paused just long enough to let the idea sink into Toby's head. Then he screamed, 'But not over here! Don't throw it over here! I don't want them after *me*!'

 Of course, Toby could just as easily have turned the torch off and hung on to it—but, when people are in a panic, sometimes they act without thinking things through. Toby did exactly that. Without a moment's hesitation—and with a scream of defiance—he hurled the torch as hard as he could, directly towards Measle. It sailed in a great arc through the air, turning end over end, its beam sweeping over the wall and the floor. Then it landed, with a soft thump, on the floor at Measle's feet.

And, by a stroke of the most enormous luck, the bulb didn't break. It was one of those big, professional looking torches, its case and lens protected by a thick layer of black rubber. Measle breathed a big sigh of relief as he bent down and picked it up.

His relief didn't last long. The moment the torch left Toby's hands, the ants seemed to lose all interest in him. Even as he was being slowly winched upwards, the ant tower began to collapse. The creatures down at the bottom—the ones supporting all the rest—turned towards the new source of light and, as they did so, the tower swayed and started to fall apart. Ants dropped from the top, landing with heavy thuds on the floor of the cave—but even those crashing down headfirst didn't seem hurt by their falls. Instead, they simply righted themselves and started to scuttle across the floor, heading straight for Measle and the light.

The last thing Measle heard from Toby, before he ducked back into the dark tunnel, was the wrathmonk's booming laughter, getting steadily fainter and fainter as he was pulled to safety.

Bent double, Measle stumbled several metres into the tunnel, before his way was blocked by Iggy and Tinker. When he saw the light in Measle's hand, Iggy's face broke into a grin. 'Ooh!' he exclaimed, sounding happy for the first time in hours. 'You has got a lighty fing, I sssee! Dat is good, dat is. Now we can sssee where we is!'

Measle pointed the torch past Iggy and on down the tunnel. The passage extended as far as the eye could see, level and straight as an arrow, so that the beam of light eventually became too weak to penetrate any further.

Behind him, there was a clattering, chittering sound that was getting louder and louder. The ants were almost at the entrance. The tunnel was low and narrow and there was only room enough for Measle and Iggy to walk one behind the other. Pushing Iggy ahead of him, Measle moved a little way along the burrow—then he stopped and turned and pointed the beam back towards the entrance.

A single ant was pushing its way through the circular opening. Its body completely filled the entrance, but there was just enough space for it to move forwards, although the only way it could do that was to shove itself along using only its back pair of legs. But there was room enough for its great jaws to scythe backwards and forwards, in steady sweeping motions, and Measle saw that anything caught in those serrated mouth parts would be cut, and crushed, and turned into ant food in an instant.

But—wait a minute! It's a bug, isn't it?

Measle grabbed Iggy's shoulder and shouted, 'Iggy! Breathe on it!'

Iggy stared wildly past Measle, his round eyes even rounder with terror. 'You *wot?*' he whispered, and Measle could feel the bones of the little wrathmonk's shoulder trembling under his hand.

'It's a bug, Iggy! You can kill bugs with your breathing spell! So breathe on it, Iggy!'

Iggy shook his head. 'Bugs is sssmall! Dat—dat is too big!' he muttered, and Measle could hear the panic rising in his voice.

The ant was moving forwards steadily now and Measle, Iggy, and Tinker were just as steadily backing away. Tinker was barking continuously, but the ant took no notice of that and simply went on pushing itself along. It seemed to have got the hang of the movement, because it was accelerating a little. Measle realized that, if the tunnel should widen at any point along this route, then the ant would be able to use all its legs. He doubted they could outrun a creature the size of a tiger with six working legs and the sort of strength and stamina that would make an Olympic athlete look like a helpless invalid.

'Just one little puff, Iggy?' he wheedled, holding tight to Iggy's shoulder to stop him racing away down the tunnel. 'Just to see if it works? I bet it does! I bet your breathing spell is one of the most powerful ones around! I bet it drops down dead, Iggy! And then—then we'll be safe, don't you see?'

'No—I don't sssee!' whispered Iggy, trying to pull away from Measle's grasp. 'Wha-wha-what about all de *uvver* ones?'

'But don't you understand?' hissed Measle, tightening his grip. 'If you can kill this one, then the tunnel will be blocked—with its own body, see?—and all the other ones won't be able to get at us!'

It took Iggy several seconds to understand the logic of this and, while his small brain was working it out, his expression went through all the usual weird muscular contortions. Then, when the penny dropped, his expression cleared and he stared at Measle with a look of admiration.

'Dat is—dat is—dat is *brilliant*!' he exclaimed. Then, remembering that he liked to pretend that it was *him* that came up with these ideas, he said, coolly, 'Of courssse, I was finkin' dat myself, Mumps. I was finkin' dat, if I breave on de nasssty fing, den it will die, and den it will stop up dis hole wiv its body, and den de uvver nasssty fings won't be able to—'

'Yes! That's *brilliant*! Clever you!' Measle gave Iggy a quick hug. Then he glanced back at the oncoming ant—it was getting closer.

'The thing is, Iggy, it'll be even more brilliant if you do it *NOW*!'

Measle flattened himself against the tunnel wall and pulled Iggy close to him. There was no room for Iggy to move past him, but there was just enough space for him to peer round Measle's body and aim his breath down the tunnel.

Iggy took a deep breath and then started to blow, as hard as he could, in the direction of the scuttling creature.

It had been a long time since Measle had been in the direct line of fire of a wrathmonk's breath. The smell of a wrathmonk's breath is horrible.

And, because of the narrow confines of the tunnel, Iggy's breath seemed even worse than Measle remembered. It was still a combination of dead fish, old mattresses, and the insides of ancient sneakers—but it seemed so much *stronger* here.

Measle wanted to hold his nose against the stink, but his free hand was gripping the heavy torch which was aimed directly at the ant and Measle needed to see what, if any, its reaction to Iggy's breath would be.

Iggy went on blowing out his foul breath, without ever taking a breath in—and the cloud of invisible, magical gases built steadily in the narrow space. The ant must have pushed itself into the outer edge of these poisonous fumes, because quite suddenly it stopped moving forward. Its antennae twitched wildly for several seconds and then they drooped down over its great round head. The whole body of the enormous creature seemed to sag downwards and, a moment later— apart from the occasional twitch from the ends of its antennae—it lay still.

'You did it, Iggy!' said Measle, and he gave Iggy a big hug.

Iggy looked pleased with himself and said, '*Courssse* I did it, Mumps. I is tocally, tocally *brilliant!*'

The ant suddenly lurched backwards, as if some-thing very powerful was pulling it from behind.

Iggy jumped in terror and grabbed hold of Measle's hand.

'Oooh, dat fing has come alive again, Mumps!'

'No, Iggy, I think it's being pulled out of the way by another ant. Come on—more of them will be here in a minute. Or they might find another way in. We can't stay here.'

Measle led the way deeper into the tunnel, bent almost double by the low ceiling. Tinker trotted along behind him and, with many fearful glances over his shoulder, Iggy brought up the rear.

The tunnel continued, straight as an arrow, leading them deeper and deeper into the mountain. And then, quite suddenly, ahead of them was a curtain of grey mist that filled the confined space from floor to ceiling. The beam of light from the torch seemed unable to penetrate this layer, so when they reached it a minute later, Measle stopped and tried to peer through it. It was like trying to see through a piece of frosted glass. Carefully, Measle put his hand up and slowly pushed it into the mist—

It was very cold. Measle thought it was like putting his hand into the freezer compartment of a refrigerator. Tinker sniffed suspiciously at the wall of mist and then poked his head through it. He gave a sudden yelp of pleasure and, before Measle could stop him, he darted through and disappeared.

At the same moment, Measle smelt the powerful stink of formic acid—and he heard the clattering, chittering sound coming from behind. Without a moment's hesitation, he grabbed Iggy and, stepping firmly into the mist, he dragged the little wrathmonk in after him.

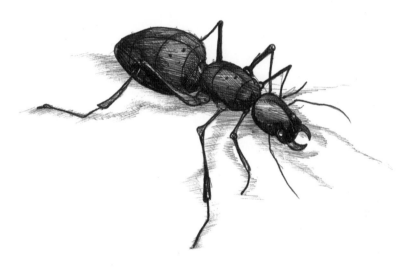

OUT IN THE COLD

After the darkness of the tunnel, the harsh white light momentarily blinded Measle and Iggy. Both of them threw up a hand to cover their eyes, and both squinted through their fingers at the world that lay before them. It was a world that couldn't have been more different from the one they'd just left.

First of all, where the tunnels and caves had been black, this world was almost pure white. As white as—well, as white as *snow*, which in fact, this world was covered with. *That explains the cold*, thought Measle, and he switched off the torch and stuffed it down the front of his jacket. Then he huddled the jacket around him and tucked his hands into his pockets.

The scene in front of them wasn't entirely white. They were standing high up, on what appeared to be the side of a huge mountain. All around them, black rocks poked up through the thick snow. Far below, high on the foothills of the mountain, there was a pine forest. The branches of the distant trees were covered in heavy layers of snow, but here and there the deep green pine needles poked through their coating of white. Even further down the slope, the trees petered out, revealing a broad field of what looked like enormous, jumbled chunks of ice. Measle's gaze traced the field backwards, towards a distant cleft in the mountains, and he saw that it had the rough shape of a meandering river—a glacier, perhaps? They'd been learning about glaciers at school . . .

An icy wind whistled around Measle's ears and even Iggy—who never seemed to feel the cold—pulled his shabby old jacket around his chest and folded his arms across the front to keep it closed. Tinker's four short legs were buried in the snow right up to his stomach and he was rapidly losing his enthusiasm for this new spot he'd discovered. Anything was better than those dark, stinky tunnels—but this place was cold!

'Er . . . Mumps,' whined Iggy, and Measle nodded and said, quickly, 'Yes, I know, Iggy, it is cold, isn't it? We'd better see if we can get out of this wind.'

Measle looked up and saw the summit of the mountain, far above. A plume of what looked like powdery snow was streaming off the rocky top of the mountain and Measle reckoned that the wind up there at the summit must be blowing at gale force. There was no point going in that direction, so Measle pointed down the steep slope and said, 'Come on—let's go that way.'

At least it was all downhill, because wading through the thick snow was sometimes a problem and, if they had tried to climb up through it, they might have found parts of it impossible. Poor Tinker, with his short, stumpy legs, couldn't get through it at all, so Measle picked him up and carried him under one arm. Iggy—who, when he wasn't happy with his surroundings, had a tendency to drag his feet (and you can't drag your feet when you're trying to struggle through thick snow)—fell over a lot, and complained bitterly every time he did.

At long last, with aching legs and wheezing lungs, they reached the edges of the pine forest. The effort of wading through the snow had warmed them up a lot and, once inside the shelter of the trees, the wind dropped to a whisper, so—while it was still bitterly cold—at least Measle and Iggy weren't being frozen to death. Tinker, huddled against Measle, was just fine, of course.

They stood there, under the shelter of the pine trees, giving their legs and lungs a rest and wondering which way to go next. Iggy sniffed loudly and said, 'Where is all de houses? Dere's never any houses in dese ssstoopid places. Where is dey, Mumps?'

'I don't think that legends live in houses.'

'Den dey is ssstoopid legends,' muttered Iggy. His toes were beginning to feel like ten ice cubes.

They set off again, trudging along under the trees. The snow was a little less deep in the woods, so the going was easier, but they still were making slow progress.

And then it started to get even colder.

For no apparent reason that Measle could detect, there was a sudden and frightening drop in temperature. Measle could feel a deep chill seeping through his body. Already, his feet were going numb.

'We've got to find somewhere to shelter,' he said.

'Yesss,' said Iggy, 'and sssomwhere what has got a nice 'lectric fire, an' a larder wiv food inssside, an' a vellytision—'

And that's when they fell through the snow.

For half a second, they fell through air—then their backs made contact with an almost vertical wall and they found themselves half-falling, half-sliding, down a sheet of what felt like smooth ice.

Iggy screamed all the way down. He must have used his wrathmonk breath, because the scream went on and on and on, with never a breath taken in. Tinker had fallen off Measle's chest and was now sliding close by him. Apart from a surprised yelp when the ground first gave way beneath him, he didn't make a sound and Measle was too startled—and then too frightened—to utter even a squeak. He saw Iggy, his arms flailing, his mouth wide open and his eyes tight shut.

The slope of the ice wall finally became less steep and now they were sliding and not falling, which was a small relief. Also, Measle could see what was up ahead. About a hundred metres down, the wall looked as if it was going to curve, quite sharply, from the almost vertical, to the horizontal, and then to level out.

A few seconds later, Measle, Iggy, and Tinker found themselves sliding, at a speed that was impossible to control, across a smooth ice floor. They were in some sort of wide tunnel, with walls that were as smooth as the floor. All three of them were spinning as they slid, their fingers or paws desperately trying to catch on to the ice in order to slow themselves down—but there was nothing to grab on to.

Slowly, very slowly, they came to a halt and it was only then that Iggy stopped screaming. He opened his eyes carefully, to make sure he wasn't dead. Then he sat up and felt himself all over to see if any part of his body hurt. Nothing seemed to be broken or even sprained. He grinned shakily and, pretending that it hadn't been him screaming all the way down, he said, 'Coo! Dat was *fun*! Where is we, Mumps?'

'I think—I think we're inside the glacier.'

'De *wot*-ier?'

'The glacier. It's a river made of ice. I saw the outside of it when we were up high—and now I think we're inside it.'

Tinker tried to stand up, but the ice was slippery and all four paws slid out sideways, dumping his stomach back onto the ice. He tried again, this time more slowly, and succeeded in standing upright. Measle had seen his efforts, so when he got to his feet, he did it very carefully before looking around at their surroundings.

The end of the tunnel was only a few metres away, so Measle shuffled his feet across the ice in that direction. Tinker, his nose twitching, was cautiously moving towards it too—and they would have got there much more quickly, if Iggy hadn't had so much trouble standing up.

There was a thump, then, 'Ow!' came Iggy's voice from behind them. Measle and Tinker turned and saw Iggy sitting on the ice, one hand rubbing his hip.

'Dat is *impossiffle*!' he announced, glaring angrily down at the floor. 'Completely *impossiffle*!'

'What's impossible, Iggy?'

'Ssstandin' up! Dat's what's impossiffle!'

Measle carefully shuffled back to Iggy, grabbed him under the armpits and lifted him to his feet. Instantly, Iggy's legs flew out from under him and he sat down again with another bone-jarring thump.

'Not only impossiffle!' he snarled, furiously. 'Dat alssso *hurts*, Mumps!'

It took Measle several minutes to get Iggy upright and balanced and, in that time, Tinker's nose was making a couple of discoveries. Somewhere up ahead, there were some interesting smells. One was quite strong—a heavy, musky odour, like that of a large animal of some kind. Equally strong was the stink of rotting meat and old bones, which—for Tinker—was slightly more interesting than the musky smell, because if you were a dog, you could eat rotten meat and you could chew old bones.

There was another smell and, while it wasn't of anything edible, it was still quite interesting in its own way—partly because it didn't seem to fit with the others. The first lot of odours had put into Tinker's mind the image of a largish animal and its lair, where it ate its food and dropped the bones and the leftovers. This third smell was altogether more delicate. It had a faint trace of some sort of flower, but not organic—more *chemical*, like you might get from some sort of soap, or possibly shampoo.

Tinker's nose twitched with the effort of identifying what, exactly, could be making this smell and he stepped a little closer to the end of the tunnel, moving his paws carefully over the ice.

'Tinker!' called Measle. 'Wait for us!'

Tinker stopped and waited for Measle and Iggy to catch up. It took a long time, because Iggy had to be supported all the way, and he shuffled his feet so slowly, and in such tiny movements, that it was a full minute and a half before they came level with Tinker's nose. Tinker's nose was sticking out from the end of the tunnel and was twitching away busily, sniffing the smells floating in the still, cold air of a narrow cave of ice.

'Oooh!' moaned Iggy. 'Not *anuvver* cave!'

Measle's nose wasn't anything like as keen as Tinker's, so he couldn't smell anything—not yet, at least. But his eyes were excellent and he saw that the soft blue light seemed to be coming from the same direction that Tinker was headed in, so he put one arm round Iggy's waist and together they shuffled along in Tinker's pawprints.

They turned a corner and found a thin layer of snow covering the ground, which made walking a little less slippery. Another corner—the light steadily brightening—and now the ground was scattered with other things besides snow.

Bones.

Bones of every size. There were several skulls of large animals, some with antlers still attached, which Measle recognized as some sort of deer. There were a few that Measle couldn't identify at all and one with a mouthful of sharp teeth, that looked positively prehistoric. Some of the smaller bones still had little bits of frozen meat sticking to them and Tinker was tempted to pick one up and see what it tasted like but Measle whispered, 'No, Tink!' and made a warning sign with one hand, so Tinker—who trusted the smelly kid's instincts when it came to sensing danger—left the bone alone and walked a little closer to his master.

Now Measle could smell the stink of rotting meat and he wrinkled his nose in disgust. Iggy, on the other hand, looked a lot happier.

'Cooo!' he said, conversationally—and Measle quickly clamped a hand over Iggy's mouth and shook his head firmly. Iggy nodded, to show that he understood he was to be quiet, and Measle took his hand away.

'I was jussst goin' to sssay, Mumps,' whispered Iggy, 'dat I *like* dis place. It sssmells *'ssstremely* nice.'

Measle didn't like this place at all. Bones in a cave meant only one thing. A meat eater lived here and it—whatever 'it' was—could be round the next corner, just waiting to pounce on any passing traveller.

Measle was leading the way now, and moving very cautiously. Every time they came to a blind corner, he would stop, motion to Iggy and Tinker to do the same, and then he would slowly poke his head around the corner to see what was up ahead.

This time, Measle paused longer than usual and Iggy, who was right behind him, tapped him on the shoulder and whispered, 'Wot is it, Mumps?'

Measle reached behind him, took hold of Iggy's hand and slowly pulled the little wrathmonk close to his side—and then Iggy saw what had made Measle stop. They were in the main part of the creature's lair. About twenty metres away was the entrance to the cave and that was the source of the light that cast the blue glow over the walls of ice. Between the entrance and the spot where they stood lay the evidence that this was, indeed, the home of something or other—and this something or other was obviously a creature that had more intelligence than a bear or a tiger or a wolf, because there were no animal bones strewn here. Obviously, the cave's owner used the rear sections of its home to store its food and to throw its rubbish, preferring to keep the section close to the entrance reasonably clean and tidy. In fact, there was nothing much there, other than a rough heap of what looked like animal skins, all piled haphazardly against one wall, and another mound of sticks and dried grass nearby, which to Measle's eyes looked as if it might be a bed of some sort.

Other than that, the cave seemed to be empty. Whatever creature inhabited this ice cave, it wasn't at home right now—but it could come home at any minute.

'Come on,' said Measle, under his breath. 'We can't stay here.'

'Why?' said Iggy, petulantly. 'Dis is a nice place. Dis is de nicest place we bin to yet! It sssmells *lubberly*! Dere is even ssstuff to eat! Nice *old* meat! Why can't we ssstay 'ere, Mumps?'

There wasn't time for a long explanation, so Measle simply started to walk briskly towards the cave entrance, with Iggy and Tinker right behind him.

They were halfway there when the mound of animal skins began to move.

The Party Grows

Tinker saw it first and he bared his teeth and growled deep in his throat. Measle and Iggy turned their heads at the sound and saw, with fast-mounting horror, the entire heap of animal skins shifting, as if something beneath them was struggling to rise to its feet. Measle shrank back against the ice wall, dragging Iggy with him.

Then a small head poked out from under a shaggy pelt of matted fur and said, 'Measle? Is—is that you?'

It was Polly. Her hair was tousled, her face had smudges of dirt on it, and her eyes were wide with a mixture of terror and relief.

'Polly!' said Measle, letting go of Iggy and running to her side. He helped pull the stack of animal furs off her and, shakily, she got to her feet. The moment she did so, she threw both arms round Measle, pressed her head against his chest and started to cry. Measle didn't know what to do. Awkwardly, he patted her shoulder and said, 'It's all right, Polly. It's all right.'

Of course, it *wasn't* all right at all but the pats and the vaguely comforting words seemed to do the trick, because Polly suddenly pulled her head from Measle's chest, swiped a grubby hand across her eyes, gulped twice, and then stopped crying.

'Sorry,' she muttered.

'It's OK,' said Measle. He glanced around the cave, looking towards the entrance. Polly saw him do it and said, in a voice that quavered with fear, 'It went out about ten minutes ago. I—I don't know when it'll be back.'

'It?'

'You're not going to believe this, Measle, but I think—I think it's a Yeti.'

'A what?'

Polly glanced at him. 'Don't you remember? We did something about them in class, with Mr Lockey—he told us about Bigfoot—Sasquatch—the Abominable Snowman?'

'Oh, yes. Right. The big hairy thing.'

'If you don't believe me, just wait a few minutes—'

Measle held up his hands and said, 'I believe you, Polly.'

Polly looked a little startled and said, 'You do?'

'Of course I do. This Yeti thing—it's all part of the stories you know, you see.'

Polly shook her head, her tangled hair dancing round her face. 'No—I don't see at all. What are you talking about?'

Measle told her, in a few short sentences, everything he knew about this place called Dystopia and, at the end of it, Polly was gazing at him through eyes wide with wonder.

'And—and we can't get out of here?' she whispered.

'I don't see how,' said Measle. 'Not unless somebody lowers a rope and, even then, who knows where the rope'll end up? There are lots of worlds here, Polly. But what about this Yeti thing? Tell me what happened?'

Polly shuddered. Then, quickly, she said, 'When Toby dropped me down that well thing—'

'The Doompit—'

'Right—the Doompit—well, I fell into a deep snow bank. I was just lying there, a bit dazed, I suppose—and then this enormous hand came out of nowhere and grabbed me—it's really *huge*, Measle, and it smells really horrible. I screamed a lot but it took no notice—it just carried me back here and dumped me on the heap of skins and then it went over there—' (Polly waved vaguely in the direction of the entrance)'—and then it just sat there, staring at me with these horrible black

eyes—I tried to get out but it wouldn't let me go
past it—'

'It didn't try to kill you? And eat you?'

'Not yet,' said Polly, miserably. 'It just seems to
want to look at me.'

Measle was thinking that he and this Yeti thing
seemed to have something in common, when Polly
suddenly looked over his shoulder and said, 'Er . . .
who's that, Measle?'

Measle turned and saw Iggy, his back pressed
flat against the opposite wall of the ice cave. Iggy's
mouth was open and he was staring, with a look of
deep distaste, at Polly.

'Oh, that's just Iggy,' said Measle, wondering how
much to tell Polly. He decided that the basics
would do for the moment. He lowered his voice to
a whisper and said, 'He's a wrathmonk, like Toby—
but it's OK, he's my friend, so he won't hurt you.
Actually, he *can't* hurt you. He's only got one spell

and it doesn't damage anybody—and his wrathmonk breath just kills bugs, so he's harmless.' Measle put his head a little closer to Polly's and, in a voice even more hushed than before, he whispered, 'And—he's not very bright, OK?'

Polly nodded. Then she put her head round Measle's shoulder and said, 'Hello, Iggy.'

Iggy was so astonished at being spoken to by this complete stranger, that he jumped several centimetres into the air. When his feet touched down again on the snowy floor, they skidded out from under him, depositing him with the usual *thump!* onto the hard ground.

'Ow!' said Iggy, loudly. Then, ignoring the pain, he struggled to his feet, pointed a trembling finger at Polly and said, 'Wot—wot—wot is *dat*, Mumps?'

'This is Polly,' said Measle, immediately sensing trouble. 'And she's a *friend* of mine, Iggy, just like *you* are. So, we're all going to be friends together, aren't we?' He turned to Polly, winked encouragingly at her and said, loudly, so that Iggy could hear, 'You'll be Iggy's friend, won't you, Polly?'

'Y-yes,' said Polly, a little uncertainly, because Iggy was still staring at her with a look of outraged bewilderment.

Tinker didn't need to be told to be anybody's buddy—as long as they were human, that is. He was pleased to discover where the soap smell came from and the small person (*the soapy kid* was what Tinker decided to call her) seemed friendly enough, because she'd bent down and had scratched the top of his head. So now Tinker was sitting at Polly's feet, gazing expectantly up at her—and hoping for another scratch quite soon.

Iggy was struggling with the concept of somebody else besides Mumps being his friend. His face had started its usual wriggling contortions as he tried to think about this odd idea—and Polly was looking at him in astonishment, because it seemed to her that Iggy was just pulling a lot of rather rude faces, and all in her direction.

'He's just thinking,' whispered Measle. 'He always does that when he's thinking.'

Eventually, Iggy's face settled down. He'd decided to be nice— well, as nice as a wrathmonk could be, which wasn't particularly nice at all.

'Polly, huh?' he said, haughtily, looking down his beaky nose at the girl. 'Dat is a funny name. Dat is de name you call dose ssstoopid birds, wot talk. I sssaw one of dose birds once. It was dead ssstoopid. All it sssaid was, "Hello, Polly," which was dead ssstoopid, because dat was its own name, sssee? And ssso it was jussst talkin' to itself, sssee? And only ssstoopid people do dat, sssee? I 'ssspect you do dat, don't you, Polly? Talk to yoursssself, huh? Do you? Do you? Do you? Do—'

'Shut up, Iggy,' said Measle.

Iggy looked deeply offended, but he closed his mouth with a snap and then just stood there, gazing sulkily at the floor.

There was no time to cope with one of Iggy's moods and Measle said, briskly, 'We should try to go before that thing comes back.'

Polly grabbed his hand. 'But—it could be right outside, Measle! That's why I was hiding in that smelly pile of skins! I thought that it might think I'd escaped when it couldn't find me, and go off looking for me, and then I could *really* escape!'

'Well, there's one way to find out if it's outside,' said Measle.

Trying not to make a sound, he walked carefully to the cave entrance. Then—centimetre by centimetre—he poked his head out, his eyes scanning the surroundings.

It was bleak out there. The glacier was below the tree line and the scenery was desolate—a jumble of ice and snow, as far as the eye could see. Measle was about to withdraw into the cave when, quite suddenly—at the edge of his vision—he caught a distant movement. He nearly didn't see it. Whatever was moving out there was almost the same colour as the ice and snow. He peered, focusing on the movement.

Two hundred metres away, and shambling towards him at a swift pace, was a gigantic creature, at least three times the height of a man. It's legs were oddly short, but its arms were very long, so that the thing's knuckles almost brushed the ground. As far as Measle could see, it appeared to be covered in a coat of long white hair—and it was this whiteness against the background of snow and ice that had made it hard to detect. In fact, what Measle had seen was the moving dark spot that was the creature's face. The contrast between face and body was marked. While the thing's head was draped with long white fur, the face itself was hairless, a blueish black colour, and so were the enormous feet and the enormous hands.

It's got hands! thought Measle. *Like a gorilla or a chimpanzee—but that's no gorilla coming up the hill towards me.*

He ducked back inside the cave and hurried to Polly. 'It's coming back!' he gasped. 'It'll be here in a minute!'

'What'll we do?' said Polly, her face going pale beneath the dirt.

Measle's mind raced. But it didn't race fast enough, because the seconds were ticking away.

Out of the corner of his eye, he saw Iggy (who obviously wasn't aware of the impending danger, or else he'd be running in small circles, squealing in panic)—he saw him idly reach into his trouser pocket, take out a red jelly bean and pop it into his mouth.

The jelly beans! Of course!

Measle plunged his own hands into his pockets and, avoiding the plastic bag with Toby's eye in it, he scooped up every bean he could feel.

Among the rest of the colours—the useless colours—there were the two remaining yellow ones, three green ones—and a single, lonely-looking pink one.

As quickly as he could, he sorted the yellow, green, and pink ones, transferred them to his other hand and then poured the rest back into his pocket.

'What are you doing?' hissed Polly.

'We're each going to eat a jelly bean,' said Measle, pushing the pink one at Polly. 'Thirty seconds,' he said, throwing a quick look towards the cave mouth. 'That's how long they last. You sort of have to count backwards and then take another one just before it wears off—'

'But—but I've only got one! What do I do when—'

Polly got no further, because a shadow fell over the cave entrance. Measle instantly raced to Iggy's side, pressed the green jelly beans into his hand, and then scooped up Tinker into his arms.

The shadow across the entrance darkened, and the light in the cave dimmed—

'Now!' hissed Measle, popping a yellow jelly bean into his mouth and biting down hard.

Polly watched Iggy do the same thing. He threw a green bean into his mouth almost as quickly as Measle had done—and, before her eyes, Measle and Iggy dissolved into a few wisps of grey smoke, which thinned and vanished in a fraction of a second. Polly didn't need any more proof than that. She put the pink bean into her mouth, bit down on it—

And nothing happened.

Polly stayed as visible as she'd ever been—and the only effect that she was aware of was the sweet and sickly taste of pink bubblegum in her dry mouth.

There was a grunt from the entrance. Polly looked up and saw the enormous figure of the Yeti, completely filling the opening. The creature glanced at her—a small girl, standing fearfully by the pile of animal skins—then it squatted down and stared at her, without expression. It sniffed, its dark eyes roaming round the cave.

Measle and Iggy were pressed against the ice wall and Measle was trying to do three things at once. He was holding Tinker against his chest, tight in the crook of his arm, with his hand wrapped round Tinker's nose to stop him from growling; he had his free elbow pressed against Iggy's skinny frame, with just enough pressure to discourage Iggy from saying something out loud about the awful failure of the pink jelly bean; and he was mentally counting backwards:

... twenty-four ... twenty-three ... twenty-two— and, why hadn't the pink one worked? Polly's just standing there—not doing anything—in full sight of that horrible great monster—nineteen ... eighteen ... seventeen ...

The monster suddenly raised one of its huge black hands and, quite gently, tossed something across the cave. It landed with a soft thump at Polly's feet.

It was a dead rabbit.

It's trying to feed her, thought Measle. *And that means it doesn't want to kill her. But it might feel differently about Iggy, Tinker, and me—and the seconds are ticking away ... fourteen ... thirteen ... twelve ...*

'Popcorn,' said Polly.

If Measle had been asked to predict what Polly would say—or even, given the circumstances, that she would say anything at all—he'd never have guessed it would be that single word, 'popcorn'.

The Yeti raised its great shaggy head and peered at her from under the bony ridge of its brows. Polly smiled at it and said, in a voice that sounded as if she was simply starting a friendly conversation with the monster, 'I'm really sorry but I've just remembered that there's a jelly bean I hate more than the pink ones. I don't like the taste of the bubblegum flavour, but I really *hate* the ones that are supposed to be like popcorn. They're white, with yellow and brown bits on them and I really, really hope you've got some of them, Measle.'

The Yeti grunted. It had no idea what Polly was saying but it liked the tone of her voice. It was very soothing . . .

Measle's mind was fizzing. What Polly had just done was very brave, and rather clever. The only problem was, there was no way to find out if he had any white jelly beans—not while he was invisible, because the beans in his hand would be invisible too. Measle tried to think—and still count down at the same time. *I've only got one yellow bean left, Iggy's only got two more of his green ones, we'll be visible sooner or later . . . nine . . . eight . . . somehow, I've got to create a distraction— maybe make the creature leave the cave for a moment or two.*

At Measle's feet were a few small chunks of ice. In one quick, impulsive movement, he bent down, picked up one and threw it, as hard as he could, towards the cave entrance. The chunk sailed over the Yeti's head and clattered onto the topmost edge of the opening. It broke into a hundred smaller pieces, which showered down onto the Yeti's shoulders. The reaction of the creature was startling in its swiftness. It leapt to its feet, whirled round, and peered out of the cave entrance—but it didn't leave!

... seven ... six ... five ...

Measle bent down, picked up another piece of ice and threw again, and it too shattered into smaller fragments, just over the Yeti's head.

It turned, its black eyes darting furiously round the cave.

That was when Tinker decided that if things were being chucked about the place, then these same things needed to be chased. He suddenly wriggled violently, slipping neatly out of Measle's arms. The moment he was free of contact with Measle, Tinker materialized—first as a wisp of grey smoke, then in a flash becoming his solid, white and furry self. As his feet touched the icy floor, he was completely visible—and the Yeti saw him. It roared—a deafening sound in the confines of the cave—and, reaching out its massive arms, it lumbered towards the little dog. But Tinker was so intent on playing the throw-and-retrieve game that he took no notice of the huge creature bearing down on him. He simply raced for the spot where the last chunk of ice had exploded and, in doing so, he darted straight between the Yeti's legs. The monster roared again and turned, reaching out one massive black paw to grab at the elusive little dog, but Tinker had reached the cave entrance and had already turned round, to wait for the next missile that was going to be thrown.

That was when he saw that there was nobody who wanted to play with him. The smelly kid and the nasty damp thing were nowhere to be seen, and the soapy kid was just standing there, with the dead rabbit at her feet, showing no sign at all that she was going to throw it for him.

But there *was* this extremely large and scary-looking monster, roaring its head off and coming towards him fast—and the creature's mouth was wide open and its teeth were yellow and long and sharp, and its great blue-black hands were reaching for him—

Tinker jumped round and, with his ears flat and his tail tucked, raced away—and out of the cave.

The Yeti, moving at a speed which was extraordinary for a creature of its size and bulk, shambled after him. It hadn't yet reached the cave entrance when Measle and Iggy became visible again—but, with its back to them, and intent on catching the small furry invader of its cave, the Yeti didn't see them. In a moment, it was gone.

Measle ran to Polly's side, his fingers fumbling in his pockets for the few remaining jelly beans. He took them all out and he and Polly craned their heads together over the small heap in his palm.

There were two white beans there, speckled with yellow and brown.

'Are you sure this time?' said Measle, as Polly took them from him.

Polly nodded. 'Actually, they make me feel a bit sick.'

'Good,' said Measle.

Iggy wandered over and joined them. 'Dat nasssty little doggie 'as gone,' he announced, with satisfaction. 'Maybe de big monsssster will eat 'im?' he added, hopefully.

'Oh, the poor little thing!' said Polly, turning and gazing anxiously at the cave entrance. 'Will he be all right?'

'I should think so,' said Measle. 'Tinker's very fast.' Privately, Measle was thinking, *Tink's fast, but so is the Yeti. And there's all that deep snow out there ...*

'Come on,' he said. 'We've got to get out of here right now. Iggy, when I say "NOW!", eat another jelly bean. Polly, you do the same thing with one of yours—and let's hope it works this time.'

'Shouldn't we test it first?' said Polly, looking doubtfully down at the two beans in her hand. Measle shook his head and said, 'We can't waste them. And they ought to work, if you're absolutely sure this time—?'

'I'm sure,' said Polly, firmly. 'The popcorn ones are completely disgusting!'

Measle led them to the cave entrance and peeked out. There was nothing to see—apart from the Yeti's huge, dragging footprints, which led away from the cave and then disappeared over a small rise in the snowy landscape. There was no sign of Tinker's tracks and Measle guessed they must have been obliterated by the Yeti's footsteps.

So, no need for the jelly beans—not yet . . .

'Come on.'

Measle led the way, wading through the snow in the opposite direction from the tracks. They had got about a hundred metres from the cave, when there was a distant roar from off to the left.

The Yeti was there, a little down-slope of them. And it had seen them. It started to lumber up towards them. It was carrying something in one gigantic paw. The something was moving—wriggling—struggling to be free. Measle could hear the high-pitched snarls and yelps as Tinker snapped at the creature that held him so tightly.

'Oh!' wailed Polly. 'It's got your dog!'

'Oooh good!' said Iggy, failing completely to keep the smugness out of his voice. 'And now de monsssster is goin' to eat 'im up!'

'Shut up, Iggy!' said Measle, sharply. He needed time to sort out a double problem—how to rescue Tinker and how to escape, themselves, from the Yeti, which even now was shambling towards them at high speed through the knee-deep snow.

The idea came to him in a flash.

'Snowballs!' he exclaimed. 'Quick—everybody take a jelly bean then make a snowball and, when the Yeti gets close, throw it at him as hard as you can! All right? *Now*, Iggy! *NOW!*'

Iggy popped a green jelly bean into his mouth and bit down on it. Polly wrinkled her nose and put one of her popcorn-flavoured beans onto her tongue and Measle threw his last remaining yellow bean into his mouth and chewed hard—and all three of them disappeared.

'Now—*snowballs!*' he yelled.

'Oh—wow!' he heard Polly whisper. Then he was down on his invisible knees, scooping together a big handful of snow. Next to him, two sets of furrows suddenly appeared, apparently digging themselves—and Measle knew with relief that Iggy and Polly were obeying his instructions.

The Yeti had stopped about ten metres away and, puzzled by the sudden disappearance of its quarry, was peering from left to right, its great shaggy head swinging from side to side. Tinker went on struggling in the creature's black paw, twisting his head and trying to snap at the massive fingers curled tightly around his body.

Measle was counting down in his head, with the sick realization that, with no more lemon-flavoured jelly beans left, once he reached zero, that was that for him. By the time he reached . . . *eighteen . . . seventeen . . . sixteen . . .* his snowball was ready. He stood up and, hoping wildly that Polly and Iggy were armed as well, he shouted, 'Now! As hard as you can! *Throw!*'

Three snowballs appeared and sailed through the air. One missed the Yeti completely but two hit the creature square in the face, exploding across its nose and eyes in a shower of icy particles. The Yeti grunted in shock, and wiped its face with its free paw—but it didn't let go of Tinker. Instead, it gave another furious roar and stepped forward.

'Quick—another one!' shouted Measle, and, a moment later, three more snowballs whistled through the air. This time, all of them hit the mark—two exploded against the monster's chest and one shattered across its gaping mouth.

The Yeti stopped and spat and coughed. Then it snarled, its beady black eyes darting all over the blank landscape—but it still held tightly to Tinker.

There was no time for another snowball.

... *nine ... eight ... seven ...*

And then Measle remembered another missile, striking another dangerous creature—and right between the eyes, too ...

'Polly!' he hissed. 'Your spell! The boxing glove! Do it! Do it now!'

He heard Polly's quick intake of breath and then—

'Pugilis Crestor Sejetto!'

The red boxing glove popped into existence, hovering at eye level above the ground. Then, with far more force and velocity than any snowball, it zipped across the eight metres that separated Polly and the Yeti and hit the monster—with a solid-sounding THUD!—smack on its nose.

The first thing the Yeti did was to drop Tinker.

The second thing the Yeti did was to utter a strange, high-pitched squeal, like the sound of a frightened pig. The third thing the Yeti did was press both its black paws to its face—and, at the same moment, it staggered backwards, its feet slipping and sliding beneath it, until suddenly it lost its balance and sat down heavily in the soft snow.

'Tinker! Here, boy!' yelled Measle and Tinker raced as fast as he could towards the sound of the smelly kid's voice. Measle struggled through the snow and met him halfway. He quickly lifted Tinker into his arms and turned away. As he did so, the jelly bean spell wore off and he reappeared—a small boy, clutching a small dog, staggering through the clinging drifts of snow, towards two other small figures, which had also just materialized out of the thin, cold air.

'*Run!*' yelled Measle, frantically waving his free hand at Polly and Iggy. He glanced back over his shoulder. The Yeti was struggling to its feet—

Polly and Iggy were already wading through the snow, desperately trying to get up enough speed so that it at least *looked* as if they were running—but running through deep, soft snow is almost impossible. Behind them, they could hear the heavy, angry grunts of the Yeti, getting louder and louder and louder. Measle risked a quick look backwards. The Yeti was only about five metres away and gaining steadily. Already its huge arms—each one as thick as a small tree—were reaching for them, the massive fingers flexing, the curved black claws glinting in the sunshine—

The ground suddenly sloped away beneath them and Measle, Polly, and Iggy found themselves half-stumbling, half-tumbling down the hill. Only the heavy, clinging snow allowed them to keep themselves on their feet—and at least they were now moving a little faster—but still not fast enough. Just before they reached the ice sheet, Measle could have sworn he felt the actual hot breath of the Yeti on the back of his neck.

The ice sheet came as a complete surprise. The snow thinned to nothing and quite suddenly they were slipping and sliding on a steep field of snow-free ice, that stretched out ahead of them in one smooth expanse of gleaming whiteness.

Iggy was the first to lose his balance. His feet slid from under him and he fell heavily on his back. Polly, who was right behind him, tripped over his body and fell across him—and Iggy, who was in the middle of saying 'OOOOOOOWWW!' suddenly found all the breath knocked out of his lungs, so all he managed was '*OW!*'

Measle, burdened by the weight of Tinker, couldn't use his arms to help himself balance, and he too found himself flat on his back a second later, still clutching Tinker to his chest.

Now they were sliding faster and faster, gathering speed as gravity dragged them across the slick ice. Iggy got his breath back a moment or two later, and he screamed, 'WHY DON'T DIS SSSTOOPID PLACE KEEP *SSSTILL!*'

There was only one thing to be said for this uncontrolled, headlong trip downwards—Measle managed to look back up the slope and he saw that the Yeti had stopped, right where the snow layer petered out, and was just standing there, its knuckles resting on the ground, glaring down in fury at its rapidly receding prey. But it made no move to step onto the ice—*and that*, thought Measle, *is a good thing!*

Polly and Iggy had got themselves disentangled and were sliding together, just ahead of Measle and a little to one side, and he looked past them, down the long, shiny hill—

—which appeared just to *stop*! There, two

hundred metres away, Measle could see a sort of lip on the ice—and beyond it, there was nothing. It was as if the hill simply ended . . .

There was nothing they could do about anything. Polly obviously saw what was coming up, because she uttered a long, wailing cry of despair. Iggy, who was far too busy being furious at this idiotic world to notice anything, kept up a stream of irritable comments.

'Ssstoopid place—can't ssstand up in it—can't sssit down in it—full of ssstoopid monsssters—I hate dis!—I hate it, I hate it, *I hate it*—!'

And, on the last '*hate it!*', Iggy, Polly, Measle, and Tinker slid up to and over the edge of the ice field. One moment they could feel the pressure of the ground against their backs—the next, that pressure disappeared, only to be replaced with the sickening sensation of falling.

Measle looked down.

Then he wished he hadn't.

Far, far below, at the bottom of the enormous ice cliff, was a tumbling, rushing river. The river appeared to emerge from a cave at the foot of the cliff. The water was white and foaming, a torrent that crashed and splashed over masses of black shiny rocks.

With the icy wind tearing at his clothes and hair, Measle held Tinker tight, closed his eyes, and waited for the end.

THE DESERT

The moment they sailed over the edge of the cliff, Iggy stopped his complaints and decided to scream instead. Once again, he seemed to be using his wrathmonk breath, because the scream went on and on and on and on—

They were falling so fast that Measle was finding it difficult to breathe at all, let alone make any sound. Polly was obviously experiencing the same, because there wasn't a peep out of her either—and Tinker was too shocked by this bizarre new experience that he simply buried his head in the folds of Measle's jacket and, like his master, waited for it all to stop.

Then, in a totally unexpected way, it did.

One minute, they were free-falling, an icy blast

ripping at their clothes and skin, and the next, they were plunging into water as warm as a bath, with no more force than if they'd just jumped off the edge of a swimming pool. It was so shocking, that Measle gasped and took in a lungful of water, which made him choke and cough and splutter. He let go of Tinker and flailed his arms wildly and then, to his surprise, his feet touched the bottom. It felt like soft mud and he straightened his knees—and found himself standing in a pond, in water up to his neck. Iggy was splashing about nearby, squealing furiously and Polly was already climbing out onto a low, sandy bank covered with tall reeds.

Another Dystopian world, thought Measle. *And, so far, a lot nicer than the last one.*

There was another difference from the world of ice and snow and Yetis—it was night-time here. A warm, velvety blackness surrounded them, the only light coming from a sky filled with billions of stars. Measle had never seen so many. He remembered being told that you saw more stars when you were a good long way from civilization, with its street lamps and its car headlights and its office blocks blazing with light bulbs, which effectively blotted out all but the brightest stars. *Well, in that case, we're right out in the middle of nowhere!* he thought.

Measle pushed Tinker towards the bank and then waded over to Iggy and grabbed him by the collar of his shabby old coat.

'Stop splashing about, Iggy,' he said. 'You're not drowning. See—you can stand up. It's all right.'

'All right? *All right?* No, it is *not* all right! All dis ssstoopid water! I is not all right at all! I is all *wet*, not all *right*!'

Together, they waded through the water to the bank. Tinker was there already, busy shaking himself dry, and Polly was peering in all directions, standing on tiptoe, trying to look over the reeds. When Measle came and stood next to her, she turned and looked at him through wide eyes.

'That was—that was—the *weirdest* thing that's ever, *ever* happened to me!' she said.

'Me too,' said Measle—although, in fact, he could think of several occasions at least as weird, if not weirder. Certainly this one had been the *luckiest*— the fact that they were all still alive and well and not frozen to death in an icy river, or shattered to death against sharp black rocks, was truly remarkable.

'Where are we?' said Polly.

'Sssomewhere really ssstoopid,' muttered Iggy. He was pulling his few remaining red jelly beans out of his pockets and trying to stuff the melting, gooey mess into his mouth before it all dissolved away into nothing. Water streamed from his soaking clothes and he looked thoroughly miserable.

There was something missing. It took a moment before Measle recognized what it was.

'Where's your umbrella, Iggy?' he said, trying to remember the last time he'd seen Iggy carrying it.

Yes! In the forest—when Iggy got stung—he'd dropped the umbrella there . . .

Iggy looked up, as if expecting to see the umbrella looming over his head. When he realized it wasn't there, he looked guilty and muttered, 'Dunno. Lossst it.'

Even in this warm dry air, Iggy's tiny wrathmonk rain cloud still hovered overhead, drizzling its droplets down on Iggy's already soaking head. Measle said, 'Why don't you whistle for it, Iggy?'

Iggy sighed heavily, like somebody who has just been asked a really silly question. 'I is *already* wet, Mumps,' he explained patiently. 'You fink my humble-ella is goin' to make me nice and dry, do you?'

'No. I just think it'll stop you getting even wetter. And, if you're not getting any wetter, then this nice warm air will dry you off really quickly. And that'll be good, won't it?'

Iggy's face wriggled about for a bit. Then he said, in a smug voice, 'Well, dat is wot I was goin' to do, before you interbubbled me, Missster Clever Clogs! I was goin' to whissstle for my humble-ella, because, you sssee, I don't want to get any wetter dan I is already, and dis nice warm air will make me dry—and I can't fink why you didn't fink of dat before!'

Iggy pursed his lips and whistled.

Tweeee—twee-twee-twee—tweeeee!

Nothing happened for half a minute—then something large and round and black blotted out a circle of stars. As the umbrella sped towards them, it obliterated more and more stars, so that it looked like a black hole in the sky, a hole that was getting steadily bigger and bigger and bigger.

Iggy held out his hand and the handle of the umbrella dropped neatly into his open palm.

'Sssee, Mumps,' said Iggy, like a teacher starting a lecture, 'dat is wot you do when you forget where you put your humble-ella—'

He didn't get any further, because Measle was staring with mounting horror up at the umbrella. So was Polly, with an expression more of wonder than horror. Tinker was also glaring up at a point above Iggy's head, a low growl rumbling in his throat.

'Wot?' said Iggy, frowning heavily. 'Whasssamatter wiv you all?'

'Keep still, Iggy,' whispered Measle. '*Keep very, very still.*'

Iggy froze. Slowly he raised his fishy eyes and looked up into the umbrella.

There was what appeared to be a nest, built into the metal ribs. The nest was made of twigs and grass and stalks of flowers, all cleverly woven together to form a sort of thick mat. But it wasn't this woven mat that was attracting attention. It was the four pairs of slanting, emerald-green eyes that were peering angrily over the edge.

There was a sudden buzzing sound and four fairies lifted off the nest and hung there, right under the canopy of the umbrella, their dragonfly wings a blur. Polly gasped in astonishment, and was about to say how fantastically lovely they were, when she saw the poison-tipped scorpion tails, arching over the fairies' heads. Her gasp of pleasure turned into a low moan of fear.

At the sight of the fairies, Iggy's nerve gave way completely. He was the only one who'd been stung by one of the things and he was not going to repeat the experience. With a shriek of terror, he threw the umbrella away. It sailed through the air and landed, upside down, on the surface of the pond, where it bobbed about, looking like a round black boat with a tall mast that curled over at the top.

The four fairies seemed a little dazed. They'd fallen back into the umbrella when it had plopped down into the water and now they climbed past the mat of their nest and, moving slowly, started to edge along the metal ribs. Their wings were beginning to flutter again, like a dragonfly that's about to take off. Measle said, quietly and calmly, 'We've got to get away from them. Come on—back away slowly.'

Keeping their eyes firmly on the slow-moving creatures, Measle, Polly, Iggy, and Tinker walked into the tall reeds. The reeds were easy to push out of the way, but they were so tall, it was impossible to see more than a few centimetres ahead. The buzzing sound of the fairies' wings suddenly became much higher-pitched, and Measle knew that they were now airborne and on the move.

'Quick!' he shouted to the others. 'Run!'

They blundered, crashing, through the reeds. There was just enough light from the stars to keep them together and, within a few moments, they were through the reeds and out—into what looked to Measle just like an oasis in the middle of a desert. There was the familiar group of palm trees, with what looked like bunches of dates hanging from them. A few low bushes stood about the place, some stunted grass—and a lot of sand.

Where the vegetation ended, the desert began—a series of undulating sand dunes, like waves in the ocean, stretching away to the horizon.

There was no sign of the fairies. The buzzing had stopped. The only sounds were Measle's, Iggy's, and Polly's heavy breathing—and some rapid panting from Tinker.

Iggy was peering anxiously back in the direction they had come from.

'Has dey gone, Mumps?' he said, nervously.

'I think so, Iggy.'

Measle wondered to himself why the fairies had given up so easily. Perhaps they'd found it impossible to fly through the dense reeds? Or perhaps they were not meant to be in this world at all? Didn't Lucian the werewolf say that legends couldn't travel between the different worlds of Dystopia? But the fairies had done just that, inside Iggy's umbrella . . . and the umbrella seemed able to pass easily between the real world and this one . . . a very useful object, perhaps?

Measle was about to whistle for the umbrella when he realized that there was a very good chance that the fairies had returned to it. Whistling for the umbrella was just too dangerous. In fact, it looked to him as if they'd lost the thing for good this time.

Measle, Polly, Iggy, and Tinker walked warily all the way round the small oasis. In the faint light from the stars, the desert looked grey and cool—but

Measle guessed that, when the sun came up, it was going to be very hot. So, if they were going to go anywhere, now would be the time to do it.

He scanned the endless dunes, looking for something—anything—that might show signs of life. He was about to give up and set off in any old direction, when Polly suddenly said, 'What's that?'

She was pointing off into the desert. Measle peered out into the darkness—and saw a faint shape in the distance. It seemed to be a small hump in the endless sand and he was amazed Polly had noticed it because, unless you looked really hard, it was easy to miss.

'What do you think it is?' said Polly.

'Sssomething ssstoopid,' muttered Iggy, still looking nervously in the direction of the tall reeds.

'I don't know,' said Measle. 'But at least it's something different from those dunes. We could walk forever across them and never get anywhere. I vote we go and see what it is.'

They set off across the rolling sand. Sometimes the going was soft, their feet sinking into the shifting grains. At other times, they'd find themselves walking across hard-packed ground. Down in the troughs of the dunes, they lost sight of the distant hump but each time they struggled to the top of the next hill, they could see it, slowly getting bigger as they moved steadily towards it.

'I think it's a building,' said Polly, panting from the exertion of climbing up a particularly steep dune. 'That looks like a sort of dome, doesn't it?'

It *did* look like a dome—perhaps the sort of roof you might see on the top of a church, or a temple. It was too dark to make it out clearly—and it was too far away to shine the torch on it. Besides, Measle was wary of using the torch—out here, in the open desert, the beam of light could attract all sorts of terrifying creatures. He tried to think what legends he knew about that lived in such a place . . .

'Polly, do you know any stories about things that live in deserts?'

Polly thought for a moment and then shook her head. 'I don't suppose you mean Aladdin, or Ali Baba, or any of those stories, do you?'

'I was thinking more . . . er . . . more *monsters*, if you see what I mean.'

Iggy sniffed loudly, to get everybody's attention. Then he said, '*I* know wot lives in puddins. *Ssstoopid* fings live in puddins.'

'Puddings, Iggy?' said Measle. 'What do you mean, "puddings"?'

Iggy frowned irritably. 'You said fings wot live in desserts, Mumps. Desserts is puddings—at least, dey wos de lassst time I looked.'

'No, Iggy, not *desserts*. *Deserts*. Places like this.'

'Oh,' said Iggy, looking uninterested. 'Well, dey is ssstoopid, wherever dey live.'

They trudged on through the sand, climbing one

minute, descending the next. Measle thought it was like walking across an ocean, in which all the waves had somehow become solid. The building loomed larger and larger. Until, at last, scrambling down the final sand dune, they reached it.

It was a ruin. The dome they'd seen from so far away had half-collapsed and there were gaping holes in the mud brick walls. Measle put out a hand and ran it over the surface of one of these bricks. It flaked and crumbled under his fingers.

Slowly, carefully, they walked round the building. There was an intact stone archway at the front, where once there might have existed a pair of great wooden doors. Now it was just a tall dark opening into what was left of the place. Measle risked using the torch. He pulled it out of his jacket and played the beam over the interior. Bricks and

part of the roof lay jumbled and scattered across a stone floor, which was covered now by a thin layer of sand that must have been blown in by the wind. There was no sign of life.

'I think we should stay here for the rest of the night,' said Measle. He pointed the torch at his watch. Eleven o'clock.

Eleven o'clock at night, it must be. But—that doesn't make sense, thought Measle. *We haven't been in Dystopia all that long, surely—unless Time has no meaning here . . .*

'I is 'ssstremely hungry, Mumps,' announced Iggy. 'I got no jelly beans left. Wot is I goin' to eat now?'

Measle was feeling the pangs of hunger too and one look at Polly's face told him that so was she. He looked around the ruined space, knowing already that there was going to be nothing there that would help them. Lamely, he said, 'Maybe if we could get some rest—'

He didn't get any further, because Polly suddenly put her finger to her mouth and whispered, 'Shh!'

Tinker's ears were pricked up and he was obviously listening intently—to something Measle couldn't hear. Polly was frowning with concentration, her head leaning to one side—so obviously she could hear whatever was getting Tinker's attention—and Iggy's head was turned in the same direction and there was a faint puzzled look on his bony face. Measle strained his own ears.

And then he heard it.

The faint sound of somebody crying.

It seemed to be coming from a long way off, and sounded muffled, as though the noises were meeting a lot of solid objects on the way to his ear drums.

'There's somebody here,' whispered Polly, moving closer to Measle.

'Sssomebody goin' boo-hoo-hoo all over de place,' observed Iggy. 'Doin' de waterworks fing— like Tilly when she is all sssad.'

'Yes—but where's the sound coming from?' hissed Measle. He'd switched off the torch and they were standing in almost complete darkness, apart from a little starlight that managed to filter down through the gaping hole in the domed roof.

'I don't know,' whispered Polly. 'Turn the torch back on.'

'I don't think so—it could be dangerous—'

Measle felt Polly grab his hand. 'Somebody's *crying*!' she muttered in his ear. 'A girl, or a woman, I think. She's in trouble—or just plain miserable— either way, we ought to try and help!'

'I *always* help Tilly when she is sssad,' said Iggy, smugly—and it was true. Iggy was the only one who could stop Tilly from crying.

Reluctantly, Measle switched on the torch. He played the beam over the littered floor and across the ruined walls—but there was still no sign of life. Polly walked away, following the pool of light, her eyes searching busily.

'Over here!' she whispered, excitedly, pointing to a spot on the floor.

Measle, Iggy, and Tinker joined her, all looking down at a circular pit, hidden behind a section of the fallen roof. The sound of crying was louder here, but still a little muffled. Measle pointed the torch into the shaft and saw that there was a rough wooden ladder extending into the dark depths. It was fastened to the stone walls of the well with massive and equally rough-looking iron nails. Polly knelt down and then put one foot over the edge of the shaft and onto the top rung of the ladder.

'Well, come on,' she said, looking firmly up at Measle.

He handed Polly the torch and watched as she started down the ladder. Then he turned to Iggy and said, 'You'd better stay here.'

'Hoo, don't you worry about dat, Mumps!' snorted Iggy. 'I is not going down no more holes in de ground—not never, not no more!'

'Right,' said Measle, wishing that *he* didn't have to go down any more dark pits either. 'Look after Tinker,' he said. Then he added, without any conviction at all, 'We—we won't be too long.'

'I don't know why you is even boverin',' sniffed Iggy, derisively. 'You is no good at stoppin' peoples from cryin', Mumps.'

'No,' said Measle. 'But Polly is. I've seen her.'

'Well, come on if you're coming,' called Polly, only her head still showing above the edge of the well.

Gingerly, Measle sat down on the edge of the shaft and dangled his legs over, feeling for a rung of the ladder. Polly was climbing steadily downwards and Measle could see the odd flashes from the torch below. He threw one last encouraging look at Iggy, who was too busy pretending not to care that he was being left alone with the nasty little dog to notice. Then he took a deep breath and started to climb, hand over hand, down the rough ladder.

Darkness

The well was very deep.

Polly was climbing down a little slower than Measle, because she had to hold the torch at the same time, so Measle had to be careful not to tread on her fingers. As they descended, the sound of crying became louder and less muffled. Measle was worried that Polly might call out, but Polly must have taken notice of Measle's anxiety, because she kept as quiet as she could and didn't say a word until her feet suddenly touched down on a sandy floor.

'I'm at the bottom, Measle!' she whispered. 'It's just a couple more metres to go!'

Measle climbed down the last few rungs and then stood by Polly. All around them was an inky blackness, the only light coming from the powerful torch, its beam pooling on the sand at their feet. Polly lifted the torch and slowly swept it around.

They were in the first of a series of square, low-ceilinged rooms. Across from where they were standing was a short passage, which led directly into what seemed to be another similar room. When Polly pointed the torch down the connecting passage, they saw that beyond the second room was a third and possibly a fourth.

Polly brought the torch beam back into the room they were standing in and swept it around the small square space. There were images painted directly onto the stone walls, and the colours looked bright and new. The pictures showed scenes of life from what Measle guessed must be the ancient Greek world. Young men throwing spears, young girls fetching water, older women spinning wool, older men fishing—

'I think it's some sort of tomb,' whispered Polly.

A tomb—oh, great! thought Measle.

Polly grasped his hand and whispered, 'Come on.'

They crept, on tiptoe, out of the first room, through the short passage and into the second room. It was almost exactly like the first, except for the wall paintings, which seemed to be more about wars and battles and heroes. There were horses galloping, armoured men clashing, corpses of fallen warriors scattered on the ground—and, all the time, the sounds of sobbing grew steadily louder.

It was when they were halfway across the third room, which had scenes of the Greek gods, sitting on their thrones on Mount Olympus, that the crying suddenly stopped and a voice called out, 'Who is there?'

Polly was about to reply when Measle squeezed her hand. Polly turned and saw that Measle had one forefinger on his lips—and a very worried expression on his face. Slowly, he shook his head.

'Who is there?' called the voice again. From the volume, Measle guessed that it was coming from the next room but one. It was too late to turn off the torch—the beam must certainly have been seen by now; but there was every reason to keep quiet and play a waiting game . . .

'I mean you no harm,' said the voice. 'But you will do harm to yourselves if you come any further.'

There was something about the voice that was beginning to make Measle feel just a little bit safer than he'd felt since he'd arrived in Dystopia. It had a gentleness about it, a warm, soothing quality—it was definitely a woman's voice and, by the tone, an older woman, even older than his mother, Lee. In fact, it reminded him of Nanny Flannel's voice, when she was in a particularly good mood.

Measle decided to risk it.

'Who are you?' he called out. Polly's head whipped round and she stared at him, her eyes wide.

'You know of me, I think,' cried the woman's

voice. 'Or you would not be here. What is your name?'

'Measle. Measle Stubbs.'

'Your voice is young, Measle Stubbs. Are you a child?'

'Yes. And I've got a friend with me—her name is Polly.'

'Also a child?'

'Yes.'

There was a pause. The woman's voice came again. 'I have no wish to harm anybody—and, most of all, I have no wish to harm children. But if you come any further, you will harm yourselves.'

'How?' called Measle, who was beginning to feel curious about the owner of this kind and caring voice. 'How will we hurt ourselves?'

'I did not say "hurt", Measle Stubbs. I said "harm". What will happen if you come further will not *hurt*—but it will *harm*. Indeed, it will kill. It would not be my *intention* to kill. I cannot help myself, Measle Stubbs—and that is why I hide, down here in the darkness. That is why I weep, down here in the darkness. I hide because nobody may see me—and I weep for the same reason.'

'But why?' shouted Measle. 'Why can't anybody see you?'

'Because, Measle Stubbs, in the *seeing* lies the *harm*.'

Measle and Polly looked at each other in

puzzlement. Polly whispered, 'How can just seeing her be dangerous? What is she?'

When Polly said that—put the question in that simple form—Measle suddenly had an idea of the possible identity of the sad woman two rooms away. The idea was extraordinary—crazy—and, given the behaviour of the woman so far, the stories about her were wildly untrue. But there was nobody else who fitted the bill.

'I've told you my name—and my friend's name,' called Measle. 'Now, we'd like to know yours.'

'I think you know it, Measle Stubbs.'

'Is—is—is your name—Medusa?' called Measle—and this time his voice was trembling a little, because if the answer was yes, then the danger that faced them was very real.

There was a long pause. Polly was staring at Measle with a look of horror on her face. Obviously she had heard of Medusa too—and knew what Medusa could do.

At last, the deep silence was broken. The voice that came to their ears was soft and sad.

'Yes, Measle Stubbs. That is my name. Medusa. Medusa—the Gorgon.'

Measle knew about Medusa because, in the past, he'd once had dealings with a bit of her hair. But, of course, it wasn't hair at all. Yes, it grew out of her head—but there the resemblance ended, for each strand was as thick as a finger—and each strand had scales—and each strand had a head, with a

flickering tongue that was forked—
and each head had a pair of
beady black eyes—and, if you
looked into any one of those
hundreds of eyes that weaved
so sinuously around the
Gorgon's face, then you were
turned, in an instant, to solid
stone.

Measle's experience had been with a single,
mummified snake's head, which (even long
dead) still had the power to turn a person to
granite in the wink of one of its cold, lifeless
eyes . . .

Now here, just a few metres away, was the
creature herself! With, presumably, a headful of
snakes that were very much alive! And yet, she
sounded so gentle! Sad and kind and gentle.
Perhaps the legends about her cruelty were
wrong? Perhaps it might be time to show the
creature a little kindness?

'Is there—is there anything we can do for you?'
called Measle.

There was a long silence. Then Medusa said, 'A
kind thought, Measle Stubbs. And yes—there is one
thing you might do, if you can. If I could cover my
head, then those who come near me would be
safe. I have hidden here, in this underground place,
a long time. I know it well. There is nothing here
that can help me cover my head.'

Measle looked at Polly. He let his eyes drift down to the long scarf round her neck. Then he looked back into Polly's face and grinned. Slowly, Polly unwound the scarf and wordlessly passed it over.

'I've got something here,' shouted Measle. 'But how can I give it to you without—well—you know?'

For the first time, Medusa's voice sounded just a little happy. 'If you cannot see me, Measle Stubbs, you will not be in any danger. Leave your light there and come to me in the darkness. Follow the sound of my voice, Measle Stubbs.'

Polly touched Measle on the wrist and shook her head firmly. 'We can't trust her!' she hissed. 'What if it's a trick?'

'I don't think it is, Polly.'

'Why?' persisted Polly. '*Why* don't you think it is?'

Measle didn't know the answer to that. It was just a feeling—a hunch—and Measle's hunches were nearly always right, which was why he relied on them so much. He shrugged and said, 'I just *think* she won't hurt us, that's all.'

'And—and, if she does?'

'Er . . . well—then you'll know I was wrong, won't you?'

He grinned at Polly again, to show her that he wasn't in the least bit anxious, took a deep breath and turned away and entered the connecting passage. The light from the torch allowed him to see a few metres into the next room, but the short corridor on the other side was as black as night. He crossed the room and, touching one wall of the passage, he began to feel his way into the darkness.

'Er . . . are you there?' he whispered, pausing for a moment, his fingers brushing the rough stones.

'I am here, Measle Stubbs. Come forward.'

It was so dark, it was like being blind. Shuffling one foot carefully in front of the other, Measle made his way into Medusa's room.

It was then that he heard the hissing.

It was a little like the sound of a whistling kettle, a couple of seconds before the steam builds up enough pressure to actually make the whistle start. There was a small difference, of course—escaping steam doesn't sound murderous, or evil, or coldly reptilian.

'Er . . . is that n-noise . . . your s-snakes?' stammered Measle, keeping very still.

'Yes,' said Medusa. Her voice sounded close by, perhaps a few metres in front of him, and a little to the left. 'But they are not snakes, Measle Stubbs,' continued Medusa. 'They are basilisks.'

'Sorry—Basil-what's?' said Measle, thinking for a moment that Medusa was referring to his horrible (and thankfully very *dead*) guardian, Basil Tramplebone.

'Basilisks, Measle Stubbs. Magical reptiles. It is their gaze that turns to stone.'

'Oh. Right. Er . . . I heard that—well—if somebody looks at your face—'

Medusa gave a small musical laugh. It sounded like water trickling over rocks.

'No, Measle Stubbs. Only the gaze of my basilisks is fatal. My face is quite safe to see. It's an ordinary face. A little old these days, a little wrinkled—but not too horrible to look at, I hope.'

So, that's another bit of the legend that isn't true, thought Measle. *Or, at least, it isn't true for me, down here in Dystopia.*

'What do you have for me, Measle Stubbs?' asked Medusa softly—and now her voice was very close. So was the angry hissing sound—it was so close, in fact, that Measle could make out many different levels of hissing, coming from many different mouths. He was grateful for the darkness. The idea of seeing a whole nest of small snakes—or basil-thingies, or whatever they were—weaving about on a lady's head was really horrible.

'Here,' he said, holding out the scarf.

Something touched his hand and Measle had to use all his nerve to stop himself snatching it away. The touch shifted to the scarf and Measle felt it being gently tugged out of his grasp. Then there was a sigh of wonder and satisfaction.

'Fine stuff indeed!' whispered Medusa.

'Is it all right?' said Measle.

'We shall see, Measle Stubbs. We shall see.'

Measle couldn't see a thing, but he could sense movement near to him by the tiny shifting currents in the air. Medusa was doing something with Polly's scarf and Measle pictured her winding it round and over her head. The image in his head was helped along by the sounds of Medusa crooning softly.

'There, there, my little ones . . . it's all right, it's all right . . . I'm just covering you over with this fine soft material . . . so warm, so soft . . . and you shall go to sleep, my pretties . . . '

Gradually, the angry hissing died away until, a moment later, it stopped entirely. Then Medusa's voice came out of the darkness.

'There, Measle Stubbs. I am covered now. It is safe to bring the light.'

Measle turned and felt his way back into the connecting passage. There was a faint glow from the torch that filtered into the next room, showing him the way back to Polly. A moment later, he was by her side.

'We can go and see her now, Polly.'

Polly gaped at him. 'What? Are you mad, Measle? Just one look at her—'

'Hang on,' said Measle. Quickly, he told Polly what Medusa had said, but Polly still stared at him as if he was crazy.

'But—but how do you know she's telling the truth, Measle?'

Measle shrugged, awkwardly. The fact was, he *didn't* know—but he had as strong a hunch as he'd ever had about anything that the Gorgon wasn't lying. Silently, he took the torch from Polly and said, 'Well, I'm going to talk to her. If you don't want to be left in the dark, you'd better come too. Just keep your back turned and don't look at her, or just keep your eyes shut, if you're worried.'

Polly was about to make another objection, but Measle was already walking purposefully into the next room, the torch beam flashing in front of him. Polly didn't want to be left alone in the dark, so she followed, screwing up her eyes so that she'd be ready to close them in a flash.

Measle paused, fractionally, before entering Medusa's room. There was no doubt about it—he was a little frightened at what he was going to see, and even more frightened at the possibility that Medusa was lying, and that one look at her horrible face would be enough to turn him to stone.

He took a deep breath and stepped over the threshold.

Medusa didn't look horrible at all. She looked a little bit like Nanny Flannel—without the glasses, of course. She was dressed in a very tight, very simple, black robe, that fell all the way to the ground. In fact, the robe was a bit *too* tight, because Medusa was quite fat and there were bulges where her waist should have been. There were lots of heavy gold rings on all the fingers and thumbs of both hands, and some big, jangly gold bracelets on her chubby arms. Polly's scarf was wound tightly round and over her head—and the only slightly disturbing thing about that was the occasional movement of what seemed to be lumps on Medusa's scalp, lumps that shifted and rippled beneath the woollen material.

Medusa's face was—well—it was really quite ordinary. She had fine dark eyes, a nose that was just a little too long, thick eyebrows, thin lips, and round, plump cheeks, and she was sitting quite still, on a chunk of masonry, right in the middle of the empty room, looking with fascination at Measle and Polly.

'Greetings, my dears,' said the Gorgon, in a friendly, welcoming voice. And then, to Polly, 'It's all right, child, you may open your eyes. Your friend Measle Stubbs is looking at me and nothing terrible has happened to him. You are safe—and I thank you for your fine garment, which has allowed me to welcome my first visitors in several long, long ages.'

Cautiously, Polly opened her eyes and, when she saw how—well—how *motherly* Medusa looked, a great sigh of relief escaped her and she smiled at the Gorgon and said, 'Hello. My name is Polly Williams.'

'Welcome, Polly Williams. Would you care for some tea?'

This was too much for Measle. *Tea? From the Gorgon?*

'That's—that's just—that's just too—' he began, and Medusa said, 'Too what, Measle Stubbs?'

'I mean—tea—from the Gorgon! And—and—you speak English! Aren't you from Greece or something?'

Medusa smiled and shook her head, making several lumps beneath the woollen scarf shift about uneasily. 'Measle Stubbs,' she said, gently, 'I am *your* story. I am *your* legend. When you heard about me, or when you read about me in a book, did you read it in Greek? Or in Arabic, the language of Libya, which is where I am from?'

'My dad told me about you,' said Measle.

'In English, I would imagine?'

Measle nodded.

'So, for you, I am an English Gorgon, Measle Stubbs. And, as an English Gorgon, would I not be expected to offer you tea?'

It was all so odd, in such a delightful way, that Measle simply grinned and shrugged and was about to say that tea—and cake and biscuits and sandwiches and anything solid really, because they were all starving—would be really, really nice, when he remembered that Iggy and Tinker were still outside, alone in the desert.

'Er . . . there are two more of us,' he said. 'Outside. Would it be all right if—'

A frown passed quickly over Medusa's face. She said, 'They are outside? No, no—they must be brought inside as soon as possible! There are dangers in the desert! Terrible dangers! Bring them in quickly, Measle Stubbs!'

'Polly—' said Measle, and Medusa held up one hand, her gold rings flashing in the torch light and her bracelets jangling as they slid on her arm.

'Polly Williams will stay here with me, Measle Stubbs. We girls like to talk—and we have much to talk about, don't we, Polly Williams?'

Measle glanced at Polly and saw, from her shy smile, that she wasn't about to object to the idea. Measle took the torch and placed it on the sandy floor by the entrance to this last room, pointing its beam along the ground, through the various corridors towards the room where the shaft up to the surface began. Then he followed the beam, hurrying through the empty rooms. It got darker and darker, but just enough light filtered through the passages to let him see the bottom of the rough wooden ladder fastened to the rocky wall. Measle started to climb up it, hand over hand.

Looking up, he could see far above him the small circular opening, filled with stars, that was the mouth of the shaft. Going up was harder than going down. By the time he reached the top of the ladder, and poked his head over the rim of the well to breathe the cool desert air, Measle was exhausted. His legs were shaking and he could barely lift his arms over his head.

Panting, Measle pulled himself out of the shaft and stood up on the sandy ground. He peered around for Iggy and saw him sitting on a rock about twenty metres away, his umbrella held over his head. Tinker was sitting at his feet. Measle walked up behind him and tapped him on the shoulder.

Iggy screamed, jumped several centimetres in the air and then fell over, flat on his back on the sand.

'Oooh! Dat was not nice, Mumps! You nearly give me a barf attack! Creepin' about like dat!'

At least Tinker's happy to see me, thought Measle, looking fondly down at the little dog, who was racing round him in small circles, his stubby tail a blur.

'Sorry, Iggy,' he said, bending down and helping Iggy to his feet. 'Now, you've got to come with me—it's not safe out here.'

'Where is we goin' den?'

'Down the well,' said Measle, pointing to the shaft.

Iggy shook his head. 'I don't wanna go down dere, Mumps,' he said, stubbornly. 'I is fed up wiv bein' all in de dark all de time.'

'It's not dark, Iggy. We've got the torch. And there's a really nice lady down there. She's got sn—' Measle was about to tell Iggy about Medusa's interesting hair arrangement, when he remembered that Iggy didn't like snakes and was inclined to scream when he saw one.

'Wot?' said Iggy, keen to hear what the nice lady had. 'Wot's she got, Mumps? Sssnails? Sssniffs? Sssnot? Wot?'

'Snacks, Iggy. She's got snacks. And tea. Come on.'

Halfway back to the hole in the ground, Measle suddenly stopped. Iggy, keen to get at the snacks, would have hurried on, but Measle reached out and grabbed his arm. There had been something bothering him about Iggy and, until that moment, he'd been unable to think what it was.

The umbrella!

Measle hadn't noticed this before, because Iggy holding his umbrella was such a normal, everyday sight, and therefore to be expected. But ... but Iggy had thrown the umbrella into the pond back at the oasis because it had contained a nest of four angry fairies.

Measle peered up into the canopy of the umbrella. All that was left of the nest were a few wisps of straw. There was no sign of a fairy and Measle breathed a sigh of relief.

'When did you get your umbrella back, Iggy?'

Iggy frowned, trying hard to remember. Then his face brightened and he said, 'Oh, well, I was sssittin' on dat rock, waitin' for you—an' I bin waitin' for a long, long, long, long—'

'Yes, all right, Iggy, I'm sorry. I just wondered—when you got the umbrella back, why you weren't frightened that there might be those fairies inside it?'

Hastily, Iggy dropped the umbrella and wiped his hands on the front of his jacket. It was as if he'd just discovered that the handle was covered in something slimy and disgusting.

'Fairies? Where?'

Measle guessed that Iggy had probably forgotten about the fairies and had whistled for his umbrella because he simply wanted shelter from the endless drizzle of his wrathmonk rain cloud.

Measle was about to pick up the umbrella and give it back to Iggy, when he saw the writing on the outside of the canopy.

The letters were white, standing out clearly against the black background—and Measle was pretty certain that they hadn't been there when the umbrella had landed in the pond . . . which meant that they must have been written some time during the past half hour.

But—by whom?

Measle squatted down and peered at the letters. They were quite small and occupied only about half of a single section of the umbrella's canopy.

The words read: 'To whoever sees this. The bearer of this umbrella cannot read or write. He is therefore unable to understand or reply to this message. Please use the attached correcting fluid to inform me where the bearer of the umbrella is at this moment. The umbrella will be retrieved in exactly 20 minutes. Thank you.'

So . . . whoever wrote this knew about Iggy, the umbrella's owner. And how many people in the world knew about Iggy? . . . And, more to the point, how many people would want to know where he was at the moment? . . . And, even *more* to the point, how many people still used white correcting fluid? . . .

Measle remembered that his dad didn't use a computer—he always used an old typewriter when he was writing stuff for the Wizards' Guild. Computers have a tendency to freeze up when they're anywhere near a wizard, so Sam bashed out his memos and reports on a battered manual typewriter—and, when he made mistakes, which was often, he always had a bottle of the white correcting fluid in a desk drawer.

'Dad?' whispered Measle to himself, and Iggy squeaked with pleasure and said, 'Where? Where?'

'No, Iggy, he's not here. I just think it was him who wrote on your umbrella.'

Iggy peered at the letters. They meant nothing to him, other than the fact that—''Ere, dat's not *nice*. Look, he's gone an' ssspoiled my loverly humble-ella wiv all dat ssscribblin'. He wouldn't like it if I went an' ssscribbled all over his car, would he? Dat is just plain *vampirism*, dat is!'

'No, Iggy, it's not vandalism. It's actually rather clever and I wish I'd thought of it myself.'

'Huh!' said Iggy, angrily folding his arms across his narrow chest and glaring up at the stars. 'Dat was a really loverly humble-ella, dat was. An' now it's all ruined!'

Measle didn't reply. He was too busy getting the little bottle of correcting fluid off the handle of the umbrella, where it had been fastened with sticky tape. Once he'd managed that, he gave the bottle a good shake and then twisted off the top. Projecting from the inside of the lid was a little brush. Measle bent and, writing directly underneath the original letters, wrote, 'Dad? Is that you? This is M—'

And that was as far as he got, because the umbrella gave a sudden jerk and, finding that nobody was holding on to it at that exact moment, it flew straight up into the air before Measle could get a proper grip on it. He and Iggy watched it as it sailed upwards into the dark desert night. It flew higher and higher— and then, quite suddenly, it was gone.

'Ooh!' wailed Iggy, angrily. 'Somebody is ssstealin' my humble-ella! Well, I is not goin' to let dem do dat! I is goin' to get it back! Right now!'

Iggy took a deep breath and pursed his lips—and

he'd just blown the first *tweee* of the whistle, when Measle, moving like a striking snake, suddenly and swiftly clamped his hand over Iggy's mouth and shouted, 'Not *yet*, Iggy!'

'Mmmmmphhhh!' mumbled Iggy, furiously, trying to pull his head away from Measle's hand. Measle shook his head firmly and said, 'Look, Iggy, I'm sure it's my dad who wrote on your umbrella and I'm equally sure that it's him who just whistled for it. I was writing a message to him myself, do you see—'

'MMMMMMPHHH! MMMMMMMPH!' mumbled Iggy, who was trying to say that his umbrella was not something you *write* on, it was something you got out of the rain to shelter under—and *he* didn't go around using their stupid sheets of paper to keep the rain off him, so why were they using his umbrella to write stupid letters on?

Measle tightened his grip and said, 'Iggy, you can have the umbrella back, but not yet. Don't you see? We've got to give it time to get back to Dad. Then he's got to get another bottle of the white stuff, because, look, I'm still holding the one he sent, and then he's got to write on the umbrella—'

'*MMMMMMMMMMMMPPPPPPHHHHH!*' moaned Iggy, trying to shake his head to show his disapproval of the whole thing—but Measle's grip was too tight for even that.

'Stop it, Iggy! This is really, really important! Don't you understand—using your umbrella, Dad and I can communicate with each other! And maybe he can help us get out of here! You'd like that, wouldn't you?'

But Iggy was too upset to listen to logical stuff like that. He continued mumbling and spitting against Measle's hand, and wriggling under the grip like an energetic eel.

'Iggy, listen!' hissed Measle into Iggy's big ear. 'You want to see Tilly again, don't you?'

The wriggling and spitting suddenly stopped. In a quieter, gentler voice, Measle said, 'If you won't let us use your umbrella, you might never see Tilly again. So, which is more important? Your umbrella—or Tilly?'

'Mmmph-mmmph,' mumbled Iggy.

Two syllables, thought Measle. '*Tilly*' *has two syllables*. '*Humble-ella*' *has got four—*

Measle took his hand away from Iggy's mouth and Iggy, rather sulkily, said, 'Okey-dokey. You can use my humble-ella to do your ssstoopid writin' on—but I want a new one when you and your dad is all finished wiv messin' it up.'

'Thanks, Iggy,' said Measle. He looked up at the sky, wondering how long he should allow before summoning the umbrella back. *Twenty minutes? Yes, twenty minutes ought to be enough time.*

'Iggy, if we wait about . . . er . . . about three squillion seconds, then we can whistle the umbrella back again.'

'Three sssquillion sssseconds?' said Iggy, who hadn't a clue about how long three squillion seconds would last.

'Three squillion,' said Measle.

'An' I get to do de ssspecial whissstle?'

'Yes. But not a second sooner, all right?'

Measle wondered whether he should leave Iggy up here alone in the desert, or take him down into the underground rooms. It didn't take him long to realize that placing Iggy and Medusa anywhere near each other could be a very bad idea indeed, so he decided to risk leaving him on his own for the few minutes it would take to bring Polly up and out of the tomb. He patted Iggy encouragingly on his damp shoulder and then hurried back to the shaft. Quickly, he climbed down the deep well and, a few moments later, his feet were on the sandy ground. He could see the torch beam lighting the way back through the successive rooms and corridors and he ran along its path, finally bursting into the space where Medusa and Polly were having tea.

Except that they weren't having tea at all.

Things Get Worse

Medusa and Polly were opposite one another. Medusa hadn't moved from her rock and Polly was sitting on another. Between them was a chunk of ancient stone, roughly square, that seemed to be serving as a sort of table.

But there was nothing on it. No cups and saucers, no plates, no cake or sandwiches—its rough surface was bare. And yet Medusa and Polly were both making the *gestures* of having tea. Measle watched as Polly lifted an imaginary cup to her lips and drank some imaginary tea—and he saw Medusa lean forward and cut, with an imaginary knife, a slice of imaginary cake and lift it to her lips. The Gorgon took an imaginary bite and then chewed, her eyes closed in ecstasy at the wonderful, imaginary taste.

Measle took the opportunity of Medusa's eyes being shut to look more closely at Polly, and he saw that she was staring at him, over the top of her imaginary teacup, through fear-filled eyes.

Something happened while I was up top, thought Measle. Something bad! Polly's been made to do this—to play this game of pretend tea party!

From the look of Polly, Measle guessed that perhaps Medusa wasn't quite as motherly as she'd at first appeared. Not only that, perhaps she was also just a bit mad . . .

'Ah, Measle Stubbs!' cried Medusa, as if he was a long-awaited guest. 'Welcome! You're just in time for some tea!'

'Er . . . ' said Measle, aware that Polly was staring at him with a beseeching look in her eyes. 'Well, thank you very much, but the thing is, we've got to go.'

'Go?' said Medusa, and now her voice was a little chilly.

'Well, yes,' said Measle. 'Something has . . . er . . . something has come up and we've got to go. Sorry.'

Grinning apologetically, Measle slowly extended his hand towards Polly. Polly rose to her feet and, forcing a smile onto her lips, she walked to Measle's side.

Medusa looked at them coldly. Then she said, 'No.'

'Wh-what?' said Measle.

'No.'

'Sorry, I don't quite—'

'I don't want you to leave,' said Medusa, firmly. 'I am enjoying your company. You will stay.'

'No—look—I'm really sorry—we both are, aren't we, Polly?—but we really do have to go. It was great meeting you—'

'Really great,' said Polly.

'But there's just no more time, you see. Not if we want to get home.'

'No,' said Medusa—and now her voice was as hard and as cold as ice. Her looks had changed, too—her expression was no longer motherly. Now her eyes were dark with anger, there was a deep, frowning crease in the middle of her forehead, her lips were pressed together in a thin line, and her mouth was drawn down at the corners in a scowl.

'No—I am tired of being alone in the dark. I want companionship. We have finished our tea and now I shall take this garment from my head, and then you, Measle Stubbs, and you, Polly Williams— you will both be with me for ever.'

'Look—'

Medusa hissed suddenly, like one of her snakes. She rose from her rock—the first time she had done so—and Measle's eye was caught by a glint of gold at her feet. He looked more closely, and saw that there was a short, but massive, golden chain around one of the Gorgon's ankles! The other end was fastened to an equally massive hasp set into the floor.

Medusa was a prisoner!

No wonder she's mad, thought Measle. *The poor thing's been chained up here in the darkness for ever!*

But now was hardly the moment to be feeling sorry for the Gorgon, because she was reaching up to the scarf on her head and was starting to unravel the end—

Measle made a single, darting movement and snatched up the torch. He thumbed the switch and a second later, the room was plunged into darkness. He felt for Polly's hand and, holding it tight, he edged towards where he knew the opening to the passage was. There was a furious hissing from Medusa, and then the hissing grew much louder, and came from many more throats than just hers.

'Give me back the light!' she screamed, her harsh voice echoing round the rock chamber. 'Give it to me!'

Measle didn't reply. Holding tight to Polly, he fumbled his way into the passage and, running the fingers of his free hand along its walls, he stumbled clear into the next room. Behind them was a heavy clanking sound as the Gorgon struggled against her chain. Then there was a long, wailing cry of despair—

'I only want a friend! And not even one that speaks! A friend of stone!'

Carefully keeping his back to the sound, Measle whispered, 'Don't look back, Polly, I'm going to turn the torch on.'

Polly gave his hand a squeeze and Measle thumbed the switch again. The torch beam was a little more yellow than before, and not quite as bright—*the batteries are going*, thought Measle, *we'd better be quick!*

He and Polly hurried back towards the shaft, the sound of Medusa's wails diminishing behind them. They climbed up quickly and reached the top, both gasping for breath. Iggy was standing there, his hands on his hips, one foot tapping impatiently at the sand.

'I 'ave been *waitin'*,' he said crossly '*Again!* Waitin' for at least twenty squillion *squillion* seconds—'

'Yes, yes, Iggy,' gasped Measle. 'You can whistle for it now!'

Iggy pursed his lips—

Tweeee—twee-twee-twee—tweeeee!

They didn't have long to wait. The umbrella appeared, flying swiftly down towards them. Iggy put out his hand and caught it.

'Oooh, look, dere is even more ssstoopid letters all over my humble-ella! Dat is not fair! Dis is *my* humble—'

Measle snatched the umbrella out of Iggy's grasp and put it down on the ground. He shone the fading torch down onto the canopy.

'Measle—is that U? Where R U? Where Iggy and Tinker? R U together? Will summon umbrella back in five mins. U do same. Write fast. Love, Dad.'

Measle uncapped the bottle of correcting fluid and, in a hurried scrawl, wrote, 'All together in Dispotier. Or Distopier. Can't spell it. Need rescuing. Toby Jugg did it. Come quick.'

They all waited, listening with only half an ear to Iggy's grumblings about the wanton destruction of his precious possession. Then, exactly five minutes after it had arrived, the umbrella lifted off the ground with a *whoosh* and sailed away into the darkness. Measle pointed the torch beam at his watch and pressed the stopwatch button. He watched as the second hand swept round and round. Five minutes seemed a terribly long time but, at last—

'All right, Iggy. Whistle again.'

Tweeeee—twee-twee-twee—tweeeee!

A few moments later, the umbrella sailed back into Iggy's hand. There was more writing:

'Spelt Dystopia. I can't come there. Only I know special whistle, so if I there with you, then nobody here able to summon umbrella back. Did Iggy and Tinker arrive on umbrella? If so, you use umbrella to come back, one at a time. Hold on tight, don't want to lose any of you. Measle—you last, obviously. Will whistle in five mins.'

Measle was so engrossed in reading his father's message, that he failed to notice that something was happening only a couple of metres behind him.

There was a sudden squeal of shocked surprise. Measle whipped his head round—and saw Polly being dragged backwards across the ground, her two heels leaving a pair of shallow furrows in the sand. She was struggling as hard as she could but there was nothing she could do. Not against the two mighty arms that were wrapped round her body, holding her as tightly as a straitjacket.

The arms belonged to Toby Jugg.

He was grinning like a wolf, exposing his two sets of pointed teeth. Out here in the open, his big wrathmonk rain cloud was directly above him and it was pouring a steady downfall over him and Polly, so that the hair on both their heads was plastered flat and dripping wet. Around his waist was the rope and, even as Measle watched in horror, Toby reached up to the string that hung parallel to it and gave it a double tug. Immediately, the rope tightened and Toby started to rise, his feet dangling.

'A hostage, Measle, old ssson!' he boomed, easily holding the struggling Polly as if she was no heavier than a puppy. 'And you can ssspend your time wondering what has happened to the girl, while I try to find you again! What fun we shall all have, eh? Bye! Be ssseeing you!'

Toby and Polly were rising very slowly. Obviously, the added weight was proving a bit much for Mr Needle and Mr Bland, because Toby and Polly were still not more than a couple of metres off the ground—

Click click click, went Measle's mind.

'Iggy!' he shouted, grabbing the little wrathmonk's arm. 'Do your spell! Do it at the knot!'

'*Not?*' said Iggy, gazing in wonder up at the pair slowly rising into the dark sky. 'Wot? *Not?* Do my spell or *not* do my spell? Wot?'

'No, Iggy! Do your spell at the rope round Toby's tummy. Quickly, before they go any higher!'

Iggy frowned in puzzlement. What good would his lock-opening spell be on a rope? But, well, Mumps had always been right about when he should do it, and at *what*, so Iggy stopped trying to work out the logic of it all. Instead, he stared hard at the rope and yelled, '*Unkassssbbbriek gorgogasssshbh plurgholips!*'

Lavender sparks flew from Iggy's eyes, zapped

across the space, and sizzled onto the rope around Toby's waist. Instantly, before Toby could do anything about it, the knot unravelled—just as Measle had hoped it would.

Toby felt the support around his middle suddenly give way. He made a desperate, one-handed grab for the rope, but the combined weight of himself and Polly was too much even for his powerful grip, and he half-slid, half-fell the two metres back to the ground. He landed heavily on his back, with Polly on top of him. For a moment, he seemed winded, because he didn't move. Then he struggled to his feet, both arms still locked around Polly. He looked up—and saw the rope steadily disappearing into the night sky. Without the weight on it, it was moving quickly and Measle pictured Mr Needle and Mr Bland hauling away, hand over hand, and probably wondering uneasily why the thing was so light all of a sudden . . .

'You idiot!' screamed Toby, glaring with fury at Iggy. 'You cretin! You moron! What have you done? Now we're all stuck here, until Needle and Bland lower the rope again—and there's no knowing where it'll end up each time! You—you—you—'

Toby's face was going purple with rage. Suddenly, without letting go of Polly, he took two huge strides which brought him close to where Iggy was cowering. Toby leaned over the little wrathmonk and took a deep breath—

'*NO!*' screamed Measle—but it was too late.

Toby blasted out his stinking wrathmonk breath all over Iggy—and Iggy froze.

Literally—he froze solid.

Measle watched in horror as a layer of white frost formed all over Iggy's face and body. Iggy's rain cloud froze as well and, instead of water, a tiny flurry of snowflakes began to fall on Iggy's head. Then, slowly, Iggy overbalanced. Dropping his umbrella, he toppled like a falling tree, thumping down onto the ground, and then lay still and silent on the sand.

Measle was too shocked to do anything. He stood there, paralysed, while Tinker trotted over and sniffed at Iggy's icy form. Then Tinker glared up at Toby, bared his teeth, and started to bark. Toby blew one contemptuous blast of freezing breath at the little dog—and Tinker's barks were silenced at once. In an instant, he became a small frozen thing, his snarl locked in place, a little icicle of dribble hanging from one corner of his mouth. Because Tinker was on all fours, he didn't fall over. He just stood there, a canine statue of ice . . .

Measle shook off the paralysis. He screamed, 'You—you've killed them!'

'Well, what did you expect, old ssson?' snarled Toby. 'That pathetic excuse for a wrathmonk has done for usss all—and you told him to do it! What do you sssupose will happen now? We're all ssstuck here, possibly for ever—'

So, Toby doesn't know about the umbrella! thought Measle, his despair lightened by a tiny trace of hope.

Toby hadn't finished. 'And you think I won't take my revenge? How little you know me, Measle! Well, sssince I've dissposed of the idiotic wrathmonk, and the irritating little dog, I might as well continue with thisss pretty girl here!'

Polly, who had stopped struggling the moment she'd seen what had become of Iggy and Tinker, was gazing up at her captor in terror. Toby took a breath—and then puffed it down straight into Polly's wide open eyes. For a single fraction of a second, an expression of disgust swept across Polly's face—and then the expression was frozen in place for ever. The frost formed quickly, covering her in a fine layer of ice. Her eyes lost all their life and her skin colour changed from pink to a cold, pale blue.

Casually, Toby let Polly's rigid body drop to the ground. Then, grinning, he turned to Measle and said, 'Do you know, old son, I really think thisss mussst be the end of the road for usss too. If I'm to be ssstuck here, at leassst I shall have the sssatisssfaction of knowing that my arch-enemy, Measle Ssstubbs, is no more! Now, which of my hundreds of hideous killing ssspells shall I use on you? Or should I reserve my major magic to ward off the dangers that lurk in thisss terrible place, and sssimply breathe on you, as I've done with your three little friends? Which shall it be, Measle?'

Toby was advancing towards him across the sand, his one yellow eye glittering. Measle looked around, wildly. There was nowhere to go in this vast desert, nowhere he could run to.

Well, there was *one* place—

Without giving the matter another thought, Measle turned on his heel and raced for the hole in the ground. He scrambled down into it, descending as fast as he could move his limbs. A moment later, Measle felt the ancient wooden ladder shudder under the weight of the wrathmonk. Toby was coming down after him . . .

Measle speeded up his descent, his feet and hands scrabbling for the rungs. At one point he misjudged a downward step and his foot slipped, leaving him dangling for a second or two before he managed to find a new foothold. It was a relief to find himself standing on the sandy floor of the tomb.

Then he realized what he'd done. He'd trapped himself here underground! The only way out was up the shaft, but Toby's massive body was coming closer every second—

It was only a matter of time now. Like all human beings who are faced with certain death, Measle's only interest at this moment was to prolong his life for as long as possible, so he switched on the torch and began to walk quickly through the rooms and passages. The beam from the torch was yellow and dim.

Suddenly, in the weak light, Measle saw movement ahead—the rustling hem of a dark robe, a pale hand—

Medusa! Quickly, before he could catch sight of her halo of writhing basilisks, Measle switched off the torch, plunging himself into pitch darkness.

'Is that you, Measle Stubbs?' called Medusa, in a plaintive voice. 'Have you come back to me?'

From somewhere behind him, Toby called out, 'Hello, old ssson, have you got sssomebody down here with you? I thought I heard a voice—who is it, Measle?'

Measle had never felt so threatened in all his life. He couldn't see a thing. Somewhere in front of him was the Gorgon, somewhere behind him was his most fearsome enemy. They were both very close—and there was nothing he could do about either.

'A man's voice! Have you brought me a companion in my loneliness, Measle Stubbs? Have you?'

'Oh, thisss is mossst interesssting, old ssson!' boomed Toby's voice, a little closer this time. 'You've got a lady friend, eh? Now, who on earth can it be?'

Measle found himself edging towards the sound of Medusa's voice. Anywhere, even at the Gorgon's side, was preferable to being near Toby Jugg!

Measle had his back pressed against a wall—he was pretty sure it was at a spot just before the final passage started and he felt for the opening, both hands brushing over the stones.

Ah—here it was! He felt the rough corner, then gingerly he took a step into the short corridor.

Quite suddenly, Measle heard the sound of hissing. It was dangerously close. Medusa must be at the very limit of her golden chain. Measle tried to picture the length of it in his mind and he guessed it was possible that she could be standing right at the end of this passageway, only three or four metres away.

'What's that noise?' muttered Toby, his voice betraying the fact that he was now no further away from Measle than Medusa. 'Funny sssort of hissing—what could that be, Measle old ssson? What's legendary, ladylike—and *hisses*?'

There was a moment when all sound, even the hissing of the basilisks, ceased, and then Measle heard the quick intake of breath from Toby and the distinct sounds of shuffling feet, and then of bone banging against stone.

'Ouch! My head!'

A few seconds passed, then Toby's voice came again and this time it sounded as if it was coming from much further off.

'Greek mythology comes to mind, Measle. I wonder—is it possible—have you found the *Gorgon*? If ssso, does she have her two sssisssters

with her? No, I sssussspect not. You might have heard of Medusa but not, I think, of Stheno and Euryale, ssso I imagine there's jussst the one. Sssounds like you've made a friend there, Measle! I wonder how you did it, eh? Without looking at her. I can't believe you wandered around down here in pitch darkness! Of coursse, you've got my torch, haven't you? And that leads me to wonder ... oh, very clever, Measle! Very clever indeed!'

Measle was bewildered by this. He couldn't think how he'd been clever. Then Toby supplied the answer.

'You're just waiting for me to come a bit closer, aren't you? And then you'll switch on the torch— probably with your eyes shut, or maybe with your back to the creature. Then, caught out in the open, I shall take one look at her terrible face and be turned to stone, eh? Oh yesss, very clever indeed!'

That is *clever*, Measle realized. *I wish I'd thought of it! But—but I didn't, and now Toby won't be caught by that trick, even if I played it right now ...*

There was the sound of shuffling feet and then another bump of bone on stone. The 'ouch!' came from even further off than before and Measle guessed that Toby had retreated back to the corridor before this one, well out of sight of the Gorgon.

The hissing began again, uncomfortably close. Then Medusa, in a cooing voice, whispered, 'Where has he gone, this friend you have brought me? Why doesn't he come forward and greet me? What is happening, Measle Stubbs?'

Toby was obviously too far away to have heard this, because his booming voice overlapped Medusa's final question.

'Tell you what, old ssson—I was going to sssimply breathe on you, and sssave my real magic for later. But sssince I daren't get any closer—and, as I sssay, that was jolly clever—I think I'll risssk it and dissspose of you with one of my killing ssspells. Now, what shall it be? Ah, yesss! Of courssse! What's the opposite of ice? Why—*fire*! I think I'll ssset fire to you, Measle! It's so dark down here—you'll make a lovely light for a few minutes. A human torch! Sssadly, I won't be able to sssee it, because of your friend—in fact, the moment you burst into flames, I shall be on my way—but I'm told it hurts really badly! Ssso—are you ready, Measle? Because here it comes!'

Overlaying Measle's utter terror was another, even more powerful emotion. An icy fury at the careless, vicious, and cold-blooded murder of his friends.

It was this frigid anger that made Measle's mind work, even at this moment of greatest danger.

Click click click . . .

It was the weirdest idea he'd ever had.

Freedom!

Measle plunged his right hand into his trouser pocket and yanked out the plastic bag. At the same moment, he lifted the torch in his left hand and, holding it up at eye level, he pointed it backwards over his shoulder. He raised the plastic bag to the same level, aiming it backwards over his other shoulder.

Then, he switched on the torch.

He was only just in time. Metres away down the dark passages, Toby had already started his spell: *'Ignidrom calorispoot—'*

But that was as far as he got.

The plastic bag was scratched and dull, and the beam from the torch, with its weak batteries, was yellow and dim—but neither of these factors stopped Toby's imprisoned eye from looking directly into the face of Medusa.

For a fraction of a second before the awful magic took effect, Measle saw her too. Very dimly, and only a fleeting impression, Measle caught sight of the Gorgon, reflected in the shiny wet eyeball encased in the plastic bag . . .

Medusa no longer looked motherly at all. Her face was contorted into a snarl, her dark eyes flashed a deep, angry red—and, on her head, scores of writhing, wriggling, hissing things, each the width of a finger, stared into the eyeball with tiny, crimson eyes.

Three things happened. First, Toby's voice simply stopped in mid-spell. Second, the eyeball dulled and the hideous reflection faded from sight—and, third, the colour of the eye changed, from slimy white, to a flat, speckled grey. It also seemed to get a little heavier in Measle's hand and, when his fingers touched its surface through the thin layer of polythene, it no longer felt squishy. Now it was as hard as—well—as hard as what it had become.

Solid rock.

Toby could close his other eye, against the Gorgon's stare. But, without lids, the eye in the plastic bag was forced to see whatever Measle wanted it to see. So, if Toby's eye in the plastic bag was now solid rock, then logically it must follow that Toby himself was also . . .

Measle switched off the torch. There was a deep silence. Even the basilisks on Medusa's head seemed to sense that something had happened, because their hissing died away. Then Medusa whispered, 'Something just took place, Measle Stubbs. What was it?'

Measle thought fast.

'Er . . . well . . . I've sort of got you a friend,' he said. 'I'm afraid he's made of stone. He's just a couple of rooms away.'

'Bring him to me!'

'Er . . . right. The thing is, that might be a bit difficult. He's . . . er . . . he's going to be really heavy.'

'But I want to see him!' said Medusa, longingly. 'If only—if only I could free myself from my chain!'

Measle had been wondering about the chain, so he said, 'Who chained you up in the first place?'

'Why, Measle Stubbs,' whispered Medusa, sadly, 'I did, of course.'

'*You?*'

'Yes. I am not evil. I have no wish to harm. That is why I imprisoned myself down here. Once, long ago, I felt the madness of solitude creep over me and I knew I would have to stop myself from wandering out of here. So, I caused the chain to restrain me for ever. But now you have brought me a companion—and one that is safe from my basilisks' stare! Now, I shall never be lonely again! You must bring him to me!'

'How about if I bring you to him?' said Measle.

Without waiting for a reply, Measle felt his way to the next room. Then he switched on the torch and hurried towards the shaft. On the way, he passed a great stone statue. It was of a big, burly man, with a beard and long, flowing hair. The statue was crouched, its back against a wall, and the head was turned, the single sightless stone eye seeming to look along the corridors towards Medusa's lair. Measle paused for a moment next to it. Then he took the plastic bag, opened it, and shook it gently. Toby's other, disembodied eye fell with a solid, stony thump onto the sandy floor.

'You can have it back now, Toby,' whispered Measle.

There was just one more thing to confirm.

Measle hurried to the bottom of the well and quickly climbed to the top. He poked his head over the lip of the shaft and stared out into the dark desert.

'I is absssolutely *freezin'*, Mumps!' said a whiny, complaining voice behind him. Measle turned round—and there was Iggy, his arms wrapped round his skinny body, shivering violently. Measle could hear his teeth chattering. Next to him stood Polly, her face blue with cold, and, at their feet, Tinker was shaking the last few fragments of ice out of his wiry fur.

It was what Measle had hoped for—hoped for desperately. A wizard's spell—and the foul breath of a wrathmonk is just another wizard's spell—could only be broken by the death of the spell-caster.

Being turned to solid stone was, of course, fatal for Toby, so, at the instant of his death, Polly, Iggy, and Tinker had become unfrozen—and had come back to life, too. Apart from feeling chilled to the bone, none of them seemed to have suffered any bad effects from the spell.

'What—what happened, Measle?' said Polly, blowing warm air into her hands and then rubbing them together vigorously.

Measle was so relieved that what he'd hoped for had actually *happened*, that, for a moment, he couldn't speak. Instead, he simply gave each one of them a big hug.

'Coo, you is ssso *sssoppy*, Mumps,' said Iggy, going a little pink.

Then Measle told them everything as quickly as he could and Polly's eyes grew wider and wider and wider. Iggy listened but he wasn't really interested, since he wasn't the hero of the story. Tinker listened too, but he didn't understand a word, so after a while, he sat in the sand and had a good scratch.

'So, Iggy,' concluded Measle, 'that's why we need you to do your spell again.'

'Wot?' said Iggy, vacantly.

Measle sighed. It was obvious that Iggy hadn't heard a word.

'Your spell, Iggy. One more time. Then we can go home—I *think*.'

Measle led them all back down the wooden ladder. Then he shouted, his voice echoing through the tomb. 'Medusa! We're coming! All of us! Please put the scarf back on—we're coming to get your chain off!'

The light from the torch was so feeble now, it was hardly any use at all. But Measle had passed through these rooms and passages so many times, he didn't need it. He used it to show the others the crouching statue of Toby Jugg then they hurried on. They all paused before the final room.

'Medusa, have you got the scarf on?'

'Yes, yes, Measle Stubbs. You are quite safe.'

They stepped over the threshold—and there

was the Gorgon, standing up to receive them, Polly's scarf wound tightly round her head.

Iggy was very nervous of Medusa. To him, she looked like a fatter version of Nanny Flannel—and Nanny Flannel made Iggy very nervous indeed.

' 'As she . . . 'as she got a mop, Mumps?' he whispered, standing very close to Measle and staring sideways at the Gorgon out of the corner of one fishy eye.

'I don't think so, Iggy.'

'An' . . . an' wot's dose lumpy fings wot is sssquigglin' about under her hat?'

'Er . . . well . . . they're . . . um—'

'They're mice, Iggy,' said Polly and she winked at Measle.

'Oh, *mice*,' said Iggy, with the air of a fellow who met people who kept mice under their hats so often, that it wasn't really very interesting any more.

'And she'll be your friend, Iggy,' said Measle, encouragingly, 'if you do your spell on that chain that's round her leg.'

Iggy peered at the chain, rather like a burglar facing an unusually difficult safe.

'But, Mumps,' he whined, 'I can't do my ssspell again. I jussst done it, on Missster Jugg. Can't do it again, not for a squillion hours.'

'I think you can, Iggy,' said Measle, reassuringly. 'There's a lot of free mana down here—that's what Mr Jugg said—so I think you can. Just try it.'

Iggy shrugged, stared hard at the chain round

Medusa's ankle, and said, with no great conviction, '*Unkassssbbbriek gorgogasssshbb plurgbolips!*'

There was a sizzle of purple light and then a heavy *clank!*—and the chain fell away from Medusa's leg.

'Oh, my gratitude! Thank you! Thank you! Thank you!' sighed Medusa.

Iggy grinned self-consciously. 'It was nuffink,' he said, airily. 'Any time.'

They led Medusa down through the rooms and passages, to the crouching statue. Medusa ran to its side and brushed her fingers over the curls of stone hair on the figure's head.

'So . . . so handsome!' she whispered.

Medusa was absorbed in her new friend and hardly noticed as Measle, Polly, Iggy, and Tinker turned away and started to make their way once again towards the foot of the ladder. They left her, crooning softly to the statue and gently stroking one of its hands, and Measle thought to himself, *Poor lady—all by herself in the darkness, with nothing but a statue to talk to!*

Once up top, they all looked around for the umbrella. It was nowhere in sight.

'Of course!' said Measle. 'Dad whistled it back. He must be wondering what's happened to us. Go on, Iggy—it's your umbrella.'

Tweeee—twee-twee-twee—tweeeee!

The added words on the umbrella were short and to the point.

'Hello? Anybody there? 5 mins.'

It was decided that Polly should go first. Since it was his umbrella, Iggy took it upon himself to show Polly exactly how to do it.

'You put dis hand 'ere—an' you put dis hand 'ere—and you hold on tight—an' you don't let go—an' you close your eyes an' take a big breaf, cos you is goin' in de water an' you don't want to 'ave water runnin' down your tubes—and den, in a bit of time, you is dere.' Iggy paused—and then he said, earnestly, 'An' *dat's* when you let go.'

Measle watched the seconds tick away on his watch. As the hand swept for the last time to the number twelve, he said, 'Ready, Polly? Hang on—any minute now!'

The umbrella gave a jerk and then settled again. Another jerk—this time stronger than before, as it tested the unexpected weight.

'It did dat to me, too,' said Iggy, watching with interest.

A third, more powerful jerk. Then the umbrella lifted off the ground. Polly clung to it, her eyes screwed shut and her arms and legs wrapped tightly around the handle.

'Hold on, Polly!'

With a sudden whoosh, the umbrella soared up into the night sky. Polly squeaked once. A moment later, the umbrella was gone.

After five minutes, Iggy did the whistle again—and back flew the umbrella. There was more writing now.

'All good this end. Polly safe. Nice girl. Iggy next.'

Iggy was extremely pleased that he was the unchallenged expert at flying about on his umbrella and, nonchalantly, he wrapped his arms and legs around the handle and then sat there, his eyes open, waiting for take-off. Five minutes later, it came—

'Bye, Mumps!' yelled Iggy. 'Sssee you sssoon! An' don't forget to keep your mouf shut—cos you is goin' in de water—an' den, if your mouf is open, you get all de water runnin' down your—'

Iggy's voice faded away into the night sky, and Measle was left alone with Tinker. The torch beam gave out one last little fluttering burst of light and then died away. Together, in the dark, they sat on a rock, looking up at the billions of stars.

Measle let five minutes go by. Then he pursed his lips and whistled.

Tweeee—twee-twee-twee—tweeeee!

The return journey was rather frightening. Measle clung tightly to the umbrella, with Tinker tucked down inside the front of his jacket. Measle's arms and legs were wrapped round the handle in a vice-like grip. The first part of the short trip was scary enough—flying at several hundred metres over the desert floor—but then the umbrella suddenly swerved sideways and up, straight towards a jet-black hole that appeared in the sky above them. It seemed to expand as they neared it.

The umbrella zipped upwards, straight into the hole, plunging them into the blackness.

Which, a moment later, turned out to be very *wet* and very *cold* blackness— and the wet and the cold was all around them, squeezing them so tight that they couldn't breathe, which was a good thing, of course, since they were deep under water. Measle closed his eyes and his mouth and pinched his nostrils shut between finger and thumb. He could feel pressure building on his eardrums, and it was getting really rather painful—and now his lungs were beginning to burn—

The pressure on his ears and in his chest suddenly released as the umbrella broke the surface of Limbo Lake and Measle took a great gulping breath of cold air. Deep in the folds of his soaking wet jacket, he could hear Tinker snuffling and coughing the water out of his chest.

'Nearly home, Tink!' he shouted, over the wind that whistled past their ears. It was night-time here, just like in the desert of Dystopia. *Only here,* Measle reasoned, *in the real world, it's probably* supposed *to be night time . . .*

They skimmed low over the dark water then rose a little to clear the tops of the gloomy pine trees that encircled the lake. Soon, the pine trees gave way to fields and then there, in the distance, were the welcoming lights of Merlin Manor.

The umbrella slowed as they neared the house and Measle looked down and saw a small knot of people clustered together in the courtyard outside the kitchen door. Before he could make out who they were, the umbrella swooped down, aiming its handle directly towards a bony, outstretched hand—

The combined weight of the umbrella, Measle, and Tinker was a bit much for Iggy's grasp and, the moment he caught hold of the handle, he discovered just how heavy it was. It hurled him backwards and he sat down with a painful thump on the gravel, with Measle, Tinker, and the umbrella sprawling across his chest.

'Ooowww!' wailed Iggy. 'You is ssso *clumpsy*, Mumps!'

A pair of strong hands lifted Measle and Tinker off Iggy, and a pair of soft hands wrapped big warm blankets around their wet and shivering bodies—and a pair of firm old hands pushed a big mug of hot chocolate into Measle's shaking grasp.

The owner of the strong hands said, 'Hello, Measle. Have a good trip, did you?' and the owner of the soft hands said, 'No questions now, Sam— we'll do all that later! Measle's wet through and exhausted!' and the owner of the firm old hands said, 'Quite right, Lee dear—it's off to bed with the whole pack of them. And Iggy can come inside for once and sleep in one of the spare bedrooms—I'm not having him catch his death of cold, even if he is a nasty, damp little wrathmonk who treads mud all over my nice clean kitchen whenever my back is turned!'

The next morning, they were all sitting round the big kitchen table, having one of Nanny Flannel's gigantic breakfasts. Iggy was there, too, sitting a little apart from the rest, surrounded by piles of old towels which soaked up the drizzle that was falling from his little black cloud and dribbling off his umbrella. Iggy wasn't eating any of Nanny Flannel's breakfast, of course—he was stuffing his face with handful after handful of red jelly beans. Tilly was sitting close to him in her high chair, leaning towards Iggy and trying—affectionately—to bash his head with a wooden spoon.

Polly was a little shy at first but soon she was telling Sam and Lee all about how brilliant and brave Measle had been, which made Measle go pink. In turn, Measle told them about how brilliant and brave *Polly* had been. And then (knowing how Iggy was going to resent anybody other than himself being a hero) he told them how brilliant and brave *Iggy* had been—and the little wrathmonk smirked and nodded and agreed with every word. When at last the story was finished and everybody had had their say, Sam put down his cup of coffee and said, 'Well, what an adventure! Fascinating! I got a taste of it with those fairies you sent us.'

'*Fairies?*' said Measle. Then, looking nervously around the kitchen, he said, 'Where?'

'Nanny managed to catch them—she threw an old towel over them. Nasty looking little brutes. They buzzed out of the umbrella and then I knew something bad was up. Don't worry—I've got them bottled up tight in a big old glass jar. Question is, what do we do with them?'

'I think we should drop them into Limbo Lake,' said Measle. 'That way, they've got a chance to get home.'

'Right,' said Sam. 'Into Limbo Lake it shall be. But nobody falls in, OK? I don't think any of us will be wanting to spend our holidays down there in Dystopia, will we?'

There was a lot of shaking of heads and murmured 'no's'. Sam grinned and nodded and said, 'And, finally, we can call off the search for Toby Jugg. What a fitting end for him, though, eh? He froze innocent people solid with his wrathmonk breath—and now he's solid too, and in good company, as well! I'm sure the Wizards' Guild will be very grateful to all of you. And, as for Needle and Bland, no doubt they'll come back eventually, with their tails between their legs. We can deal with them then.'

Nanny Flannel said, 'And we can certainly sort out some orange jelly beans for those fearsome werewolves. *You'll* have to throw them into Limbo Lake, Measle dear, because I don't trust Master Niggle not to eat them all on the way there!'

Sam turned and looked at Polly. 'Now, the question is—what are we going to do about Miss Williams here?' he said gravely.

Polly blushed and muttered that she didn't know.

'Well, I think I do,' said Sam. 'I'm going to have a word with your parents, Polly, and see if they'll agree to your staying here with us for a few days. Since it seems you're a real wizard, I think you need to learn a few things about the wizarding world—and, since I'm the Prime Magus of the Wizards' Guild, and my wife is a great and glorious Manafount, then who better than me and Lee to show you the ropes, as it were? Would you like that?'

Polly said she would like that very much—and Measle was just thinking how very much he was going to like having Polly around, if only for a few days, when the telephone rang. Lee got up and answered it.

'Hello? . . . Oh, yes, hello . . . well, thank you for taking the trouble to call . . . '

Lee glanced back over her shoulder at everybody sitting at the kitchen table. Then, taking the phone with her, she walked out into the passage beyond and her voice became indistinct.

A minute later she returned and put the phone back in its cradle.

'That was the school,' she said. 'The headmaster himself. Mr Crusoe wanted to know if you were all right, Measle. If you'd recovered from that nasty illness he heard you'd got.'

'Ah,' said Measle, hoping for the best. 'And . . . um . . . what did you tell him, Mum?'

'Well, I was very careful not to lie, of course. I said that whatever had been the problem was now resolved and you seemed to be just fine—'

'Oh, Mum!' squealed Measle. 'What did you say that for? I could've got out of lots of school! I could've been off sick all week! I could've—'

'School is important, Measle!' said Sam, trying hard to sound severe.

'But—but—but—' Measle spluttered. *It was so unfair! The only nice thing Toby Jugg had ever done for him—given him a fantastic excuse to stay home from school for a few days—and now his mum had gone and ruined it all!*

Lee was trying hard not to laugh. 'Oh, and another thing, Mr Crusoe thought you'd be happy to know that Miss Patterson is much better, too, has recovered from her chicken pox, and will be back in class on Monday morning—'

'Oh, Mum, no!' wailed Measle, burying his face in his arms. 'Not Miss Patterson!'

'Why?' said Lee, with an innocent look on her face. 'Don't you *like* Miss Patterson?'

'That's not funny, Mum!' said Measle crossly.

'Ssstoopid ssschool!' muttered Iggy, who wasn't sure what was going on, but he'd heard the hated word and now his best friend Mumps was looking really unhappy.

'Ssstoopid, *ssstoopid* ssschool! Ssstoopid Miss Pooplessson! I'll *breave* on her, dat's wot I'll do!'

The thought of Iggy breathing on Miss Patterson cheered Measle up for a moment, but then he relapsed into despair again. *Why haven't I got any magic?* he thought miserably. *If I had magic, I could really have some fun at school! But I* haven't *got any, have I?*

But ... wait a minute! I know somebody who has ...

Measle turned to Polly and muttered, 'Er ... Polly?'

'What?'

'Well, you know that boxing glove thing you do?'

'Yes?'

'And ... um ... you know Miss Patterson?'

'Yes?'

'Well ... '

Polly frowned in puzzlement. Then her face

cleared and her mouth widened into a broad, beaming smile.

'Oh . . . yes . . . right . . . ' she said, nodding slowly and delightedly at Measle.

'Not actually directly *at* her,' said Measle, grinning as broadly as Polly.

'Oh no, not directly *at* her,' said Polly.

'But quite *close,* don't you think?'

'Oh, yes, I think so—quite *close.*'

Sam put his coffee cup down with a clink and, peering suspiciously down the table at Measle and Polly, he said, 'Now then, now then—what wickedness are you two plotting?'

'Oh, nothing, Dad,' said Measle, airily. 'Nothing at all.'

Maybe, he thought, *just maybe—with Polly Williams at my side going back to school might not be so bad after all.*

Ian Ogilvy is best known as an actor—in particular for his takeover of the role of The Saint from Roger Moore. He has appeared in countless television productions, both here and in the United States, has made a number of films, and starred often on the West End stage. His first children's book was *Measle and the Wrathmonk*, followed by *Measle and the Dragodon*, *Measle and the Mallockee* and *Measle and the Slitherghoul*. He has written a couple of novels for grown-ups too: *Loose Chippings* and *The Polkerton Giant*. His play, *A Slight Hangover*, is published by Samuel French. He lives in Southern California with his wife Kitty and two stepsons.

Measle Stubbs is best known as a bit of a hero—in particular for his triumphant role as the charge of the evil wrathmonk, Basil Tramplebone, his defeat of the last of the Dragodons and his escape from creepy Caltrop Castle. Measle's last adventure was his struggle against the slobbery Slitherghoul. Now he has defeated the Doompit, he can relax at home with his family—for a while, at least.

There are lots more **MEASLE** adventures to discover!

Measle Stubbs is not a boy known for his good luck.
He's thin and weedy and hasn't had a bath for years—
and he has to live with his horrible old guardian,
Basil Tramplebone.

Just when Measle thinks things can't get any worse,
he's zapped into the world of Basil's toy train set.
There's something lurking in the rafters and a giant cockroach
is on his trail—it's times like these you need a few friends . . .
and a plan!

'Stink is what Ogilvy does best.
This is a book that smells superbly foul.'
Michael Rosen, *Guardian*

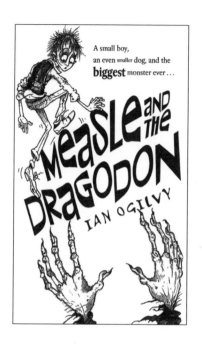

A small boy,
an even smaller dog, and the
biggest monster ever...

MEASLE AND THE DRAGODON

IAN OGILVY

Things are looking up for Measle. He's been
reunited with his parents and they're making up
for lost time and having lots of fun.
It seems too good to last.

And it is. The mysterious Dragodon and his gang
of wicked Wrathmonks have cast a spell on Measle's dad
and snatched his mum. Measle and his dog, Tinker,
have only one clue, and it leads them to a deserted
theme park—The Isle of Smiles.

Being hunted down by horrors in a dark, wet
funfair is anything but fun! Measle is on a mission
with more twists and turns than any rollercoaster—
can he save the day once again?

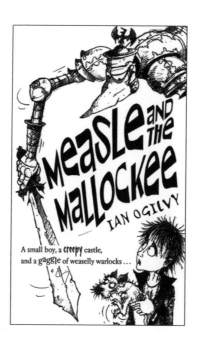

A small boy, a **creepy** castle,
and a **gaggle** of weaselly warlocks …

Measle's on his own again. Some double-crossing
wizards have locked up his mum and dad and
now they're after him.

He's got his baby sister with him—a baby sister with
amazing magical powers—and every warlock in the place
wants to get his hands on her.

Measle has to hide, and Caltrop Castle seems safe.
But there's something strange about it. The creepy
castle can keep the wizards and warlocks out …
but what is locked inside with Measle
and the mallockee … ?